A GHASTLY SPECTACLE

A Regency Cozy

LYNN MESSINA

D1496249

Beatrice Hyde-Clare Mysteries

To everyone who clutched their books so tightly their knuckles turned white to get through the pandemic

Chapter One

Having endured the collective concern of friends and family members on several previous occasions, the former Beatrice Hyde-Clare decided to take the preemptive step of inviting all interested parties to Kesgrave House to address candidly and forthrightly her investigation into the death of Mr. Réjane.

It was necessary, she thought, because the account reported by the scurrilous Mr. Twaddle-Thum in the *London Morning Gazette* had contained several significant inaccuracies. For one thing, Bea had not stood over the remains of the unfortunate victim and coolly examined the spot where his head had been detached from his neck.

Whether she would have been able to maintain her composure while scrutinizing that grisly spectacle was unknown to her precisely because she had been denied the opportunity. By the time she arrived at the kitchen where the inventor of *la grande cuisine* had been murdered, no trace of the incident remained. Every speck of blood had been ruthlessly scrubbed from the floorboards, and it was impossible to know for sure exactly where he had fallen. At best, the butler could provide only an approximation of the location.

Bea felt compelled to correct this point in particular because it still irked her that she had not actually seen the body. If she had been able to inspect the incision, she might have learned important information about the murder itself.

That arrangement, however, was obviously untenable. No gently bred lady could request access to a severed cadaver without rousing the disgust of the *ton*. As a spinster with an excess of curiosity, she would have been roundly derided as an unnatural female whose inability to nab a living man had driven her into the arms of a dead one. And that response, even with all its sneering contempt, would have been kind compared with the torrent of gossip she would have unleashed as the Duchess of Kesgrave. It would have been expressed as concern for the duke, of course, the poor man leg-shackled to a baffling oddity who seemed determined to expose him to every humiliation.

Was it not enough that she had debased him thoroughly by ensnaring him in a marriage he had neither wanted, nor sought? Must she bring him to yet another new low? Was there no depth to which the wretched girl would not sink?

Knowing the scorn that lay in wait for her new husband, she had withstood the desire to seek out the remains. Whatever insight she might have gleaned from the corpse itself was not worth the scandal it would have provoked.

It was precisely because she had restrained her inquisitive nature out of deference for society's delicate sensibilities that she found Mr. Twaddle-Thum's erroneous account to be so vexing. If she had to listen to Aunt Vera lecture her on the ghoulish impropriety of examining decapitated chefs, then she would have at least liked to first have the privilege of actually examining a decapitated chef.

She knew that correcting her aunt's understanding of the

situation would do little to improve that of the *ton*'s, and she certainly could not invite each and every member of society to Kesgrave House for tea to address their mistaken beliefs.

Not only was that plan impractical, but it was also exceedingly tedious.

Bea found it challenging to make conversation with the *beau monde* under the best of circumstances and was always grateful when the weather did something interesting to provide a benign topic. ("Why, yes, the wind was particularly strong in the park yesterday. It knocked down several branches and rather boorishly removed Miss Graybill's hat.")

Furthermore, the damage had already been done, as demonstrated by the print of her holding Mr. Réjane's head aloft that was hanging in Hannah Humphrey's window in St. James Street. In the picture, she was examining the dead man with interest while he begged for a private moment to pull himself together.

"Errant nonsense," Lady Abercrombie had written in her note accompanying the caricature. "Best forgotten immediately."

Bea wanted to follow the countess's decree, but the image was somehow more vicious than even she had anticipated.

It was her chin, she decided, the way it jutted out in a monstrously intrusive manner, as if advancing before her by several feet.

Suddenly self-conscious about the size of the feature, Bea cynically applauded the artist for forcing her to consider yet another deficiency. She had long ago realized her eyes were too drearily brown to be compelling and her nose too weak for interest, but the defects of her chin had never occurred to her. If she had considered it at all, it was only to confirm that it curved in the right angle and did not dimple jauntily. Her chin was certainly not her best feature, for that was an endearing spray of freckles across her nose, but it was also not her worst.

That Bea had spent a full ten minutes at the mirror that morning examining the protrusion for signs of obstinacy was a credit to the artist, and it was only picturing his satisfaction at that development that convinced her to pull herself away. Having decided to mock her grotesque curiosity, he would be delighted to know he had pricked her vanity.

It had been shocking, really, to discover she had any left.

But Hannah Humphrey and her printshop were beyond Bea's reach and she resolved to focus only on the things she could control, such as the tea service. Although she had been a duchess for little more than a week, she had already exploited the absurd lavishness of the home's tableware on several occasions, most notably in intimidating the neighbors' servants during her most recent investigation. Cowing Aunt Vera varied only in the speed with which it would be accomplished. One look at Kesgrave's impressively fine silver and her relative would fall silent, providing Bea with an opportunity to correct the misunderstanding regarding Mr. Réjane's body before her aunt launched into one of her rambling tirades.

At least, that was Beatrice's hope.

There was always the possibility that the notion of her niece inspecting a headless corpse was so appalling, it would overcome her instinctive awe of grandeur.

A desire to forestall the tedium of her aunt's outrage was not the only reason Bea extended the invitation.

No, she also wanted to keep her family from stumbling into a dangerous situation that could almost certainly get them killed.

It sounded grandiose, Bea conceded, and, yes, a little hyperbolic, but that was exactly what had happened two days before.

Her cousin Flora, deciding with irrational determination that Mr. Theodore Davies's entirely reasonable death bore all the hallmarks of murder, thrust herself into a misadventure that had come heart-stoppingly close to claiming her life.

Bea knew Davies's death was entirely reasonable because she had devised it herself, tossing him under the wheels of an oncoming carriage in the middle of a busy street because such accidents were commonplace in London. The notice she had written for the newspaper announcing his tragic passing had been deliberately vague, but on the whole it had not varied muchly from the other items that ran in the *London Morning Gazette* that day.

Flora had absolutely no cause to be suspicious.

Even without evidence, she had managed to convince herself that the law clerk had been cruelly murdered by one of his associates to protect a dark secret he had unwittingly discovered. Concocting a lurid tale of greed and betrayal out of thin air, Flora somehow blundered across an actual lurid tale of greed and betrayal.

Bea would never forget the frantic race up those ramshackle stairs in that decrepit house where Flora's would-be killer had brought her. Terror hitched in her throat as she imagined her cousin's unseeing eyes staring blankly at the ceiling. Climbing, she heard the pounding of her heart alongside her aunt's desperate screech, a wail as infinite as her chatter but pitched toward misery and despair.

And then the shock of seeing Flora with her hands desperately clutching a two-foot-long floorboard and her eyes preternaturally calm as she turned to address Bea.

That sight alone was already the single most astonishing thing Bea had ever seen in her life—truly, the serene look on her cousin's face, as if the scene itself had unfolded to her precise specifications—and then Flora uttered unfathomable words: *There. There is the man who killed Theodore Davies.*

Struck by the horror of what she was seeing, although she could scarcely comprehend it, Bea denied it.

Obviously, the unconscious man at Flora's feet was not the man who killed Theodore Davies. Bea knew this fact irrefutably because Theodore Davies did not exist. He was a fiction conceived with little consideration to cajole a suspect into making an indiscreet confession.

The suspect was indiscreet, yes, but in revealing Bea's love affair, not her own. Within hours of hearing the tale of doomed romance, she had shared it with every member of the small house party gathered in the Lake District.

Her family was astonished to discover that the drab spinster had managed to secure any man's attention and did not at all mind that he was a lowly law clerk.

Indeed, as far as Aunt Vera was concerned, the lowlier the better.

Given her relatives' interest, Bea had no choice but to arrange Mr. Davies's demise in *an entirely reasonable* manner.

And yet, despite the seeming rationality of all her actions, her cousin still somehow wound up at the top of a ramshackle staircase in a decrepit house with a gun to her head.

It was almost two full days later and the thought still made Bea's knees buckle.

But focusing on a tragedy that did not occur served no purpose, and furthermore Flora had acquitted herself beautifully. Keeping a cool head, she successfully wielded her wooden plank and rescued not only herself but also Mr. Holcroft, the gentleman who had lent his assistance to her investigation.

Bea really could not quibble with how her cousin handled herself.

Except...her cousin should not have needed to handle herself, for launching the investigation into a fictitious man's murder had been an act of madness.

To be sure, Bea's own inquiries into the various deaths that seemed to surround her did not fully rise to the height of sanity. When the Earl of Fazeley, for example, fell at her feet in a newspaper office on the Strand, there was no reason she could not leave the matter in the hands of the authorities. The dagger protruding prominently from his back made the fact of his murder plain. There could be no mistaking it for suicide or an accident.

In truth, she would have remained utterly uninterested in the famous dandy's violent demise if she had not recognized the dagger. But having recalled seeing it in the collection at Montague House, there was nothing she could do but visit the museum to confirm her suspicion.

Then, when she discovered that the antique blade was one of a pair, she had no recourse but to pay a call on its last known owner.

Flora, it would seem, felt the same tug of inevitability when she observed the evasive expression on Bea's face in response to her query about Mr. Davies's death—which was hardly surprising, given that she had been trying to evade the subject.

It was horrifying that a lie told in passing and almost immediately forgotten by its author could keep rearing its ugly head over and over again.

Keenly aware now of the potentially dire consequences of even a minor fabrication, Bea resolved to confess every last detail of her investigation into Mr. Réjane's death.

Well, not *every* last detail, she amended, as Marlow entered the drawing room followed by her family. The manner by which she had learned of it did not bear repeating, for she had been tucked behind the door in the butler's own bedroom at the time. She had not meant to eavesdrop, but it was by far the lesser evil than being discovered where she did not belong.

Marlow's opinion of her had been low enough without adding a tendency to invade his privacy to her list of objectionable character traits.

Flora, striding into the room with an air of familiarity, thanked the butler by name and affected a sort of world-weary determination not to be impressed by the magnificence all around her. The imposing marble columns and gilded ceilings might as well have been piles of sand for all the interest she showed in them.

Her mother, in stark contrast, inhaled sharply as she beheld the graceful proportions of the room, with its ornate plasterwork and masterful frescoes depicting scenes from classic Greek literature. Penelope plied her loom while her stern son stood over her reproachfully.

Although usually given to chatter when anxious or overcome with nerves, Aunt Vera remained silent as her eyes darted from the mirrored alcove to the statue of Athena.

Observing her aunt's unusual reticence, Bea thought with wry amusement that she should have married a duke with a palatial home in Berkeley Square years ago.

Uncle Horace, unconstrained by the awe that gripped his wife, greeted Bea warmly and observed that it was lovely to see her looking so well. "Marriage agrees with you, which I was confident it would. You are certainly busy with other activities at the moment, but I hope when you have settled comfortably into your new situation, we will have time to resume our discussion of Kepler. I have undertaken supplemental reading material to improve my understanding of heliocentric astronomy. Next, I will attempt *Epitome Astronomiae*."

"An excellent tome and a concise delineation of Kepler's laws and theories," Bea said approvingly.

Russell, realizing that his father and cousin had established some sort of reading club with an exclusive membership policy, began to recite the facts of the universe as he understood them. Firmly, he positioned the sun in the center of the solar system but wrongly described it as Ptolemaic.

While his father winced at the inadequacies of his education, Russell owned himself to be particularly fond of Mars. "I think red is a very becoming color for a planet."

Flora, overhearing this comment, seconded the opinion by citing as supporting evidence coquelicot's versatility, for it suited ball gowns *and* pelisses. "Naturally, that adaptability must extend to planets as well."

Although his own argument lacked academic rigor, Russell rejected his sister's reasoning and thanked her not to demean his scientific observations with her superficial comprehension of the world.

Flora responded hotly that his inability to grasp the hugely significant importance of color on one's social success indicated *he* was the superficial one. "Do explain it to him, Papa," she said.

Her father, as if to demonstrate the versatility of the color red, turned a bright fuchsia shade, at her directive, and Bea, observing his discomfort, could not discern for whom he was embarrassed: himself or his children. Ordinarily at this juncture, Aunt Vera would interject with her own trivial observation, compounding the problem instead of solving it, and her uncle would raise the newspaper with an impatient flourish and resume perusing the articles.

Now, however, Aunt Vera could only stare at the sterling-silver teapot, with its egg-and-dart border, ivory finial, and engraved family crest.

It was, Bea imagined, the detailed craftsmanship of the tiger that dismayed her rather than its fierceness. Aunt Vera had at once an undaunted eye for quality and a fearful reverence of it.

Before Bea could urge her relatives to make themselves

comfortable, Marlow entered with the Dowager Duchess of Kesgrave, who, despite the long walk from the front door, was still berating the butler for the overt familiarity of his reception. It had been appropriate, she conceded, prior to her grandson's marriage. "But now that you have a new mistress, you must treat me with the excessive courtesy of a stranger."

Although Bea felt more like an interloper than a mistress despite holding the position for ten and a half days, she applauded her new in-law's appeal for formality and advised the butler to request her calling card before admitting her to the house in the future. "We cannot allow the rabble to roam freely, however well turned out they might appear."

Marlow, unable to respond to this mischievous suggestion with anything but earnest deference, said only, "Yes, your grace."

The dowager, however, laughed with pleasure and thanked Bea for including her among the rabble. It was, she insisted, an inconsideration for which she had waited her whole life.

Bea assured the septuagenarian it was her pleasure as she escorted her to the settee. "Next I shall call you *riffraff* and *tag, rag and bobtail*."

Aunt Vera, who was standing beside the settee with an uncertain expression on her face, failed to chide her niece for making such a disrespectful remark. It was, Bea thought, the greatest indication yet that her relative was deeply unsettled by the circumstance.

"Ah, yes, the de Lamerie," the dowager said with an appreciative nod as she observed the tea service laid out on the table. "Very elegant, my dear. That pot has always been a particular favorite of mine. Damien's mother, knowing how fond I was of it, hid it away so that the housekeeper could not use it during my visits. Nasty creature."

It was an intriguing tidbit—indeed it was—for Beatrice knew very little of Kesgrave's parents. The fault was hers, of course, for she had been continually reluctant to dig into what she could only assume was a deep well of pain.

His father was clearly a tyrant.

According to Lord Tavistock, who was a villain in his own right, the previous duke would never have allowed his son to marry her.

Tether the Matlock name to a spinsterish nonentity of common descent?

No, not ever.

He would have thwarted the engagement easily enough by making her disappear.

It was an ominous description, and Bea had no idea what it meant in practical terms. Would she have been kidnapped and shipped off to some far-flung colony for a life of slavery or simply murdered in her sleep?

Both options were horrifying to contemplate and implied terrible things about Kesgrave's upbringing.

Her own childhood had been far from ideal, but her relatives' cruelty had been of the offhand variety. Thrust into a terrible situation, her aunt and uncle behaved terribly. Bea resented them only somewhat because neither one possessed the grace or kindness to rise above the situation.

And why should they?

They were Hyde-Clares, whose family motto was, "*Si non est molestum.*" If it's no trouble.

Transcending their own pain to comfort the orphan in their midst could have been an awful lot of bother.

Deliberate cruelty, however, was a different beast entirely, and Bea could not believe Kesgrave, if subjected to it, would have escaped unscathed.

From almost the very beginning she had been struck by the duke's gleaming perfection. She teased him often about his pedantry and arrogance as if they were in some way outrageous flaws, but in truth they were not. For a man of

Kesgrave's standing those traits were not so much faults, as the inevitable consequence of being alive.

And yet he had responded to her taunts with good-natured humor, an act that set him apart from ordinary dukes.

Indeed, his insouciance set him apart from ordinary *humans,* for any other man would have lashed out in defensive anger at her presumption.

His attitude was even more astounding given his physical appearance, which was highly attractive by any standard: brilliant blue eyes, strong jawline, curly blond hair, lithe form that hinted at power and strength. A small part of her—a very small, teeny-tiny, minuscule part—worried that there was something seething and ugly beneath it.

She recalled the first time she had met him, during their stay in the Lake District, over the corpse of a swindling spice merchant. It had occurred to her then that there was something slightly nefarious about his perfection, and she had found herself wondering if faultlessness was sometimes compelled to seek out corruption as an antidote to its own intolerable excellence.

Naturally, she no longer suspected anything so dire. Even before she figured out who had murdered Mr. Otley, she had ceased to distrust the duke.

He was wholly good.

Even so, pain itself was ugly, and the surest way to unleash her own agony was to broach the subject of her parents.

She had no idea if it was the same for Kesgrave, but during one's honeymoon did not seem like the appropriate time to find out.

Of course, one's honeymoon was also not the ideal time to investigate the decapitation of one's neighbor's chef and she had definitely done that. But a different standard applied to the things that scared her, which she felt was reasonable.

Nonetheless, it could not hold, her reluctance, and as she invited the dowager to sit down, she resolved to address the matter of his parents soon, for his mother sounded as unpleasant as his father.

"I am glad you approve," Bea said smoothly, with a glance at her aunt to see if the dowager's fondness eased any of her anxiety. Surely, a beloved teapot was significantly less daunting than a sterling-silver heirloom with expert engraving. "I hope you will come often to tea so that I may visit with you while you visit with the de Lamerie."

"You are very kind to offer, but I cannot visit too frequently or I will lose my cherished standing as rabble," the dowager said, before looking inquisitively at Aunt Vera. "May I offer you some tea, Mrs. Hyde-Clare, to help calm your nerves? You appear as agitated as a deer standing in the middle of the Great North Road."

Aunt Vera jumped slightly at this observation—not, Bea was convinced, at the prospect of appearing so blatantly apprehensive in company but at the notion of such an august personage performing a service for her.

If anyone in the room was going to pour tea, it would be she, not the Dowager Duchess of Kesgrave.

Aunt Vera, scurrying around the back of the settee to assume the cushion next to the dowager, said that a cup of tea would be lovely. "I realize now that I am actually parched. I do hope you will allow me the pleasure of pouring. You are right, your grace, the teapot is lovely. De Lamerie, you say? We have a pair of candlesticks by him at Welldale House. They are quite superior," she announced proudly, before rushing to explain that *superior* was a relative term and that her candlesticks were actually quite inferior. "They were made by a lesser silversmith under the de Lamerie mark, I am sure of it, as his practice was known to hire subcontractors. The superb craftsmanship of your teapot indicates that it was

LYNN MESSINA

done by the master himself. And the condition—it is so pristine. You are fortunate it was hidden away for so long." She paused just long enough for the statement to resonate in her head before clarifying that it was *un*fortunate. "What are a few nicks and scratches compared with the joy of using a beloved object? Indeed, the more nicks and scratches the more beloved, I always say."

In fact, she did not.

If Vera Hyde-Clare could somehow contrive it, her family would live belowstairs and only emerge from the servants' quarters to receive guests. She resented every chip, scratch, mark and abrasion suffered by her possessions.

The dowager owned herself to be of the same mind, which caused Bea's aunt to blush as she lifted the pot to pour.

"Your grace," Vera said, presenting the teacup to the dowager, who immediately deferred to Bea.

'Twas only an act of courtesy, the offer, not an obligation of decorum, and yet Aunt Vera responded as if sharply rebuked. Her breath hitched and her face turned a bright shade of red as she stared down at her fingers grasping the sterling-silver handle of the de Lamerie.

She could not have appeared more horrified if she had done something genuinely shocking, such as remove her shoes in the presence of the prince regent.

As she watched the other woman's cheeks darken, Bea wondered if she had misunderstood her aunt's objection to her marrying Kesgrave. Given her family's timidity, she had assumed Vera was unnerved by her flagrant disregard for the natural order. If some upstart spinster had to have the temerity and poor conduct as to nab a duke from under the nose of a dozen more worthy young beauties, then let it be someone else's upstart spinster, not the Hyde-Clares'.

Why must they be forced to suffer the indignity of outrageous success?

Now, however, Bea considered the possibility that her aunt's opposition sprung from a far more personal concern. Perhaps her anxiety was not how the *ton* would receive the Duchess of Kesgrave but how *she* would. The informality of a niece rushing headlong into the formality of the aristocracy—nothing in Vera's life had prepared her for the collision and now she was at a loss as to how to behave. The simple act of pouring tea had proved slightly wrong, and her composure deserted her.

How vexing it must be for Aunt Vera, having to think about her niece so much when she was accustomed to not thinking about her at all.

Bea knew her assessment was unfair because her relative had done the best she could for the child of an adulterer and a murderer. That her best was woefully inadequate was a defect of character.

It was not Vera's fault that she lacked spirit *and* generosity. If she had been granted one it might have compensated for the absence of the other.

Bea thanked the dowager for her offer as Lord Nuneaton entered the room in the company of Kesgrave. Excusing herself, she strode to the doorway to welcome the viscount, who was dressed to perfection as always. Although his appearance was familiar—pristine elaborately tied cravat, embroidered waistcoat, light-colored pantaloons—the expression on his handsome face was not, and he looked at his hostess with uncharacteristic interest.

"I must congratulate you, your grace, on an act so shocking I cannot even pretend to affect indifference," he said, causing the duke to chuckle. "I am unaccountably eager to hear every last detail of your latest endeavor and count myself unduly fortunate to be among the select group to whom you would deign to discuss it."

Perhaps so, Bea thought with amusement, but he was also

disgruntled by his own enthusiasm, if his tone was any indication. "I hope you will accept my apology for foisting a new experience on you. Overturning a lifetime of carefully cultivated ennui was most assuredly not my intention."

His lordship regarded her sternly and announced there was nothing careful about his ennui. "It is rash and reckless."

Bea was instantly contrite, lowering her eyes and saying, "Yes, of course," to the claim, which was patently false. Everything about the viscount's presentation was ruthlessly planned to within an inch of its life, his blank expression as much as his elaborate cravat.

Not fooled for a moment, Nuneaton asked Kesgrave if he had grown weary yet of his wife's disrespect.

Presuming to speak for the duke, Bea replied that he had not. "But it has been little more than a week, and it takes time for familiarity to breed contempt. We must wait a fortnight or so before he starts to chafe at my impertinence."

"Surely, a full month," Kesgrave said, his lips twitching with familiar humor.

Bea laughed and shook her head. "Even now, he underestimates me," she said, before offering the viscount tea. "Please make yourself comfortable while we wait for Lady Abercrombie."

No sooner had Bea mentioned the name of the beautiful widow who had been her mother's dearest friend than she appeared in the entranceway, her elegant features set in a staunchly disapproving frown as she berated the young woman for making such a muck of things.

"One week," her ladyship said reproachfully. "You could not maintain the facade of a dignified duchess for one whole week. I begin to despair of you, my dear."

"Begin?" replied Nuneaton humorously.

"You are your mother's daughter so I understand your desire for adventure," Lady Abercrombie continued as though the viscount had not spoken. "And, truly, I would not have raised an eyebrow if you had decided to immerse yourself in an intriguing domestic matter such as discovering if there was any truth to the rumor that the duke's butler once won a bout against Dan Mendoza. I would have questioned Kesgrave's ability to entertain his new wife, yes, and worried about the long-term prospects of your union, but I would have never raised an eyebrow."

Astonished, Bea stared at the countess. "Marlow was a bare-knuckle boxer? Our Marlow?" she asked, incapable of comprehending how nobody in the household had mentioned this fascinating tidbit before. She could understand the maids being reluctant to gossip and Mrs. Wallace certainly did not seem inclined to share confidences, but Jenkins, the duke's groom, was a keen follower of the Fancy and knew she would delight in the information.

Her ladyship refused to indulge her. "Seeking out a decapitated corpse, however, is beyond the limit, young lady, and as your maternal surrogate, I must insist that you cease all such activities at once."

Aunt Vera, returning the teacup to the table, protested this description by sharply insisting *she* was Bea's maternal surrogate.

As factually correct as this statement was, its accuracy had no bearing on the situation as Lady Abercrombie understood it and she duly ignored it. "I must accept some of the blame because I did not perceive the danger in allowing you to seek out capitated corpses. I see now that was a mistake."

Although Aunt Vera remained generally awed by nobility, her reverence for the countess in particular had lessened with repeated exposure to her. Angrily, she rose to her feet and objected yet again to her ladyship's assumption of surrogacy. "Beatrice is *my* niece. She is *my* responsibility. If anyone is to accept blame for allowing her to seek out capitated corpses, it is I."

"For goodness sake, Mama," her son said impatiently, "*capitated* is not a word. The opposite of a decapitated corpse is just a corpse."

"Is it?" his sister wondered thoughtfully. "Or is the term *headful* to contrast with *headless?*"

Russell scoffed at the absurdity, while his father observed that it appeared to him as though nobody allowed his niece to do anything. "As far as I can tell, she abides by her own authority without concern for anyone else," he explained. Then, fearing the slight of selfishness, he quickly added that he found her intellectual independence to be quite admirable. "Your father was the same way."

Determined to win his sire's favor, Russell proclaimed himself also to be a freethinker, to which his sister observed that he was just free of thought.

"There is a difference," Flora said with grave condescension.

Mortified at the prospect of her children bickering in the stately drawing room of Kesgrave House, Aunt Vera reversed her stance on the countess's complicity and said more loudly than necessary, "If only Lady Abercrombie had not encouraged Bea to find out what really happened to her parents, then none of this would have happened."

Obviously, that statement could not stand, for Bea knowing the truth about her parents was the best thing for her, especially as it allowed her to understand why her aunt and uncle had treated her poorly for all those years. She did not excuse their fear but could at least comprehend it.

Aunt Vera, realizing her faux pas the moment the words left her mouth, colored brightly as she stammered an apology. "Of course I don't mean...Bea's investigative skills are so... without them we would never have learned...and I would still think...her parents were unfortunate victims...naturally, I do not wish anything to be...I am grateful for her ability and..."

Unable to bear her aunt's flustered explanation, Bea interrupted to ask her to pour tea for her ladyship. "No doubt she is parched."

"Delighted, yes, please," Aunt Vera said, her cheeks flushing even more hotly at the request, which she clearly interpreted as implied censure of her behavior.

'Twas an absurd reaction, Bea thought, as her aunt was a guest and could not be expected to host the Countess of Abercrombie.

Smothering her impatience, Bea thanked her aunt and escorted the countess to an armchair adjacent to the settee. Then she waited while the rest of the company settled in. Flora took the seat opposite her ladyship, and Uncle Horace assumed the bergère next to her. Russell strode several steps toward a chair with scrolled arms, then promptly changed direction when Nuneaton positioned himself against the fireplace. Struggling to match the viscount's insouciance—studied as always, Bea noted with humor—her cousin placed his elbow on the mantelpiece, where it rested just a little too high for comfort.

With a glance at Kesgrave, who had made his belief in the futility of her endeavor known, Bea folded her hands in her lap and said with more portentousness than she had intended, "Let us begin."

Chapter Two

Her aunt startled at the words, as if afraid something further would be required of her, and seeking to calm her nerves, Bea offered the other woman a reassuring smile. But of course, nothing distressed Vera Hyde-Clare more than the implication she should be at ease and her posture straightened fitfully, causing her cup to rattle and a small amount of tea to spill over the side.

"Oh, dear," she said softly.

Bea, deciding the best course was to ignore her aunt, thanked everyone for responding so quickly to her summons. "You adjusted your schedules to attend to me, and I am grateful for the consideration. As my note mentioned, I wanted an opportunity to explain my actions in regard to Auguste Alphons Réjane's murder because I know some of you are troubled by my investigative habit. It is true that I inserted myself into the Mayhews' personal business. No invitation was extended. However, my presence ensured that a grave miscarriage of justice was averted, and I think that is important to keep in mind."

Obviously, Aunt Vera could not be made to care about the

integrity of the judicial system, but her uncle was an educated man who studied the principals of the Enlightenment even if he did not personally subscribe to them. He would respect a rational argument.

Indeed, Bea was much gratified by the expression on his face, which displayed mild interest.

Intentionally, she did not look at her aunt because she did not want to see her horrified disapproval.

Smoothly, she continued. "If you are particularly concerned now it is because Mr. Twaddle-Thum's account contained several shocking details, and I am sure it will ease your mind to know that a good many of them are wrong. Most glaringly, he claims that I examined the victim's decapitated corpse. This is not true. By the time I arrived at the room where the murder had taken place, Mr. Réjane's body had been removed by the constable and the kitchen floor scrubbed clean."

Having clarified what she considered to be the most significant point, Bea allowed herself to look at her aunt. She was aghast.

"That is your concern with the account?" Vera asked before repeating shrilly, "*That?*"

Bea smiled placatingly. "It is one of my concerns, yes. According to the *London Morning Gazette*'s report, I stood over Mr. Réjane's decapitated corpse and coolly examined it for evidence of how he was killed. In fact, I did neither. It is a necessary distinction to make because Mr. Twaddle-Thum paints me as utterly ghoulish and I don't think that portrayal is fair when I was not given the opportunity to discover the extent of my ghoulishness."

"Those are just details," her aunt said angrily as she jumped to her feet with surprising agility.

Slightly taken aback, Bea nonetheless remained calm. "Yes, inaccurate details."

"Inconsequential details," Aunt Vera countered, stopping to clutch the back of the settee. It was a measure of her agitation that she did not notice how close her fingers were to the Dowager Duchess of Kesgrave's elegant chignon.

Ordinarily, proximity was a presumption she would not dare.

Uncle Horace, perceiving the depth of his wife's anxiety, rose to his feet as well and explained, "What your aunt is trying to say is that the particulars of your investigation do not matter so much as the investigation itself. The *beau monde* cares only about what you did or did not do. *How* you did it is immaterial."

Incapable of adding anything to her husband's concise summation, Aunt Vera whimpered and tightened her grip on the settee.

"It is true, my dear," Lady Abercrombie said. "As much as it pains me to agree with anything Clara's atrocious sister-in-law says, Mrs. Hyde-Clare is correct if incoherent. Nobody cares if you examined the dead man's decapitated corpse."

"I care," the dowager said.

Grateful that someone comprehended the distinction, Bea smiled appreciatively at the septuagenarian, who immediately added that she thought it was very dashing of her new granddaughter. "When I was a child, one of the cows on a tenant's farm lost its head in an accident with a plough and it was quite dreadful. I could not bring myself to look upon it."

Lady Abercrombie murmured consolingly in the general direction of the dowager duchess and amended her statement to be that almost no one cared. "I trust it goes without saying that we are all deeply concerned about your welfare, and that is why we have gathered here to discuss it. The situation is dire regardless of the details. If your investigation into the chef's death were a singular event, it would be easy enough to explain away. We could have, for example, attributed it to the anxiety of a young bride unnerved by her new situation or the expectation of marital relations. Unfortunately, Mr. Réjane's murder is not the first one you have investigated. As you yourself just said, you make a habit of it, a habit of which society is now well aware. If only the victim had been one of Kesgrave's own servants...."

Sighing prettily, her ladyship trailed off and lifted her shoulders.

Noting the implied criticism, the duke announced that he would not apologize for overseeing a well-run establishment lacking in seething resentments that drove its inhabitants to violence.

Although he had explicitly not sought forgiveness, Lady Abercrombie granted it, observing that it most likely would not have made a huge difference in the end who employed the murdered chef. "Bea's history of detection is too firmly established to draw attention away from it. The only way forward is to draw attention *toward* it. To that end, I have arranged a dinner party for next week in which the entertainment will be a play about a murder and all the guests will take a part. I will come up with the clues and assign the roles and decide who is the victim and who is the culprit. It will be delightful fun and utterly charming."

Aunt Vera, stepping back from the settee, shook her head and announced that she could not be party to making a May game of murder.

"Well, naturally, no," her ladyship said with a warm laugh. "As the point of the event is to foster a sense of exclusivity, the guest list will be limited to only the most illustrious members of society. I cannot imagine how your presence would further the goal of attaining the *ton*'s acceptance of the new duchess. But you are thoughtful to assure me of your lack of interest. Thank you."

Flora, however, was very interested and leaned forward in her chair. "A friendly face," she said eagerly.

Lady Abercrombie barely turned her head to acknowledge the comment. "Excuse me?"

Withering slightly under the lovely widow's vague dismissal, Flora leaned back in her chair. Nevertheless, her voice was strong with conviction as she elaborated on her remark. "Bea is brave, to be sure, when it comes to confronting murderers on terraces, but she is actually quite a timid woman. Having a friendly face at the party would help put her at ease and increase the likelihood of her success."

It was, Bea thought, a cogent argument.

Tossing her into a sea of influential society matrons, Incomparable beauties and Corinthians and expecting her to charm the company was not a plan that was likely to prosper.

Indeed, it seemed carefully calculated to do the exact opposite.

Breezily, the countess dismissed Flora's concern by saying Bea would have Kesgrave.

Flora was not so easily deterred. "A *few* friendly faces," she amended.

"Nuneaton will be there as well," her ladyship said.

Her most persuasive argument rebuffed, Flora settled back in her seat with a disappointed frown. A moment later, however, the viscount stepped forward and offered to escort her to the dinner party as his guest.

"I trust that option is available to those of us deemed sufficiently illustrious to warrant an invitation?" he asked, raising one elegant eyebrow.

Although Lady Abercrombie offered a tight smile in response, she could not refuse the query and agreed at once.

Flora clapped happily, which, Bea noted, did little to endear her to the lovely widow, who pressed her lips together at the display. Russell glared at his sister as a scowl darkened his face, and Bea, observing all their reactions, decided that it was time to put an end to her ladyship's absurd notion.

Although Bea would never voice her disconcertion in the same stark terms as Lady Abercrombie, she felt no more comfortable being in agreement with her aunt than the countess did.

On this point, however, Aunt Vera was correct. Murder was a serious consideration, literally a matter of life and death, and she could not allow her ladyship to turn it into a parlor game, especially not in service of a cause that was almost certainly lost.

Dissuading the beautiful widow would not be easy, for she was impetuous, determined, and disinclined to weigh the consequences of her actions. This was a woman, after all, who had adopted a lion cub as a pet without giving any consideration as to what would happen to the creature when it outgrew its babyhood.

Overwhelmed by the prospect, Bea sought out Kesgrave's gaze and was surprised to discover he was already watching her. His eyes, steady and patient, indicated that he was prepared to abide by her decision.

Proceeding with Lady Abercrombie's harebrained scheme, scotching it—whichever she preferred.

She appreciated it, the show of respect, for it was always gratifying to have one's opinion deferred to, particularly by a man whose lineage allowed him to ignore the preferences of a vast swath of the population. At the same time, she wondered how he could have any doubt which option she favored.

Naturally, she found the countess's proposal repellent.

Even if she did not object to turning the viciousness of murder into a pleasant diversion, she would never consent to a plan that positioned her as the focus of a dinner party. Large or otherwise, it was still too intimate an introduction.

If she must be launched into society as the Duchess of

Kesgrave—and Bea was not yet convinced such an event was necessary—then let it be a lavish ball with several hundred guests, all vaguely indistinguishable, milling around a dance floor as an orchestra played.

Exclusivity, she decided, was among the most terrifying words in the English language, and hoping to evade a situation that she found intolerable, she fulsomely thanked the countess for her consideration.

"Knowing you extend it as much out of a fondness for my mother as for me makes it particularly meaningful," she added, tilting her head at what she thought was a gracious angle. "I am sure she would have been pleased. I am less certain that your murder mystery dinner party play is the right note to strike at this time. It is an intriguing idea, but perhaps this moment calls for a more conventional approach. Previously, you had mentioned hosting a ball in our honor, and I will admit that I was less than enthusiastic at the prospect. But I realize now that it is exactly what the situation requires, and I do hope you will accept my apology for not lending my full support when you originally proposed it. Shall we discuss dates? I cannot speak for Kesgrave, but my own commitments are few."

Bea looked pointedly at the duke, but before he could lend his support to this alternate plan, Lady Abercrombie trilled lightly and called her a silly goose.

"Of course we are going to have a ball in your honor!" she said firmly. "That was never in doubt, my dear. My murder mystery play will be in addition to the lavish party I intend to throw. Now, there is no reason for you to worry about it striking the right note because that is my responsibility, not yours. All you need to worry about is impressing everyone with your ingenuity."

All, Bea thought, in horror.

Unaware of the terror she had struck in the duchess's

heart, her ladyship continued. "It would be unsporting of me to give you inside information, but I am sure we can all agree you have a natural advantage and if you require help Kesgrave will be there to assist you."

"And I," Flora insisted.

"Ah, yes," Lady Abercrombie said with significantly less zeal. "And your little cousin. So, all will go swimmingly on Saturday."

"On Saturday?" Bea asked, alarmed by the specificity.

Her ladyship nodded and advised her to arrive at her townhouse by seven. "So that we may have a tête-à-tête before the other guests appear."

"The other guests are not going to appear," Bea said sharply, "because we have not consented to the plan."

"But they are," Lady Abercrombie insisted. "I have already received half a dozen eager responses. Not a single guest has declined."

"Tilly," Kesgrave said warningly, as he stepped forward.

The countess looked at him with her light-brown eyes opened wide with helpless wonder. "I do not know what you expect me to do now, for the matter is completely out of my hands. The invitations have been sent. Even Nuneaton has replied positively and with a guest. I apologize if I have acted with undue impetuosity, but it simply never occurred to me that either of you would object. You, Kesgrave, have attended several dinner parties at my townhouse without complaint, and you, Bea, coolly examine wretched headless corpses without flinching. It is perverse that you would balk at enjoying light conversation in my drawing room."

"I did not examine Mr. Réjane," Bea reminded her irritably, darting a glance at her aunt. "As I mentioned previously, his body had been removed from the premises before I arrived. That is among several inaccurate details included by

Mr. Twaddle-Thum in his account, and that I invited you here to correct."

"Hush, darling, hush. You are getting worked up over nothing. Thanks to our friend at the *London Morning Gazette,* the whole of London knows the truth and we must proceed from there. What can no longer be denied must be embraced," her ladyship explained matter-of-factly. "It is, I think, for the best because no matter how often you are advised against continuing with your strange proclivity, you appear incapable of abiding."

"She is correct," the dowager said. "The moment the newspaper printed the story, denials became useless. Her solution is elegant if ostentatious."

Lady Abercrombie bowed her head in gratitude and assured her grace that she strove for that exact combination in all her endeavors. Then, turning to Bea, she urged the duchess to consent to her plan. "Like your mother, you are far too practical a woman to chafe against the inevitable. Truly, I do not know why you are so resistant to my idea, for it solves several problems at once. It furthers your acceptance by society *and* affirms your viability as an amateur Runner. Surely, that is all to the good. The only other option is for you to halt your investigative practice altogether, and I am far too sensible to wish for that unlikely solution. Come, your grace, I do not comprehend why you are so resistant to the idea. If everything goes according to my plan, you shall be summoned all over London to coolly examine dead bodies. The way my name is synonymous with elegance and ostentation, so yours will be with murder and violence. Does that not sound above all things marvelous?"

Flora clapped her hands in appreciation while Aunt Vera gasped in horror at the thought of her niece scrutinizing corpses all over the city.

Bea's own response was somewhere in the middle, for the

countess's description held obvious appeal. It would be lovely to pursue investigations without worrying about the judgments of the *ton* and how they might fall on Kesgrave. Eyebrows, of course, would never cease to rise and some sticklers would always be appalled, but if her strange proclivity was accepted as just another eccentricity of the gentry, like Mr. Mytton's fondness for riding bears, then life would be more comfortable for all of them, including her aunt.

Oh, but the terror Lady Abercrombie's proposal unleashed in her stomach was undeniable. Even as she sat comfortably in her own drawing room, a horde of butterflies began to flutter restlessly and her hand clenched tightly at her side.

For all the plan's many advantages, it was, at its core, an utter nightmare for Bea—literally, in fact, for she had returned often in her dreams to the evening of her come-out. It always began well enough, with her in the receiving line next to her aunt and uncle, happily exchanging bon mots with members of the *ton*, and then her thoughts growing ever more leaden as the guests rose in importance until at last, she was standing in front of the Prince Regent completely silent. At that point, she usually changed into something inanimate like a carriage wheel or a vase. Once she turned into a turnip, which she felt was a little too accurate.

As uncomfortable as her presentation to society had been, it did have one thing to recommend it: It was a singular event allowing no encore.

A young lady could be introduced only once.

It was a thought in which Bea had taken much comfort in the years since her debut, and now the Countess of Abercrombie was stating the categorical opposite: She must suffer the ordeal again.

And her ladyship's version was all the more excruciating

for its informality and intimacy. At the very least, a ballroom provided the benefit of a crowd of people among whom she could hide, even during her come-out, but a small gathering would afford her no cover. She would be open and exposed, the focus of everyone's attention as they watched and waited for her to reveal her true self: glittering diamond or lump of coal.

Verily, it made her blood run cold.

And yet what the countess said was true: Something had to be done. Mr. Twaddle-Thum's article required a response and clarifying a few inaccuracies to a small contingent of intimates was not an adequate reply. Plying a coterie of influential members of the *ton* with food and drink, on the other hand, was a time-honored method of courting approval. And the idea of rousing their interest with an intriguing puzzle was a genuinely clever stroke, for it not only put the new duchess's odd investigative habit at the center of the event but also provided her ladyship's guests with a small measure of its appeal.

As viscerally appalled as she was by the widow's scheme, Bea was too reasonable to deny its merit. The wholeness of her ambition could not be attained, for there was no world in which the Duchess of Kesgrave would be routinely called upon to inspect cadavers.

Some things were pure fantasy.

But even modest success would be an improvement, Bea thought, if it spared Kesgrave some ridicule.

Unclenching her fist deliberately and nodding at her husband calmly, she accepted her ladyship's offer, and it was an indication of her agitation that she experienced no hint of amusement at her aunt's gasp of horror.

Chapter Three

Although Bea had intended to arrive to Lady Abercrombie's murder mystery dinner party early enough to acclimate herself to the unfamiliar surroundings, the duke's carriage turned into Grosvenor Square a full half hour late.

It was her own fault, of course.

Unaccustomed to the high grooming standards of the *haut ton*, she had allotted only thirty minutes to the preparation of her hair. In Portman Square, it took half that time to press her limp strands into half-hearted curls, and she expected her maid to provide the same cursory service.

Dolly, however, refused to allow her to rise from the dressing table a moment before every last ringlet was perfectly twirled.

It was an odd new experience for Bea in a fortnight of odd new experiences, being unable to convince her own maid to relinquish custody of her. As the Duchess of Kesgrave, she had dozens of servants at the ready to fulfill her every desire, and yet, when all she had wanted was permission to leave her own dressing room, she had been roundly rebuffed.

The poor girl had been hugely apologetic, yes, and deeply embarrassed by her own intransigence, but she remained firm in her determination to turn her mistress out in the highest style.

Obviously, Bea appreciated her efforts, for if she was to be inspected by a begrudging assortment of society's most illustrious members, then of course she wanted to look her best. The gleaming curls showed her to advantage as did the gorgeous rose sarcenet grown trimmed with silver satin.

Examining herself in the mirror, she felt an unexpected tinge of confidence and thought perhaps the evening would go well after all.

And then Kesgrave ruined it all by securing a glittering strand of priceless jewels around her neck. "The Matlock rubies," he explained softly, laying one kiss, then two and three, on her neck before standing back to admire his handiwork. "Perfect."

He spoke mildly, simply, as if the intricate band of oval-shaped gems surrounded by diamond clusters were not astonishingly beautiful, and it was a measure of her discomfort that she did not feel a familiar shiver of delight at the touch of his lips to her skin. Rather, she felt only panic at the thought of wearing something so outrageously expensive and her fingers itched to tear it from her throat, but obviously she could not indulge in behavior so excessively childish. Kesgrave's no-nonsense attitude toward the necklace made her keenly aware of how unextraordinary it actually was to a man of his wealth and position.

Objecting would have only called attention to her own inadequacies, and she was determined not to do that anymore, for if she herself was tired of it, then Kesgrave must be weary to the bone.

Furthermore, it served no purpose, because there was nothing he could do to alleviate her insecurities. They lived in a cold little box in the deepest heart of her, and she was the only one capable of rooting it out.

Rooting it out, Bea thought as Kesgrave helped her down from the carriage, or allowing the cold to consume her.

She was being utterly histrionic, she knew, and yet she could not quite free herself of the sense that some aspect of her entire future rested on her performance this evening. If she could just manage to charm everyone in the room, then her acceptance would be assured.

It was an unlikely ambition for even the most erudite young woman and seemingly impossible for one who possessed a history of timidity and incoherence.

As these thoughts served no purpose other than to unsettle her further, Bea ruthlessly pushed them aside. In some part of her, she was still a drab spinster, yes, but she was also the woman who had stared more than half a dozen murderers in the eye.

And she was counting her husband in that tally, for when she had raised her gaze in the darkened library in the Lake District to see the Duke of Kesgrave standing threateningly before her, she did not know yet that he was innocent.

In that moment, she had been fully prepared to meet her death.

It was in a similar frame of mind that she entered Lady Abercrombie's fantastic drawing room and observed the fashionable coterie assembled by the beautiful widow to either approve or reject her.

Greeting her warmly, the countess threaded her arm through Beatrice's and assured her she looked quite lovely. "And you are wearing the Matlock rubies. That is good. Nothing gives a woman more confidence than a string of exquisite gems."

Although Bea knew the opposite to be true, she made no comment and submitted anxiously to a series of introductions: Lord and Lady Bentham, Mr. and Mrs. Fawcett, Lord Bredbury and his niece, Miss Petworth.

In fact, the last guest was already known to Bea, and although she had found the Incomparable to be unbearably forward during their previous dealings, she was grateful now for the familiar face.

Nevertheless, she could not help but flinch when the chestnut-haired beauty with large gray eyes and rose-blossom cheeks claimed a deep and abiding friendship. "I cannot properly express my delight at being here to support you during your first public appearance as the Duchess of Kesgrave. It is such an honor, and although I know it is not at all the thing to take pleasure in another person's misfortune, I am so happy my uncle's betrothed was feeling too poorly to attend."

"My niece eagerly offered herself as substitute when Miss Hathaway came down with a head cold," Bredbury explained.

Lady Abercrombie remarked on the perfect dreadfulness of such a condition, and Bea felt some of her apprehension ease at the insipidness of the exchange.

Surely, she could spend a few hours discussing physical complaints and the weather without embarrassing herself.

Her calm was short-lived, however, for almost immediately after, Kesgrave was pulled away by Bentham. Before consenting to leave, the duke sent her a questioning look, as if to confirm she would be all right on her own, which obliged her to indicate with a smile that, yes, she would be fine.

But her arm trembled at her side with the desire to tug him back—to actually reach out her hand, grasp his wrist and yank him to her side.

She restrained the impulse, of course, and engaged in a benign conversation with Miss Petworth on the delights of the theater. A few minutes later, however, the final guest arrived, Lord Pudsey, and the young lady excused herself to speak with Lady Bentham.

As the host of a popular political salon she had attended with Nuneaton and his sister, his lordship was already known to Bea. They spoke briefly about their mutual acquaintance, whom Pudsey had seen at his most recent gathering.

"Mrs. Palmer was much displeased with my latest proposal," he said with a laugh, then proclaimed that that was the usual state of affairs. "She considers most of my positions to be wide of the mark."

Bea, who was familiar with some of his ideas, refrained from pointing out the accuracy of the other woman's assessment and merely smiled blandly as he launched into an explanation of his most recent legislation, an importation tax, for Bredbury's benefit.

She was rescued from the tedium by Flora, who giddily insisted that she come talk with her and Nuneaton.

Apologetically, Bea excused herself from the small group and accompanied her cousin to a red silk settee at the opposite end of the room. Although the Grosvenor Square residence was several times smaller than the pavilion at Brighton, Lady Abercrombie was determined to rival its excess and grandeur, creating a lush fantasia in the Oriental style with lotus-shaped chandeliers, gilded serpents coiling around the coved ceiling, a bamboo canopy and trompe l'oeil paper with dragons, dolphins, birds, and flowers.

Somewhere roaming the halls was Henry, the lion cub the countess had adopted in an extravagant bid for attention.

Everything she did, Bea thought, was designed to increase the *ton*'s interest in her. Upon first meeting her—in this very room whilst investigating Fazeley's stabbing—she had assumed the need was spurred by an overweening fear of being ignored or overlooked by a society that craved youth and novelty. Now, however, she understood that the other woman's acts of outrageousness were merely attempts to alleviate her own boredom.

Having ascended to the height of social success, Lady Abercrombie had discovered there was little to do at the peak but examine the view.

Hence the outlandishness of this evening's program.

Bea did not doubt for a moment the sincerity of Lady Abercrombie's intentions. Without question, she desired the wholehearted acceptance of her dearest friend's daughter. But it was the enormity of the challenge itself that truly interested her, for only an exceptionally skilled operator would succeed in dragging the unappealing new duchess up to the summit beside her.

"I have been consigned to the kitchens," Flora said cryptically as they sat down.

Although Bea had felt the weight of several curious stares as they crossed the floor, she held her shoulders straight as she contemplated her cousin. "A temporary arrangement only, I trust. I am sure Uncle Horace can purchase your freedom."

Flora giggled. "In the game, silly. Lady Abercrombie is quite churlish about my presence and tells me I have been given the role of a kitchen maid in her play. I won't pretend I am not disappointed, for I *was* hoping for a more illustrious character such as an empress. But servants are observant and capable of carrying large trays, so I shall take it as a compliment. It could have been worse, as her ladyship might have stuck me in the scullery."

Even with her nerves so tightly wound, Bea found it impossible not to smile at her cousin's understanding of the situation. "An empress? Whose murder did you think we would be investigating? Napoleon's?"

"Well, yes," Flora said with a matter-of-fact tilt of her head. "If you could rid the world of any single person, even in pretend, would you not choose the greatest scourge of our time, who has killed such a large number of our own countrymen? Who would you rather—Caligula?"

Amused, Bea examined her cousin, whose light blue dress beautifully complemented her hazel eyes and auburn hair. "What do you know about Caligula?"

"Not as much as you, I am sure," Flora admitted agreeably. "But I am aware he tried to make his horse a magistrate and I cannot approve. That might be a useful way to rule over a farmyard, but it is a terrible way to govern a country. Now, darling, I know you are worried about this party, but you must not be. Nuneaton and I have discussed the matter between us and have decided the only way forward is to present a united front. No matter which one of us discovers the evidence or figures out a clue, we will present it as your doing. Regardless of how the mystery actually unfolds, you shall be perceived as the heroine of the evening."

Flora spoke reassuringly, her tone gentle and benevolent as she placed a comforting hand on her cousin's shoulder, and Bea smothered the laugh that rose swiftly to her lips. In the week since her encounter with a murderous law clerk, Flora had adopted a sort of avuncular attitude toward her cousin. Styling herself as a learned elder with wisdom to impart, she seemed perpetually on the verge of donning spectacles, decanting a bottle of port and addressing Bea as "dear boy" or "old chap."

It was, she thought, utterly delightful.

Striving for a suitably somber reply, Bea thanked Flora for her consideration and assured her it was not necessary for her to identify the villain of Lady Abercrombie's mystery. "It is just a game."

Flora's manner altered at once as her heartening expression turned deeply serious and she spoke with earnest concern. "Oh, but it *is* necessary. We have been given an opportunity to solidify your reputation as a preternaturally gifted investigator and we must take *full* advantage of it. You are not at all what one hopes for in a duchess," she announced with brutal honesty, before rushing to assure her cousin that she did not say that to hurt her. "But there is no point in pretending otherwise. It is not merely that you are so old or so plain, although"—she broke off to examine Bea with almost quizzical confusion—"I must say that you are looking remarkably well tonight. That necklace is stunning. I must confess *entre nous* that my fingers are itching to caress it."

"Please resist," Bea said, "as I am already uncomfortable enough in it."

"Yes, my dear, precisely *that*," Flora said as if her cousin had made a salient point on an interesting topic. "Your manner is so forbidding. You scowl when you should smile and make no effort to ingratiate yourself. If only you *tried* to trill lightly while fluttering your lashes! Granted, it would look a little strange at first, but I am sure you would settle into it and it would soon become natural. And then the *ton* would embrace you eagerly. Even without these necessary skills, you have some appeal, for there is an air of originality about you, which few women possess. It is a firm basis for popularity, I am sure of it, and all you have to do to cement your position is perform brilliantly tonight in an area in which you famously excel. Everyone expects it. I trust you comprehend now the utter necessity of your identifying the culprit. This is our only chance, and we must not squander it."

Flora smiled amiably as if to soften the harshness of her words, but Bea, responding to their urgency, felt her trepidation increase tenfold. It did not help that her cousin echoed her own thoughts about the evening.

There was one significant difference, however, in their understanding and that was the mechanism by which Bea would earn approval. It would not be through the astute examination of evidence and clues, for the expertise required to figure out the identity of a murderer was not prized by the *beau monde*, at least not in a woman. No man wanted to tether himself to a rational creature who possessed the ability to outthink him. Schoolroom misses were tutored in the fine art of simpering—and make no mistake, Bea genuinely believed simpering well *was* an art form—not in the science of logic. The ability to look at an assortment of bottles and jars on a lady's crowded dressing table and figure out which item indicated a suspect's guilt did not help a young lady secure a husband.

No, society valued only those skills that helped it perpetuate itself, and to win over the company Bea would have to excel in a way that was deemed appropriate for a female. As that category was vexingly narrow, she would either have to flutter and trill, as her cousin had said, or display excessive rhetorical wit.

Everyone adored clever repartee.

Unquestionably, Bea possessed some gifts, for she had an agile mind and could see connections between seemingly unrelated objects. In addition, she had an excellent memory and could marshal facts and figures to her defense at a moment's notice.

If drawing room banter consisted of noting the increased yield in the wheat harvest from 1705 to 1765 (83.5 million quarters), then she would be well established before the soup course was ladled.

Alas, it entailed the consistent production of amusing bon mots interspersed with deceptively mild slights and the occasional epigram delivered with cynical good humor.

All of these things were beyond her ability.

She was clever, yes, but not the right sort of clever, which was why the spiteful Miss Brougham had been able to undermine her confidence so easily during her first season. A more adept young lady would have issued a cutting rejoinder in response or simply acted as though the insult did not rise to her attention. Bea, however, could manage neither. Instead, she folded in on herself in mortification, collapsing suddenly and ineffably like a house of cards.

If it had happened once, it could happen again.

And nothing was more likely to ensure that outcome than focusing on it, Bea reminded herself. "Very well, I accept your offer of help. Thank you."

"You have decided to be sensible. I am glad," Flora said with an approving nod as she spotted her fellow conspirator approaching their tête-à-tête with three glasses of wine. "And here is Nuneaton. Very good. We may begin."

The viscount, turned out with impeccable precision in a ruthlessly tailored coat in deep purple velvet and inconveniently high shirt points, greeted Bea with a warm smile as he distributed the drinks. Then he sat down in an armchair next to the settee. "Delightful as always, your grace. I trust you are enjoying your first foray into society as the Duchess of Kesgrave."

Before Bea could respond, Flora leaned forward in her seat and chastised his lordship for wasting time on pleasantries. "The game will begin at any moment, and we have yet to review the players," she said, turning to her cousin to explain that Nuneaton would now brief them on the dossiers he had compiled on their fellow guests.

"Brief us on the dossiers," Bea repeated in bemusement. "Are you Wellington now, planning the Siege of Burgos?"

"As I have never heard of that confrontation, no, I am not," Flora said. "But if you want to draw a comparison to a famous battle where there was much glory to be had, such as Waterloo, then I am happy to reconsider my answer. In the meantime, I do wish you would cease being frivolous, my dear, so that Nuneaton may share the information he has gathered."

Having been accused of frivolity infrequently in her life, Bea found it impossible to comply with her cousin's request and turned to the viscount with humor gleaming in her eyes. "I am humbled, my lord, that you would exert yourself so much on my behalf. I wonder how you came to be here tonight, for surely you are exhausted from the effort."

"I understand your alarm," he said calmly, "and would share it if what Miss Hyde-Clare said were true. However, she disserves me gravely by implying I have been industrious, and I would beg her not to repeat anything so repellent, for I have a reputation for idleness that I have worked hard to cultivate. The truth is, I compiled nothing. Rather, I have lived among these people for more than a decade and can tell you anything you would like to know about them without any effort at all. With whom shall we start? Pick one, your grace, and I will happily provide all the pertinent and impertinent facts."

While Bea surveyed the occupants of the room, Flora apologized to the viscount for overstating the level of his industriousness, which drew the immediate rebuke that she had just repeated the offense.

"I do not know why you continue to abuse me like this," he lamented, "for I have done everything you asked, even accompanying you on a drive through Hyde Park so that we may settle on a strategy for this evening."

Hanging her head in shame, Flora sighed heavily and owned herself at fault. He had been generosity itself, and she had repaid him poorly.

But kindness no more befit the image Nuneaton wished to project than diligence, and he was forced to issue yet another complaint.

Flora laughed, and Bea noted how thoroughly at ease her

cousin was in the presence of the viscount. Previously, Flora had been awkward and unsettled in his company, which Bea understood, for there was something off-puttingly fragile about his lordship's perfection.

Exhale too sharply and you might dislodge a hair from its place.

Bea smothered a smile and, examining the inhabitants of the room, decided to begin with the man who had carried Kesgrave off soon after they had arrived. The gentleman in question was engaged now in conversation with Pudsey, discussing a topic that seemed to animate them both. Poor Mr. Fawcett, who clearly sought to participate, stood at his shoulder trying with little success to insert himself.

Nuneaton winced at her choice but gamely replied, "John Codington, Earl of Bentham, founder of the Henley Sporting Club, which is exactly as it sounds—an organization devoted to the furtherance of the manly arts of hunting, driving and fishing. He is a strict adherent to all his club's dictates, including donning the drab coat with mother-of-pearl buttons and three tiers of pockets that is the group's required uniform. I trust I do not have to explain to you the problems of such a garment, for its adequacies speak readily for themselves."

Indeed, the former Miss Hyde-Clare needed no further explanation, for she was well familiar with the designation of *drab* and all it denoted.

"Membership is highly selective and capped at eighteen, so you can imagine how ardently his favor is curried," his lordship continued. "Unlike with the Four-in-Hand, it is not extended permanently. Members have to apply for their position every two years, and most do not make it. They are put through their paces, as if skill and proficiency are the deciding factors, but in the end, it comes down to Bentham's whim. Some days he likes the cut of your coat, and you are in.

Some days he finds your breeches a little too snug and you are out."

Examining Bentham from across the room, Bea noted his appealing face, with its aquiline nose offset by round cheeks, and waistcoat, which was vibrantly colored despite the demands of his sporting club. With a bright smile, he nodded at something Pudsey said, and as she watched his dark head tilt backward, she realized she had no idea if her husband was a member of such a club, or indeed any club.

If she were to enumerate the things she knew about him, the list would be mortifyingly brief, extending to only a dozen or so items. Half of them pertained either to herself—his inexplicable attraction, for example, to impudent scolds—or the condition of his tenants' roofs.

Unnerved by the discovery, Bea asked if Kesgrave was a member.

Nuneaton's dismissive scoff was reassuringly disdainful. "Truly, my dear, I do not know which is more implausible: your husband in drab or his racing to a posting house in order to prove his worthiness," he said with genuine amusement. "No, he has never shown the least bit of interest in Bentham's little club, which has endeared him to the earl. He harbors, I think, a faint disgust for the members of his own organization."

Bea was not at all surprised by this information, for it was always the fruit that was just out of reach that appeared to be the tastiest. "Obviously, I know Lord Pudsey, having attended his political salon in the company of yourself and your lovely sister."

"Yes, his attendance here was inevitable, given his position as a leader among the political set and relationship with Lady Abercrombie," he said.

"Relationship?" Bea asked.

"Yes, they are engaged in a dalliance," he said.

"I thought she was currently dallying with Mr. Cuthbert," Bea said, repeating information she had gleaned from her aunt. That conversation, however, had occurred several weeks ago, which was more than enough time for the countess to change romantic partners.

"And so she is," Nuneaton replied. "The countess is generous with her attention and manages to apportion her time so that she is able to dally with both men. But she is also a woman of the world and the consummate hostess, which is why Pudsey is here. His approval would go a good distance in earning you the esteem of the political elite, a dubious accomplishment, to be sure, but one worth pursuing. Cuthbert, on the other hand, would contribute nothing to the evening save a strong jawline. Undoubtedly, a strong jawline has its uses but none that are discernable for helping to establish an unusual duchess in society."

Having seen Mr. Cuthbert only in passing, Bea could not speak to the strength of his jaw, but she recalled a dark-haired gentleman three decades younger than Pudsey's fifty-five years. In dallying with both, the beautiful widow seemed to be satisfying a demand for youthful vigor as well as a need for aged wisdom.

By all accounts it was a sensible arrangement, and Bea was too pragmatic to disapprove. Nevertheless, the topic's intimate nature discomfited her and a warm blush suffused her cheeks.

Resolutely, she looked away from Pudsey toward the third member of the trio, who remained incapable of making the contribution he desired. "What do you know about Mr. Fawcett?"

"Ah, yes, Owen Fawcett," Nuneaton said. "A genial man of even temper who is among Prinny's inner set. He is terrible at cards, which explains much of his appeal for the regent, good with a blade and excellent at choosing horseflesh. He has a pair of prime goers that Petersham has been sighing over for months."

Observing the frustration on Fawcett's face as he attempted yet again to insert himself, Bea wondered if perhaps he was too genial for his own good. A more forward man would have shouldered his way into the conversation by now.

"I assume he has petitioned for membership of the Henley Sporting Club," Bea said.

"But the fees, your grace, the fees," Nuneaton replied with a hint of severity. "Perhaps if he were better at hazard or worse at horses, he could easily stand the expense. Alas, even the cost of the Henley hat—which is so rudimentary in its design, coachmen up and down the London Road can afford it without flinching—is a little too dear for his purse."

"Even without the financial constraint, there is still the matter of the great discord between the families," Flora said portentously.

Amused by her cousin's intensity, Bea repeated her words. "The great discord?"

"Lady Bentham and Mrs. Fawcett are sworn enemies," Flora said. "For years they have been plotting against each other, with one or the other coming out on top at various times. It is the most fascinating feud in all of England."

Although Nuneaton caviled at this description, insisting that their enmity, like most mutual grudges, was tedious to bystanders, he allowed that it did keep things interesting for those who laid wagers in the betting book at Brooks's. "Alvanley, for example, bet Goddard one hundred guineas to ten that Mrs. Fawcett would intercede on Miss Yates's behalf with the patronesses of Almack's."

"Because Lady Bentham had made sure Mrs. Yates was denied vouchers after her daughter had the misfortune to splash mud on her ladyship's slippers when disembarking from her carriage at the Haymarket last year," Flora explained. "It was quite cruel because Miss Yates *did* apologize at once and Lady Bentham *professed* to accept it. Of course she was welcome to take a pet, for I understand the silk on the slipper was *very* fine, but then she should not pretend that all was well only to spring an unpleasant surprise a full year later."

Knowing the importance of entrée to the assembly rooms to a young lady's success, Bea could not accuse her cousin of exaggeration. "Did Mrs. Fawcett succeed?"

"She did, yes," Flora replied, "by securing Lady Jersey's approval."

"How fortunate for Alvanley," Bea said, "and Miss Yates, of course."

Flora nodded emphatically, then added that the machinations ran both ways. "When Mr. Dibdin failed to be impressed with Mrs. Fawcett's daughter, she arranged for his expulsion from Whites. So Lady Bentham took up *his* cause and he now is the MP for Sudbury."

"And how many guineas did Alvanley make on that appointment?" Bea asked.

"Fifty, I believe," Nuneaton said.

"Then there is Prince Adriano," Flora said eagerly.

Despite her cousin's air of expectation, Bea did not know the name. "Prince Adriano?"

"He is the ruler of a minor Italian principality," his lordship explained.

"Formerly affianced to Lady Bentham's daughter," Flora said with excited delight, "and *currently* betrothed to Mrs. Fawcett's eldest."

Drawing the obvious conclusion, Bea asked how Mrs. Fawcett had arranged that favorable outcome.

"Fluorspar," the viscount said succinctly.

Flora's brow wrinkled in confusion, but Bea was familiar

with the mineral and recalled that some regions on the Continent were rich in it. Although she could not remember its exact application, she knew it served some purpose in the production of steel. "Mrs. Fawcett arranged lucrative partnerships or contracts with foundries in Sheffield for the sale of it?"

"Middlesbrough," he said, then added with an admiring smile, "but otherwise correct. Very good, your grace."

Delighted, Flora clapped her hand as if her cousin had just performed some impressive feat of daring or skill. "You see, darling, you have no reason to be alarmed. You will solve this murder handily and take your rightful place among the *ton*."

As Bea never doubted her ability to draw a logical conclusion based on a preponderance of evidence, she took little comfort in her cousin's assurances.

"That leaves Bredbury," she said, gesturing to the gentleman sporting an amethyst waistcoat and the Titus. "What can you tell me about him other than he is uncle to Miss Petworth?"

"Ah, yes, the divine Miss Petworth," Nuneaton said admiringly. "She is the embodiment of grace and elegance."

Flora, incapable of concealing neither her disgust of the Incomparable who had made her presentation to the court in the same month as she nor her envy, frowned at this statement. Then she snidely added that it was no surprise to find her at the same affair as Lord Pudsey after her behavior at Mrs. Reddington's rout three nights ago. "She is quite dogged in her pursuit of him, even though he appears not the least bit interested."

As Bea was not as apprised of town gossip as her cousin, she could not respond to this statement other than to point out that Miss Petworth had moved to the other side of the room as soon as Pudsey arrived. It was, she thought, an indication of the opposite desire.

Unpersuaded, Flora replied that the beauty was merely being coy in stalking her prey.

"She is here at the behest of her uncle, whose betrothed's illness precluded her attendance," Bea added, then paused a moment to allow Flora to imply that Miss Petworth had somehow arranged for the other woman to be sick. When she made no such claim, Bea asked Nuneaton to continue.

"Bredbury is a nonesuch," he said. "A former captain of the Coldstream Guards, he served with distinction on the Peninsula and sold out when his father and older brother died in a fire, leaving the estates and two siblings in his care. He is a skilled gambler, an expert swordsman and a bon vivant. He hosts a monthly dinner at his home in St. James, an intimate affair with never more than six guests, and it is the most coveted invitation in London."

"Oh, yes, I believe I know of him," Bea said thoughtfully as she examined his lordship, whose frame was short but lithe. "He had a duel recently, with swords, if I am remembering it correctly. It was over something remarkably trivial like a berry tart."

"Banana," Flora said.

Bea accepted the correction but noted that the type of fruit did not increase its significance. "Any tart is a poor reason to run a man through."

"But it was not just *any* tart," Flora rushed to explain. "Bananas are excessively difficult to cultivate, and only his family has managed to attain the ideal conditions to produce a steady supply. And the recipe itself is a family heirloom. His many-times-great-grandmother made it for William the Conqueror."

Bea was incapable of containing her amusement. "Nonsense. The first banana did not arrive in England until 1633. Are you sure it was not a berry tart? It would be an equally absurd pretext for calling a man out but would at least have the advantage of being factually possible if still utterly unlikely."

As Flora had read few books on the agricultural history of Europe, she was unable to address this claim specifically and instead observed that it was a moot point because Bredbury did not harm his opponent. "Ferryhill disgraced himself by actually slicing Bredbury's arm, but Bredbury's control of a rapier is so masterful he was able to overcome his opponent without leaving a mark."

Although Bea believed his lordship's opponent was correct to defend himself against a man whose erraticism was so acute it led him to issue challenges over minor and invented slights, she refrained from further comment. Flora clearly found Bredbury's integrity and caprice to be charming.

Nuneaton, whose opinion on the matter was neither sought nor given, felt compelled to address another indignity. "It hardly seems fair to me, Miss Hyde-Clare, that I am subjected to the charge of industriousness for simply observing the actions that happen around me and your cousin cites the precise year bananas came to our shores and you level no so such indictment against her. It seems as though there are two standards in play, and it is to my detriment."

It was, Bea thought, an outrageously flirtatious thing for the viscount to say, and she expected her cousin to color prettily and look away. Despite being out for more than a year, the other girl was not accustomed to the attention of peers. She was a Hyde-Clare, after all, and possessed the entrenched deference of her parents and grandparents.

The idea of a viscount flirting with her should mortify Flora.

And yet her gaze remained steady and her voice was even as she explained that Beatrice's industriousness was too widely known to elicit comment. "It would be like noting that the sky is blue, and then you would be repulsed with my banality."

Duly appalled by her understanding, Nuneaton insisted he would never bestir himself to rise to the level of repulsion, and Flora observed that he had already roused himself to disgust.

"Can repulsion be far behind?" she asked, her brow furrowed in a simulation of genuine concern.

Observing her cousin's exchange with the viscount, Bea realized the situation was more dire than she had imagined. Aunt Vera and Uncle Horace would be furious at her, yes, for exposing their daughter to mortal peril by holding fast to her lie about Mr. Theodore Davies. If her relatives had an inkling how close Flora had come to dying in a sordid little house in Tuttle Lane, they would have Bea drummed out of the family, duchess or not.

And yet the danger to life and limb was only the second-worst consequence of Bea's dishonesty.

Far more troubling was the profound bolster of confidence Flora's escapade appeared to have given her.

Bantering with a viscount!

Her aunt and uncle would never forgive her if they learned the truth.

It would come to naught, Bea knew, for Flora was quite smitten with the gentleman who had assisted her in her investigation into the fictitious law clerk's death. But even the merest hint of her daughter making a match with a viscount would be enough to send Aunt Vera into a dither, for the prospect of two titled in-laws was more than the poor woman could bear.

Mrs. Hyde-Clare had once thought to nudge her daughter in the general direction of a baron's heir at a country party, but since Bea's needlessly extravagant success with the duke her ambitions had undergone a dramatic reconsideration.

Now she felt a more modest arrangement for Flora was required in order to restore balance to the universe.

Mr. Holcroft did not quite align with her vision of a thoroughly ordinary suitor, for he possessed a lavish fortune and at least one disgraced family member, but Flora was not overly concerned with her family's preferences. After decades of listening to her mother's breathless chatter, she had developed the neat trick of allowing her parent to feel heeded while not actually hearing a word.

Nuneaton rousingly scoffed at the suggestion that his demeanor was anything but indolent just as their hostess called for everyone's attention.

"And now," she said with high drama, "the game begins!"

Chapter Four

❦

To Bea's horror, however, the game did not begin.

No, first Lady Abercrombie had to welcome her guests en masse to her murder mystery dinner party play, given expressly in honor of the new Duchess of Kesgrave.

Having ensured that everyone in the room turned to look at Bea, her ladyship continued. "We are delighted that you are here and humbled that you chose to make our little gathering your first outing as a duchess. You have my best wishes, your grace, and my utter devotion."

Knowing that a dignified nod was not a sufficient response, Bea pressed her lips together tightly as she stood up and raised her glass. The beat of her heart ticked upward as her gaze swept the room too quickly to land on any one face, not even the duke's. Struggling to appear insouciant, she forced a smile and thanked her hostess for devising such a unique evening. Then, her voice quavering lightly, she suggested a toast. "To Lady Abercrombie and to her endlessly inventive mind."

The room dutifully echoed her call, and Bea, sitting down, was petulantly annoyed to discover her hand was shaking.

If either Flora or the viscount noticed, neither was unkind enough to comment.

Her ladyship blushed prettily at the compliment, a skill that impressed Bea, who had no control over her own unbearable flushes, and announced that in a few minutes she would have the pleasure of introducing their victim to the company. "But first you must familiarize yourself with your prescribed roles. At this very moment, my footmen are distributing portfolios that detail your character's personal history and unique traits. You will be able to keep these files on hand to consult with whenever necessary, so there is no need to memorize the details."

As she spoke, a pair of liveried servants began to circulate around the room, handing out leather-bound folders about the size of a pamphlet. Eagerly, Miss Petworth accepted hers, and as Bea watched her open her portfolio, she was struck by a horrifying prospect: What if the young beauty was assigned a role of greater social standing than Flora's kitchen maid?

If? Bea thought in amusement. Of course Miss Petworth's role would be superior to her cousin's. The countess would never have risked alienating Lord Bredbury's affection by dispatching his betrothed to the scullery. Rather, she would have created a properly exalted part for Miss Hathaway to assume, such as a society matron of significant standing or a young lady launched into society with considerable fanfare.

The only thing truly in doubt was how Flora would respond to the provocation. An unseemly outburst struck Bea just as likely as a dainty foot strategically placed in the unsuspecting girl's path.

Both possibilities were equally embarrassing for everyone.

Determined to avoid a scene, Bea accepted her folder,

then immediately tossed it to the floor, making sure the sheets scattered across the rug.

"Oh, no," she said, turning to her cousin with her eyes opened wide with simulated distress. "I am so frightfully clumsy. Would you mind helping me collect my cards?"

"Of course, darling," Flora said soothingly as she placed her own unopened portfolio on the cushion next to her. Lowering herself daintily, she retrieved all three sheets and handed them to Beatrice, who tucked them carefully back into the folder. "I believe that's all."

But Beatrice, who had taken the cards from Flora's file the moment her head was turned, tossed that assortment onto the floor as well and shook her head. "Oh, dear, I see a few more. Goodness gracious, I have made such an awkward mess. I do not know how I accomplished it."

"Nerves, I expect," Flora said as she leaned forward again.

"Yes, that must be it," Bea replied, putting the portfolio she had been handed on the settee next to her cousin and graciously accepting the cards that had previously been given to Flora. "Thank you."

"I am happy to help," Flora said graciously. "Both Nuneaton and I are here for that precise reason, and of course Kesgrave will be of some assistance. With our support, you will win this game, impress all of London and rightly take your place among the leaders of society."

Naturally, her cousin's attempt to calm her nerves had precisely the opposite effect, for she would never dream of trying to impress all of London.

Convincing a narrow sliver not to resent everything about her would be more than enough.

Amused by the unlikeliness of even that modest goal, Bea opened her folder and read the first card, which contained several basic facts about her character: Ida Potts, palace kitchen maid, eighteen years old.

As Bea flipped to the next page, her cousin let out a happy squeal.

"She was teasing me," Flora explained with breathless excitement. "Lady Abercrombie. She was only teasing me about being a kitchen maid. Look! I'm a princess!"

Giddily, she held up a cream-colored card identifying her as Princess Catherine of Summerland. "I have crown jewels. Heaps of them. A whole royal treasury full of them. *And* I am beloved by the people. I am a kindly princess who rules with grace and love. I wonder who my prince is. Is it Nuneaton?"

Pleased with the success of her maneuver, Bea tipped her head to the left and read the viscount's portfolio from over his shoulder. "No, he is the high clerk of Seasonton."

"Perhaps I am a widow," Flora said thoughtfully. "Perhaps my dear prince died heroically in battle and I have been forced to govern alone, guided by only the memory of his royal wisdom and my own well-honed instincts."

"Perhaps," Bea said, her lips curving into a smile.

"What about you?" Flora asked.

"Alas, I am not your prince," Bea replied.

Flora shook her head. "No, I mean, which character do you play? Are you also a clerk? Or one of my ladies-in-waiting? Ooh, are you a princess from a rival kingdom? Maybe you killed my prince in an attempt to seize control of the kingdom. I'm warning you, villain, I will not let you get away with it! My royal army will fight to the last man!"

Beatrice laughed, delighted by her cousin's absurdity, and did not flinch when the other woman took the portfolio from her grasp to read the description.

Flora gasped in horror. "You're a kitchen maid."

"A royal kitchen maid," Bea corrected.

"No, no, this cannot be right," Flora said, her brows drawn in confusion. "You are the guest of honor, and the countess adores you because you remind her of your mother.

She would never treat you so shabbily. Clearly, something has gone awry."

"I expect one of the footmen mixed up the cards," Bea said reasonably.

But Flora would not be fobbed off with a facile explanation and shook her head stridently, for she comprehended at once what had actually happened. Bea was not at all surprised by her cousin's acuity. The maneuver with the cards had not been the most subtle of ploys, and despite Flora's frothiness, she was not a bit of foam.

As disappointment washed over her features, Flora said with firm resolve that she could not allow the exchange to stand. "It is not at all the thing for you to debase yourself before the elite of the *ton,* especially at an event designed to—"

Abruptly, however, she halted her speech and her expression lightened. "Actually, I *can* allow the exchange to stand, for nothing could improve your standing with the elite of the *ton* better than lowering it. Think about it, Bea. Their leading complaint with your success is how high you have risen. From nothing spinster to duchess—it is a rather dizzying ascent and one could understand why they're so surly, for it goes against every rule of nature. You are an aberration."

"Yes, well, every young miss fresh from the schoolroom dreams of standing out," Bea observed humorously.

"If you compound your good fortune by assuming the role of princess in Lady Abercrombie's play, you would only be implying that you feel you deserve an even *higher* rank," Flora continued as if her cousin had not spoken. "But just think about the message it would convey if you played the part of a menial kitchen maid with good-natured humor. It would demonstrate that you are an excellent sport who does not hold herself too high. The Duchess of Kesgrave does not stand on her consequence, no, she does not!

It is perfect, Bea, absolutely perfect—which you already know because you are the clever one who thought to switch our portfolios. Obviously, I have no cause to worry about your performance tonight. You are, as always, as sharp as a tack."

Perceiving no value in revealing her true motivation, Bea accepted the compliment with calm equanimity. Nevertheless, she felt more unsettled than ever by Flora's confidence.

A moment later, her cousin added, "Oh, dear, Princess Catherine sounds a tiny bit tyrannical. It appears she sent a destitute father to the dungeons for stealing a loaf of bread to feed his starving children. It goes without saying, I trust, that thievery should not be condoned, for then dressmakers would have to cease selling their garments for lack of funds to buy new material and then I would never get a lovely red gown from Madame Bélanger. But the punishment must fit the crime and I do want to be beloved by my people, so I would most likely consign him to the stocks for a few days. And of course I would have one of my servants send food to his home. Not bread because that would be as if to reward him. Perhaps gruel since it has all the sustenance of porridge but none of the pleasing texture."

As Flora turned her attention to evaluating the fundamental problems in Summerland that might cause her people to suffer unspeakable poverty, Bea reviewed the second card in her portfolio. It provided salient facts about Ida Potts's history: She was deposited on the steps of a church as an infant, raised in an orphanage and sent to work in the palace kitchens at age eleven. The third sheet outlined her movements at the time of the murder, reporting that she claimed to have been trimming fat off an endless succession of grouse when the event took place.

That was it—the sum total of information Lady Abercrombie provided about Ida Potts.

Clearly, the countess had not intended for Flora to play a significant role in her staged investigation.

Naturally, her cousin would have been quite miffed to find herself relegated to the background, but Bea was delighted with the assignment. Indeed, the only thing that would have pleased her more was being part of the literal background, such as a statue or a tree.

But playing a minor character would suit her nicely, for it would allow her to remain above the fray and examine the evidence coolly.

The prospect of examining the countess's manufactured clues made Beatrice smile, for she had little faith that the mystery itself would follow a logical course. Her ladyship was charming, and she had shown herself to be remarkably kind to Bea long before it became apparent that a duchy was in her future. But she was not the most rational creature, yielding often to impulse and frequently following the course that felt right to her. Any narrative she created would reflect those traits, defying the obvious and twisting capriciously.

It would be more fruitful, Bea thought, to solve Lady Abercrombie herself rather than the mystery. Her prejudices and assumptions would be far easier to follow than her logic.

Ida Potts was the perfect example of that.

Her ladyship had not wanted to invite Flora to her party, and as a consequence, she assigned her an inconsequential and subservient role. Making her cousin the killer would draw too much attention to a guest she would rather pretend was not present.

Although few would relish being the murderer, the countess would consider it an honor she bestowed on a worthy subject.

But not too worthy a subject, she thought.

For example, Bea was confident Lady Abercrombie would not make her the culprit because the purpose of the event was to endear her to her fellow guests. Casting her as a literal villain would undermine that goal.

Additionally, the new duchess was supposed to impress everyone with her well-honed deductive skills, which would be more difficult to do if she was obliged to identify herself.

No, her ladyship would not have made Bea the killer.

Perhaps Kesgrave?

Thoughtfully, she looked across the room to where he sat next to Mrs. Fawcett, who was smiling amiably at something he said.

It was a possibility, yes, for Lady Abercrombie would consider it very dashing to have a murderous duke. His crime, of course, would be done in the service of a greater good—rescuing a widow in distress, for example, or avenging a wronged pensioner. Easily, she would stand the plot on its head, turning the villain into the hero and the hero into a heartless crook who stole mementos from kindly old ladies.

As much as that scenario would appeal to her ladyship's sense of drama and sentiment, Bea quickly spotted the problem in having a newly married woman identify her husband as the culprit. It was not that such an arrangement would set them at uncomfortable odds to each other at an affair designed to showcase how well they were suited; it was rather that the event would descend into a two-person play. The surest way to bore her guests was to render them irrelevant to the action.

Lady Abercrombie was far too accomplished a hostess to make an inexperienced misstep like that.

Very well, then, Bea thought, whom to consider next?

Nuneaton was a viable prospect, for he was respected by the *ton* and favored by the countess. His goodwill, however, had already been secured so there was no purpose in courting it by bestowing the honor.

Indeed, that was central to the question, was it not?

Her ladyship would only bestow the honor to someone who would be flattered by the distinction.

By that token, Bea decided Miss Hathaway—via Miss Petworth—was out of contention. She was a newly engaged young woman who was probably still adjusting to her change in status. The prospect of being the center of attention at an event to which she was invited only as an appendage of her betrothed was no doubt horrifying to her. Bredbury was the more logical choice, for he was, by Nuneaton's account, an amiable gentleman with a good sense of humor.

Ah, but would not Lord Bentham make even more sense? At once arrogant and insecure, he seemed like the sort of gentleman who would consider any honor his due, and if being the perpetrator at a murder mystery party was the pinnacle of the event, then he would want to perch there.

Yes, Bea thought, but so too would his wife.

And that would make for an awkward carriage ride home, and an awkward carriage ride home would ensure that the evening was remembered with churlish dissatisfaction.

By the same token, the murderer could not possibly be Mrs. Fawcett, for any favor conferred on her would be deeply resented by Lady Bentham, once again undermining the evening's success.

Similarly, Lord Pudsey was out of consideration. It would never do for a hostess to assign the best part to her own lover.

Subsequently, that left Mr. Fawcett.

"Good people of Summerland, Wintersburg, and Seasonton," Lady Abercrombie said from the front of the room, where she towered over a petite woman a good many years her senior. "I welcome you to the international summit to finalize the details of the Treaty of Seasonton to end the decade-long war between Summerland and Wintersburg. Furthering Summerland's interests we have its prince and princess"—she gestured to Kesgrave and in the general direction of Bea—"as well as its ambassador Lord Fairweather and his assistant, Miss Fairweather, played graciously by Lord Bredbury and his niece Miss Petworth."

A smattering of applause accompanied these introductions, and the countess paused momentarily to allow it to subside. "Here to represent Wintersburg in lieu of its monarch, who is still a small boy, are Lord and Lady Sunshine, portrayed by Lord and Lady Bentham. Assisting them in their pursuit of peace is Mr. Moonstone, a special emissary accompanied by his wife, Mrs. Moonstone, brought to life by Mr. and Mrs. Fawcett. Finally, coordinating the peace talks on behalf of the great kingdom of Seasonton is high clerk Lord Concisely and his assistant Lord Rambling, played by Nuneaton and Pudsey, respectively."

Another polite ovation followed this explanation, and Bea, noting that Ida Potts was left out of the introductions, was more pleased than ever that she managed to switch roles with her cousin.

"Now that you know who you are," Lady Abercrombie continued, "I would like you to meet your victim for the evening. She is Lady Rambling, wife to Lord Rambling, special attaché to Lord Concisely of Seasonton. Those of you who think Lady Rambling looks vaguely familiar, I am delighted to assure you that you are not wrong. Lydia Simon, one of the great actresses of our age, has kindly consented to play the part of Lady Rambling. Mrs. Simon, do curtsey now in expectation of a wonderful performance."

As the Hyde-Clares rarely attended the theater, neither Bea nor Flora was familiar with Mrs. Simon's work, but Nuneaton said quietly, "Brava," and several guests applauded lightly.

Lady Abercrombie nodded in approval as the actress sat down in an overstuffed armchair beneath the bamboo canopy. "We are indeed very fortunate to be graced by her presence. Now here is how the game is to be played. It will proceed in three acts. In act one, which will begin shortly, you will each have the opportunity to ask Lady Rambling two questions about her life and death. That limit will be strictly adhered to, so I advise you to think carefully about what you would like to know and listen carefully to the queries posed by your fellow suspects. It would be a shame, would it not, to ask her to repeat information already provided."

"Are follow-up questions permitted?" Bentham asked.

"If the examiner has a second question remaining, yes, of course," the countess replied. "If he does not, he must hope that one of the succeeding interlocutors asks it. Act two of the game will convene over dinner, where you will converse freely with each other to discover information about your fellow suspects, which you will use to try to figure out who the murderer is. During this portion, you are welcome to ask as many questions as you like. Answers, however, must adhere to the facts provided in your portfolio. But to the facts only. If there is no information that directly relates to the question, then you may deceive and mislead to your heart's desire."

"Does the killer know who he is?" Mrs. Fawcett asked. "Or is he in the dark like the rest of the players?"

"The latter," Lady Abercrombie said, then added with pointed emphasis, "*They* do not know they are the guilty."

Several heads nodded thoughtfully.

"For act three you will adjourn to separate rooms to make your determinations in private. You will write down whom you think is the murderer, how they did it and why. Then we will reassemble here, in the drawing room, and one at a time level our accusations and provide the evidence to support them. I promise you, everything pertinent to the discovery of the murderer is contained in your portfolios. The question is, will you be able to discover it?"

Judging by the almost intolerable air of satisfaction her ladyship possessed, Bea could only conclude that the answer was no. Enamored with the challenge of creating the perfect murder, the countess had concocted a puzzle so twisty and arcane none of her guests would be able to decipher the clues and arrive at the truth.

"Now, if everyone is ready"—the countess's gaze swept the room, looking for dissenters, of which there were none—"let us begin. Princess Catherine, please do the honors and ask the first question."

Lady Abercrombie was looking directly at Beatrice as she spoke, and her brow furrowed with confusion when Flora rose to her feet. Disconcerted, she opened her mouth to protest or clarify, then promptly closed it to glare censoriously at the pair of cousins.

"Good evening, my lady," Flora said hesitantly, her bearing more awkward than regal as all eyes in the room turned to look at her, even the footmen, who were standing rigidly near the far wall. "Thank you for calling on me *and* for arranging such an interesting diversion. I am delighted to be here and am deeply gratified by the privilege you have bestowed on me. Thank you."

The poor girl, Bea thought with genuine sympathy as her cousin struggled to order her thoughts amid the sudden onslaught of attention. If Flora had realized that being the Princess of Summerland would put her immediately on the spot, she might have been a little less eager to assume the role.

"And you as well, Mrs. Simon," Flora continued, directing her words to the actress. "Thank you for being here, too. I trust you are well."

It was a statement, yes, but her voice lilted just a little bit upward at the end, nudging it slightly toward an interrogative, which she realized almost immediately. Breathlessly, she sought to fix her mistake by saying, "No, no, I did not mean to ask that, Mrs. Simon. I hope I can begin again."

But in making her clarification, Flora succumbed to the same mistake—that minor modulation in the wrong direction —and the declaration bore a faint resemblance to a question.

Bright red suffused her cheeks as she struggled for coherence. "I did not...that should not...I was not asking for permission...that is, I did not mean..." she said, stammering painfully.

Neither of these remarks counted as a question, and Bea felt certain that nobody in the room would categorize them as such. Clearly, they had been directed at the actress, not her character, and furthermore, denying Flora her two questions would serve to penalize all of them, for theirs was a collective project, at least during phase one of the game.

Flora, however, was too flustered to realize that yet, and Lady Abercrombie was enjoying her discomfort too much to explain it.

Resolutely, Bea rose to her feet and announced that she had a question.

"Yes, I thought you might," the countess murmured approvingly. "Ladies and gentlemen, the *other* Princess of Summerland, Princess Katerina."

That her ladyship appeared to have an endless supply of royal family members on hand amused Bea, and she was tempted to go along with the hastily devised substitution just to see how quickly the other woman could produce a portfolio of biographical facts. She resisted, however, because Flora's observation was correct—the Duchess of Kesgrave did not stand on her consequence—and playing an inconsequential character would allow her to focus on the mystery itself, thereby helping her fulfill the true purpose of the game: impressing her fellow guests.

Indeed, she already felt more relaxed knowing she would not have to endure interrogations about her character.

Surely, that alone increased her chances of succeeding.

Plus, she was fairly certain she already knew who the murderer was.

For the first time since Lady Abercrombie coerced her into agreeing to attend her murder mystery dinner play, Bea felt almost confident that the evening would not end in dismal failure.

"Actually, no," Bea said, blinking innocently at the countess. "I am Ida Potts. I work in the palace kitchens."

Lady Abercrombie shook her head. "I'm sure that cannot be correct. A kitchen maid would not have had access to Lady Rambling to cause her harm. You are Princess Katerina, sister to Princess Catherine."

Flora, recovering some of her equanimity in time to hear this comment, respectfully disagreed. "Princess Catherine is an only child. It says that right here." Then the color rose in her face again, although not as intensely red as previously. "On, no, did I just reveal information that was supposed to be coaxed from me during the conversational portion of the game?"

"Yes, but it is only a small detail, I'm sure," her ladyship said soothingly, determined now to smooth over her own ruffled feathers, "and a welcome reminder, for it had completely slipped my mind. How thoughtful of you to refresh my memory. Now, your grace, I believe you had a question for Lady Rambling? Do ask it so that we may proceed with our game."

Bea began in a manner similar to her cousin, bidding the actress good evening and wishing her well. Then she asked the victim the first thing she asked every victim: How did you die?

Mrs. Simon, whose matronly figure was not shown to advantage in the jonquil dress she wore, raised her head as if startled by the query, then laughed self-consciously, clearly in character now. "Goodness gracious, yes, yes, of course you would ask me that. I should have anticipated it and yet somehow I am surprised you want to know. Oh, it was an elegant death. So lovely and clean, which is a relief, for one is loath to leave an ugly corpse, such inconsiderate behavior. But my death was gracious. Even so, I cannot bear to think about it. It happened here," she said, shifting slightly to retrieve an embroidery sampler from a basket at her feet. She began to stitch. "Right here while I was working on this lovely pattern of a toad from my family's heraldic shield. Someone snatched the scissors from my embroidery basket and punctured some artery, but I cannot recall its name— warta, orta, porta. It is something silly like that."

Although Bea would have preferred for Lady Rambling to plainly state that she had been stabbed in the heart, she recognized the artistry in Lady Abercrombie's approach. Having the victim work her way around to the information made it more like a play and loosely mimicked the frustration of trying to understand what a dead body was telling you.

"Thank you, Lady Rambling," Bea said because she could not bring herself to treat a living person entirely like a dead one. "Where is 'here' precisely?"

Lady Rambling fluttered her lashes as she examined her surroundings, her fingers continuing to ply the needle grace-fully as she explained that she was in the state apartment in the Summerland palace. "In the sitting room, most specifi-cally, which is very, very grand," she added, before launching into a detailed description of its interior, lingering with an almost reverential awe over the quality of the silk curtains and the plastered ceilings and gold-edged vanity. It was only when she began to expound giddily over the fine veins of the marble floor that Bea realized that Lady Rambling was in fact a caricature of Mrs. Hyde-Clare.

Well, Bea conceded, not truly a caricature, for much of the behavior portrayed by the accomplished actress aligned with Aunt Vera's actual conduct. If her relative ever did receive an invitation to Windsor Castle, it was very likely she would spend the whole visit marveling over the quality of the furnishings.

Only two weeks before she had gasped in wonder at the fine marble in the Dowager Duchess of Kesgrave's Clarges Street home.

As accurate as the depiction was, however, Bea thought it was in rather poor taste for Lady Abercrombie to mock Mrs. Hyde-Clare so mercilessly.

Without question, her aunt had done much to earn the countess's disgust, starting with her treatment of Bea's mother when she was alive and continuing with her treatment of Bea after her mother was dead. Aunt Vera had acted in response to egregiously inaccurate information about Clara Hyde-Clare and her husband, Richard, but her ladyship hardly considered that to be a mitigating factor. If anything, she found it even more infuriating that Vera could have believed such hideous lies in the first place.

Aunt Vera knew the truth now and was trying to repent for two decades' worth of mistreatment, but Lady Abercrombie refused to be mollified.

Bea could not entirely blame her.

Although she was determined to forge a new path with her family, Aunt Vera made it difficult, as old habits were ingrained and she seemed incapable of treating Bea with dignity.

Nevertheless, the ridicule, even in absentia, was cruel, and as Mrs. Hyde-Clare was not there to bear the brunt, the only one it hurt was her niece, who felt her cheeks grow uncomfortably warm as Lady Rambling prattled poetically about the even stitching on the drapery.

Glancing at Flora, Bea could not tell if her cousin also recognized the impersonation, for her face held no expression at all, but Kesgrave, several feet across the room, obviously did because he interrupted Lady Rambling's scripted rhapsodizing to ask when she was killed.

The answer was simple—on Good Friday—but in true Aunt Vera fashion Lady Rambling rushed to explain that she herself did not consider it good because it was literally the worst day of her life.

"Which is not to say that I think the whole day is ruined for everyone," she added anxiously. "I would never presume to overturn almost two thousand years of Christian theology with my own insignificant little murder."

Mrs. Simon captured the tenor of Aunt Vera's speech so perfectly, Bea could only conclude she had somehow engaged in extensive conversation with her.

For his second question, Kesgrave sought to discover when on Good Friday Lady Rambling met her end.

A dissertation on the extravagant breakfast options at the palace followed.

The victim was informative, Bea had to concede, and as someone who had investigated several murders, she realized it was impossible to know which details were important and which details were irritating distractions.

In her experience, it was not until the end that the difference became apparent.

When Lady Rambling finished gushing over the delightful hint of nutmeg in the plum cake, Bentham insisted on questioning her next. He stepped forward, his hands clasped behind his back, and asked her to state her age and the country from which she hailed.

"And be brief about it," he ordered. "There's no need to blather on."

At his exhortation, made while towering over her, Lady Rambling jumped anxiously and stuck herself with her embroidery needle. "Yes, yes, of course, I will be brief about it. I value concision highly. Many people I know do not and simply assume that everyone else has as much time as they do to linger in leisurely conversation, but I understand what it is like to be busy, for Rambling is always running off to attend one important meeting or another. He is such a distinguished man, so vital to Lord Concisely, who could not function without his support. The world can be such a busy place and people who do not respect that can be such a bother. Yes, such a bother. But I am determined not to be that way. No, I have the utmost respect for the time of others."

Bentham growled irritably and bared his teeth.

Unmoved by the display, Lady Rambling finished her ode to brevity by describing several noteworthy geographic features of the Summerland's southern border, which separated it from her own country, Seasonton.

Finally, she said that she was sixty years old.

After Bentham retreated, his wife leaned forward in her seat to pose her two queries, followed by the Fawcetts, then Miss Petworth, Flora, Nuneaton, and Bredbury. Pudsey went last, and rather than discover more of Lady Rambling's personal details, he asked about Seasonton's political system.

Bentham, listening to the actress employ as many words as possible to say the country was a constitutional monarchy like England, muttered that if Pudsey used his second question as stupidly as his first, he would run him through with an embroidery needle himself.

Hearing him, Pudsey good-naturedly offered a correction.

"You mean you would run me through with embroidery *scissors*. I do not believe the needle would do excessive damage save in the hands of an expert swordsman like Bredbury."

Bredbury accepted the tribute with a dignified nod as Bentham scowled ferociously. Judging that her guests' patience was at an end with Mrs. Simon's true-to-life portrayal, Lady Abercrombie rose to her feet to applaud the actress.

"Thank you, Mrs. Simon, for executing the first act of our play so wonderfully," she said, clapping lightly. "I cannot think of a single aspect of your performance to criticize. You were a delight."

A consummate professional, Mrs. Simon accepted this praise modestly and assured her patron that it was the part itself that was great, not she.

Unable to refute the simple truth of this statement, the countess dipped her head in gracious acceptance and allowed the butler to escort the actress from the room.

"And now, my dear suspects," Lady Abercrombie said with relish, "we commence act two!"

Chapter Five

lthough their hostess told the company that they were welcome to sit wherever they wanted, she refused to allow Bea to take the seat next to Kesgrave. Similarly, she insisted on separating her from Flora and Nuneaton.

"No, no, your majesty," her ladyship said, slipping smoothly between Bea and the chair. "That is not appropriate for someone of your stature. Miss Petworth, why don't you sit here?"

But Miss Petworth, on the other side of the table, announced that she was quite satisfied with her spot between Pudsey and Nuneaton.

Hearing this, Flora fluttered her eyes meaningfully at Bea, who ignored the display as she reminded Lady Abercrombie that she was not a princess but a kitchen maid. Peevishly, she was told that the seat was then doubly wrong, as servants belonged at the other side of the table, near the sideboard.

Consequently, Bea found herself settled between Bredbury and Bentham, who was still nettled by a scuffle he had had with Fawcett en route to the dining room. Desiring the opportunity he had been unable to attain prior to their inter-view with Lady Rambling, a disgruntled Fawcett had grabbed Lord Bentham by the wrist and restrained him as the others departed the room, leading to the tussle.

It had been a shocking act of impertinence, causing Lady Bentham to gasp at the rough treatment of her husband, and Bea, embarrassed for all of them, quickly turned away. She had no idea what words were exchanged between them, but Fawcett had left the encounter in better spirits than Bentham.

Bea, making an attempt to draw the earl out of his sulks, noted that the weather in Summerton was unseasonably cold. It was not, she knew, the cleverest of observations but she thought it was an adequate opening salvo for the game. Bentham, however, looked at her as though she were slightly addled and pointed out that it was only April. Then he turned to his left and addressed a comment to Mrs. Fawcett.

Bredbury was more solicitous of her well-being and asked a series of benign if uninteresting questions about her evening so far, making no attempt to engage with her character.

Kesgrave sat opposite her—a circumstance, she realized, that had not occurred since her fateful stay in the Lake District. Now, like then, she could look across the table and see his handsome features arranged in a faint sneer. On this occasion, the source of his displeasure was Lady Bentham, who, engaging perhaps a little too enthusiastically in the game, was treating him as though he were actually the prince of a large European territory. Intrepidly, he tried to abide by the rules of play by asking her questions about her character. In place of coherent answers, she complimented him on the benevolence of his rule and the wisdom of his policies.

Bea, amused by his predicament, caught his eye during the soup course, angled a dinner roll in his interlocutor's general direction, and raised her brow as if seeking his permission to fling the small loaf across the table. Kesgrave laughed heartily in response, a sound so startling to everyone at the table that Miss Petworth actually spilled her soup, dousing Pudsey's waistcoat.

Mortified, her lovely ivory cheeks besmirched suddenly by red blotches, she lurched toward him, serviette in her grasp to mop up the liquid. "I'm sorry. I lowered my hand so forcefully and it toppled over the bowl and now this happened. I'm so very sorry, my lord."

All eyes in the room shifted to see how he would respond, except Flora, who fluttered her lashes pointedly at her cousin again.

Although Bea could easily empathize with Flora's feelings of resentment toward the Incomparable, she could not bring herself to believe any young woman would spill a bowl of pea soup as a romantic gesture. It was just a unfortunate accident, and, watching the girl struggle to regain her composure, Bea was absurdly relieved it was Miss Petworth and not herself.

Pudsey, an experienced politician, smoothed the incident over easily, assuring the embarrassed Incomparable that it was naught but a minor inconvenience and allowing the servants to dry the table.

"You see," he said as he gently moved his spoon through the soup, "no harm done."

Her gaze fixed determinedly on her own bowl, Miss Petworth murmured, "I am relieved, my lord."

A brief moment of silence followed this statement before Lady Bentham resumed her fawning compliments of Kesgrave's rule. Mrs. Fawcett, meanwhile, succeeded where Beatrice had failed, effectively easing Bentham out of his sullen mood and into the game. Zealously, he questioned her on her movements on the morning of the murder, pounding his fist on the table when she claimed not to recall where she was while Lady Rambling was in the drawing room being stabbed.

"You are a liar and a fraud, Mrs. Moonstone," he snarled.

Mrs. Fawcett fluttered her lashes and confessed that was true. "In fact, I am the lost Queen of Wintersburg and I have been hiding in the wilds of Summerland to foil a plot on my life. You, one of my loyal subjects, have figured out the truth and are now obligated to protect me with your life. If you fail to keep me safe, I will have you thrown into the dungeon."

Lady Abercrombie, hearing this bold pronouncement, explained that the queen had been killed two years before in a tragic hunting accident. It said so in several portfolios.

"That was a ruse to thwart my would-be assassins," Mrs. Fawcett replied.

"Impossible, for I identified the body myself," her ladyship countered, thrusting herself into the action.

"My maid Carmen, who bore a striking resemblance to me, died heroically in my stead," Mrs. Fawcett said with a mournful pout.

"Yes, Carmen, I know her well," the countess replied, refusing to be outdone. "She lives still. Unable to bear the shame of having failed her mistress, she took holy orders and buried herself in a convent along the northern edge of Wintersburg."

But Mrs. Fawcett would not be so easily maneuvered. "That is her twin sister, Carla."

Bentham, clearly feeling left out of the exchange, affirmed this seemingly outlandish claim by announcing he had overseen the swap himself. "I was determined to save the life of the queen because I am the Archcardinal of Wintersburg and consider all life sacred."

"Except Carmen's," Mrs. Fawcett amended. "But she was a necessary sacrifice. We honor her every year with a celebratory feast at the castle. All my ladies-in-waiting wear black ribbons in their hair. It is very charming."

Whatever surliness Lady Abercrombie felt at their recasting of their parts, she hid behind a serene smile as she congratulated the pair on figuring out their secret identities. "You are so both so clever."

As delighted at the countess appeared, Bea could feel her displeasure across the width of the table. It was not as easy to gain the compliance of one's guests as it was a hired thespian's.

Bea was, to be sure, fully sympathetic to the countess's plight. She could only imagine how frustrating it was to conceive an elaborate mystery play and have the actors undo all your fine work by rewriting their roles. All the same, she could not quite smother her amusement, for open rebellion seemed to be just what her ladyship deserved for arranging the event directly against the wishes of its guest of honor.

Lady Bentham, learning of Mrs. Fawcett's elevation, proclaimed herself Empress of Autumnia, a kingdom neighboring Summerland to the south. Flora gasped at her audacity —either in admiration or envy—and darted another meaningful look at her cousin. Kesgrave, seizing the opportunity, announced himself unworthy of her imperial attention and promptly turned to his left to discuss less august matters with Lady Abercrombie, whose smile remained firmly in place, though its edges had started to fray. At the abrupt dismissal, a petulant expression swept across Lady Bentham's face and for one humming moment Bea thought she would order the duke to attend to her. But Bredbury, also entertained by the antics, announced that he too desired his own country but all the good seasons had been taken.

"I cannot be the King of Spring," he said.

Nuneaton agreed the title undermined his dignity and proposed Prime Minister of Springville as a reasonable alternative. Pudsey, finding the suggestion most excellent, claimed the position for himself. "I trust you understand, Bredbury, that I have no choice. Taking advantage of a rival's momentary disconcertion is the defining feature of statesmanship."

Bredbury graciously allowed the usurpation and asked if anyone would object if he styled himself as an archpope of an as-yet-to-be-discovered religion.

Naturally, Bentham did, for he had made himself an archcardinal and had not thought to look higher, toward some nonexistent realm wherein he could create his own exalted position.

While Bredbury sought to outline the general parameters of his fictional new faith, which bore a striking resemblance to modern-day Catholicism with a few minor tweaks, including the replacement of the communion wafer with a banana tart, servants cleared the assortment of plates from the table. Turbot with lobster and Dutch sauce made way for plover eggs in aspic jelly, and lamb cutlets were exchanged for mayonnaise of fowl. The service was smooth, Bea noted, if a little uneven, as a few of the footmen who had originally tended to the table had retired from the room to be replaced by staff who were not as deft in their duties. Mr. Fawcett's request for the platter of sardines was aired twice before it was fulfilled.

Bea, whose contribution was largely absent from the conversation, as Ida Potts had no startling revelations to make about her true origins because she was exactly as she appeared, imagined some interesting drama playing out in the kitchens that required the footmen's attention. Regardless, the dishes were exquisite, and she enjoyed every aspect of the meal, the food as much as the posturing. It helped, certainly, that her hostess was too busy trying to keep her guests in line to try to draw Bea out.

When dinner was over, each of them was escorted to a

private room to evaluate the evidence they had gathered. They had fifteen minutes to make their determinations.

Bea, who was led to a cheerful study with yellow paper on the walls, remained firm in her conviction of Mr. Fawcett's guilt, although she had no clue why he would want the fictional Lady Rambling dead. Nothing she had heard during the second act had provided a motive, which was not at all surprising given how wildly the conversation veered from its intended purpose.

The one time she had tried to engage Fawcett on behalf of his character, he reminded her with patient condescension that he had only *pretended* to be the special emissary from Wintersburg to hide his true identity as its ruler—he, too, of course, faked his death in a scheme more elaborate than his wife's—and as such knew nothing of that gentleman's movements. He advised her to apply to the real Mr. Moonstone for information.

Mrs. Fawcett, applauding the regalness of her husband's reply, reminded Bea to address the King of Wintersburg as "your majesty."

"Yes, my liege," Bea had said softly, amused by how thoroughly the pair of them inhabited their characters—as if to the theater born.

Knowing the other players were in similar straits, she assumed that several would implicate Nuneaton's Lord Concisely because Lady Rambling accused him of stealing several thousand pounds in jewelry from her. Or perhaps some would point a finger at Lady Sunshine, played by Lady Bentham, who lured the victim's husband away from his happy marriage. Whether it was possible for either of the suspects to have actually performed the deed was unknown to Bea and, she suspected, her fellow guests as well.

Although little progress was made in discovering the villain of the piece, the players had had a merry time establishing their rule and overthrowing their neighbors. In that respect, Lady Abercrombie's murder mystery dinner party play was a resounding success, for several of her guests professed to being unable to recall a more diverting evening.

Alas, the purpose of the affair was to establish the Duchess of Kesgrave as a wit and a leader of fashion. To that end, it had fallen well short of its objective.

Bea was disappointed, of course. Even the most practical-minded former spinster of six and twenty years longed to achieve effortless success, and she would have made no objection if fate had seen fit to fall in line with Lady Abercrombie's plan by providing her with an opportunity to impress the company with her intelligence and daring.

Nonetheless, she was only mildly chagrined because she had known better than to expect anything else. The fact that she had managed to scrape by without mumbling in embarrassment or stumbling over her own words struck her as an encouraging sign.

At the next dinner party, perhaps, she would add a few erudite sentences to the topic under discussion.

The important thing, she thought, was she did not get tongue-tied. She responded correctly to every comment directed at her.

A brisk knock on the door signaled that it was time to return to the drawing room and folding the sheet of paper in half, she turned the knob. On the threshold stood Kesgrave, and her heart, ridiculous organ that it was, tripped lightly at the sight of him.

"Good evening, your grace," she said as if they had not arrived at the house together. It had been mere hours since their last conversation and she had spent much of the previous one silently mocking his predicament, and yet somehow it felt as though an age had passed since she last beheld him. She did not know to what to attribute the sensation other than the fact that she had spent the past two weeks practically living in his pocket and was disconcertingly unaccustomed to being away from his side. "I trust you did not allow your awe of her imperial majesty to undermine your ability to think clearly when making your assessment."

"I did not, no," he said firmly, taking her arm as he led her down the corridor. "I found it shockingly easy to disregard her entirely."

"Likewise the Archcardinal of Wintersburg?" she asked

Kesgrave's lips quirked and he informed her if she would like to know whom he suspected, she need only ask.

Bea shook her head and assured him that was not at all necessary. "I know you chose Miss Petworth."

Kesgrave stopped only slightly, just the merest hint of a pause, but his surprise was evident. "Why do you think that?"

"Her character is the only one who possesses a motivation that is even remotely political in nature, and you are far too logical to accept wild emotionality as a justification for murder," she explained.

"I cannot tell if that is an insult or a compliment," he said.

"The highest compliment," she replied. "A less rational man would have taken a diamond of the first water as his wife and the gracious assortment of cherubic children she would have inevitably supplied."

It was a reference, fleeting only, to a conversation they had early in their acquaintance at Lakeview Hall when he discovered her searching his room for evidence of his guilt. Fearing for her life, she had threatened to scream, compromising them both and utterly destroying the tidy future he no doubt imagined for himself: a stunning creature and their beautiful progeny.

Bea did not expect him to remember it. The only reason she recalled it so vividly was it had been a watershed event in her life—an unprecedented moment of audacity, a defining instance of absurdity.

Many would follow.

Dozens, in fact.

But she had had no inkling of that then.

"You astonished me then," he said, surprising her, "and you astonish me now, for you are correct. I did make Miss Petworth my guess."

Although impressing the duke was not on the agenda for the evening either, she felt her dissatisfaction lift at his words. Lady Abercrombie could devise as many elaborate schemes as she desired to transform the new Duchess of Kesgrave into a dashing highflier, but they would all come to naught. Bea's wings were too leaden to ever take flight.

But that did not signify.

Oh, indeed, it did not.

The only thing that mattered, she realized, was that she not sink further in society's estimation. If she could contrive to stay exactly where she was—quiet, presentable, just under the line of sight—then the damage to Kesgrave would be minimal. She had been so worried about the *London Morning Gazette* article. Mr. Twaddle-Thum's report made her sound like a depraved creature who bore no respect for the privacy of others or the sanctity of life, and she detested the idea of the *ton* using her depravity against the duke. But in placing her next to the decapitated corpse, the writer had overplayed his hand. The implausibility of that embellishment cast the whole story in doubt.

Given how little attention was paid to her that evening, Bea felt certain no one at the party believed a single word of the account.

It chafed a little, their incredulity, because figuring out who chopped the head off the greatest chef in Europe had required considerable ingenuity and she thought that deserved a little recognition.

Not at the expense of Kesgrave, of course.

Although maybe just a small, harmless nod of acknowledgment.

Amused by the pair of thoroughly incompatible desires, Bea smiled as she turned to enter the drawing room. Miss Petworth, her attention focused elsewhere, swept briskly past, forcing Bea to dart quickly to one side. Curious, she turned her head to watch the Incomparable hurry away down the hallway just as a wrenching cry split the air.

Bea darted into the room in time to see Mrs. Fawcett drop heavily to the floor in a faint. Alarmed, she strode briskly forward, but her movements were halted by Lord Bentham, who insisted that she go no further.

The sight, he said, was not suitable for a lady's eyes, and over his shoulder she saw the bloody corpse of Lord Pudsey, embroidery scissors protruding from his heart.

Mr. Fawcett dropped to his knees out of concern for his wife as Lord Bredbury entered the room to ask why his niece seemed so distressed. "I just saw her running out to the terrace, but she would not speak to me."

Bentham moved to the side and said, "She was disturbed by this terrible sight."

Baffled, Bredbury stepped deeper into the room and gasped when he saw Pudsey. "Good God, Bentham! What are you thinking to expose my delicate girl to something like that? I ought to call you out for your temerity!"

Bentham, sputtering at the insult, replied angrily that he did not expose Miss Petworth to anything and furthermore, his own wife had been subjected to the same awfulness. "And she remains in the room too shocked to even move. She is frozen in terror."

"And my wife is unconscious," Mr. Fawcett said angrily, "so do not ride your high horse in here, Bredbury."

His lordship objected to the characterization of his concern, and the three men began to argue loudly with each other. Wincing at the noise, Lady Abercrombie entered followed closely on the heels by Flora.

Bea, skirting around the recumbent Mrs. Fawcett, made her way to Nuneaton, who was standing next to the body. Closer now, she could see the bright red blood staining the pristine white of Pudsey's shirt mingling with the green soup splotches and the slack expression on his face.

Squeezing his arm in comfort, for she knew he had liked the man, for all his posturing about the deadly dullness of political affairs, Bea asked, "What happened?"

"I cannot say," Nuneaton replied softly, his tone calm despite the tightness in his face and the rigidity of his body. "I entered from the far door, from the anteroom adjacent, because that is where I was shown to make my guess, and when I came in, I saw Lady Bentham standing next to the settee with a completely ashen face. I did not realize what she was looking at until I drew closer. When I comprehended what was amiss, I rushed to her side and tried to lead her away, but she resisted. Mr. Fawcett entered next and chastised me for what he perceived as my harassment of Lady Bentham. A moment later, his wife came in and *she* began to chastise *him* for harassing *me,* which was fairly comical because neither one noticed Pudsey. Then Bentham arrived and thanked the three of us not to fuss over his wife. It was only when Miss Petworth came over to see what the commotion was, gasped in horror and dashed out of the room that the three of them looked down. Mrs. Fawcett screamed and fainted. You and Kesgrave arrived, and that brings us to this moment."

His lordship sighed and said irritably, "None of that is

helpful. I was in the room adjacent and should have information that is helpful. But I did not hear a thing, I swear. Not a thing. If Pudsey cried out, he did it far too softly for my ears."

"You judge yourself too harshly," Bea said, with a darting glance at Kesgrave. She was not sure how one went about consoling a viscount. "We are dealing with a diabolical murderer who is as clever as he is confident."

The bewildered look that swept across his face was quickly replaced with a perverse sort of amusement. "Yes, of course you'd know that. For months I have been plaguing you to share your investigative process, and now that I have seen it firsthand I understand everything. Tell me, duchess, what else do you know about the murderer that I do not?"

Bea leaned forward to get a better look at the puncture. "He knew exactly where to stick the scissors to make the kill as clean as possible. There is very little blood splatter. I do not think looking for blood on his clothes will help us."

He nodded, processing the information, and in the momentary pause they could hear Lady Abercrombie trying to calm the three bickering men. Flora appeared suddenly by her side, and Nuneaton suggested that perhaps the scene was too gruesome for her delicate sensibilities.

"I am an investigator, too," Flora said firmly. "The details are too shocking for me to reveal, but know that I have solved my own mystery, wrested from my cousin's stubborn hands. Ah, I see we are dealing with an experienced assassin. The person who did this was assured and proficient. Notice how there is only the one wound? That means he knew he had hit his mark on the first go."

Beatrice, who had heard a similar description of Mr. Gorman's killer from Mr. Holcroft himself, smothered a smile at the authority in her cousin's voice. It was disrespectful, she knew, to feel any sort of amusement in the presence of the freshly slain victim, and yet she could not help it. Flora's confidence was endearing.

"I am not sure what to say, Miss Hyde-Clare," Nuneaton observed.

"Impressive, my lord," she replied simply. "You are supposed to say my ability to draw deductions is impressive."

Lady Abercrombie, abandoning her efforts to calm the thunderous gentlemen, sighed wearily as she examined the cooling corpse of her lover. "Oh, George, what have you done to yourself?"

Kesgrave placed a hand on her shoulder and said, "I am sorry, Tilly."

Softly, on a sigh, she said, "As am I. He was not the great love of my life, but he was a pleasure to spend time with and I shall miss him. But that is neither here nor there at the moment. We have a wretched mess to deal with now. The constable will have to be sent for, but he will be of little use."

"Yes," Kesgrave agreed.

An expression of utter weariness flitted across her face, and seeing it, Bea wondered if perhaps Lord Pudsey meant a great deal more to the countess than she admitted. It was possible, yes, but death itself, especially one that was violent and unexpected, was also exhausting.

A trio of shouting gentlemen certainly did not help the situation.

The look of fatigue passed, replaced by resolution, and the countess said, "Very well, Bea, I have no choice but to refer the matter to you. How do you propose we proceed?"

Bea was about to suggest they start by calming the squabbling men, but before she could speak, Miss Petworth returned and gained her uncle's attention by quietly speaking his name.

At once, Bredbury fell silent.

Mr. Fawcett and Bentham continued arguing without him for a few seconds, then also allowed their words to trail off.

"I must leave, Uncle," Miss Petworth said, her voice shaking. "I cannot stay in this house with...with...that. I simply cannot."

"Of course you cannot," Bredbury affirmed consolingly, "and only a beast would insist that you do. We will leave immediately."

"Yes," Bentham said firmly in agreement. "That is the only recourse."

Something in his tone finally roused his wife from her trance, and she turned her head to look around, her eyes blinking frantically. Bentham rushed to assist her, holding her arm as if to steady her before she toppled over. "My wife requires the comforts of home."

Mrs. Fawcett, groaning loudly and fluttering her eyelids, also regained her senses. Disoriented, she stared blankly at the ceiling for several seconds from her prone position before crying out Pudsey's name. "Help him! We must help him before it is too late."

"It is already too late, my dear," her husband said gently. "There is nothing to be done for him. But you are not yourself and must be attended to. We shall go home, and I will send for a doctor immediately."

"We should go," Mrs. Fawcett agreed, her voice growing stronger with conviction. "I am not feeling well, and it is not right that we remain, for we are intruding on Lady Abercrombie's grief. I am sure she would prefer to be alone."

A chorus of agreements followed her observation as the group of guests settled on this point as their overriding concern.

Poor Lady Abercrombie, encumbered by company during her time of grief!

It was, Bea thought, a rather astonishing display, for not

only had they decided that leaving their hostess with a corpse to dispose of was the only courteous thing to do, they seemed to consider their involvement entirely at an end. Mr. Fawcett took his wife by the hand to lead her to the door as Bentham tucked his spouse under his arm. Bredbury, seemingly the only one to realize they could not depart without in some way acknowledging their hostess, apologized to Lady Abercrombie for lingering so long.

"We will of course see ourselves out," he added before promising to send a freshly baked heirloom tart in the morning. "It is a source of comfort in my family."

The countess, who appeared not to be listening, responded with an absent wave, which his lordship considered to be sufficient recognition of his generosity. Verily, he turned on his heels and in the company of his niece, proceeded toward the room's entrance. The other two couples followed, their pace slightly slower to accommodate the women's frailty, and Bea, whose constitution remained strong, breezed briskly past them as she strode to the door and shut it.

"I cannot allow you to leave," she said firmly, "for one of you is almost certainly the killer."

Chapter Six

Having acted without thinking, it took Bea a few seconds to comprehend the magnitude of her deed. It was right in front of her, of course, in their faces, which were contorted with shock, and their deep inhalations of breath, and yet it was only when she heard the words repeat in her own head that she truly understood that she had just accused six of the *ton*'s most influential members of murder.

Well, she thought, not all six.

Just one.

Alas, it was a distinction she did not expect anyone to appreciate.

Bentham, recovering his wits first, roared with outrage. "How *dare* you!"

"Yes," his wife growled, "how dare *you*, a nibbly little ant at the feast of life, elevated to the high table when you should have been left to root around in the dirt. I said this evening would be a waste of our time, did I not, Bentham? I said Lady Abercrombie's mission to turn her into a fashionable creature was the greatest lost cause since Napoleon escaped Elba. But

I agreed to come because I am a generous woman who endeavors to show kindness to those beneath me. And this is how my benevolence is repaid!"

"Lady Bentham is right," Mrs. Fawcett added, taking several steps forward so that her nose was an inch from Bea's. Her voice was even, but her eyes seethed. "I had my own reservations about this evening but allowed my belief in Lady Abercrombie's good sense to overcome them. I see now that was a mistake. You are a disgrace to the Matlock name, and I will not hesitate to say so if anyone asks. And I am confident many will when word of these proceedings gets out."

"Ladies, ladies," Bredbury said soothingly, raising his hands to shoulder level and slowly lowering them again in an effort to calm their outrage. "There is nothing to be gained with an uncharitable response. Her grace is a novice in social niceties, having been a pariah for more than a decade, and has no idea how to comport herself properly. Come now, we must pity her, not berate her. We are all open-minded individuals and should be commended for graciously attending an event that we knew would end poorly. For myself, I assumed she would prove to be the inert thing she was during dinner, silent and dull, but even that role she could not sustain, descending, instead, into this bizarre state of accusatory mortification. Although we have been subjected to these hideous insults, it behooves us to remain calm."

Bentham, his cheeks still bright red with indignation, agreed with this assessment. "Calm, yes, that is the only way forward, for we are civilized people and to devolve into name-calling would be to prove that we are no better than she."

Mindful of the rebuke, Lady Bentham nodded solemnly and sought to correct her behavior. "I apologize, your grace, for speaking so plainly," she said, directing her comments to the duke, not Bea. "My only excuse is that the events of this evening are so disquieting my good sense has been undermined. I should never have called your wife a nibbly little ant. She is a grasping schemer well past the first blush of youth, and I can say that"—a quick darting glance to her husband —"because it is factually accurate. I am sorry if that displeases you, but it is what I and the rest of the *ton* know to be true. Now, if you would kindly ask your wife to step aside, we will return to our home, where Bentham and I will endeavor to forgive this grave injustice."

The color drained swiftly from Beatrice's face. The moment Bentham bellowed with fury, she had known what was coming and felt herself go pale in that instant. The particulars of their venom had eluded her, its precise shape and cast, but its depth and intensity were immediately apparent.

Even so, it was slightly worse than she could have ever imagined, standing there by the door listening to them voice their scathing judgments, their withering verdicts, Mrs. Fawcett so close her breath brushed Bea's cheek.

She had been deluded, only a few minutes ago, when she thought she could hold the line at quiet and presentable. The truth was, there was no line to hold. Their opinion of her had been firmly fixed before they even walked through the door, and there was nothing she could have done to alter it. Her timidity at dinner offended them as much as her audacity did now.

Of course they had known what Lady Abercrombie was up to with her little game. That was not at all surprising, for society moved along narrow parameters and her scheme fit well within the boundaries.

But the realization that they had gone along with it only as an act of begrudging altruism was transfixedly humiliating for her.

Bea stood there unable to move.

Ultimately, it would not have made a difference in her

actions. If she had known in advance how ugly their response would be, she still would have thrown herself against the door to halt their progress.

A man was dead, and they were scurrying away.

Someone had to stop them.

Kesgrave, she supposed, would have been a better messenger, and she knew he would have interceded at a speaking look from her.

Lady Abercrombie, too, could have intervened on her behalf. Her status as hostess would have made the demand seem a little more like a request.

But Bea had not considered these options because she had not considered anything, and now she was standing there, under a gilded serpent in the Countess of Abercrombie's opulent drawing room, a figure of scorn, an outcast on the edge of an abyss.

It sounded precarious, she thought, her toes dangling over the void, and yet it was exactly where she had been for six seasons. From the moment Miss Brougham had called her drab in that sneering tone, she had been perched there, and although it frequently felt as though the slightest push would throw her into the chasm, in reality not even a very hard shove could dislodge her.

Despite its proximity to the brink, the ground beneath her feet was solid.

The worst of her humiliation eased at this revelation, and Bea pressed herself firmly against the door, conveying more clearly than words her determination not to give way.

Kesgrave, seemingly unconcerned by the insults dealt to either his wife or himself, said, "The grave injustice, Lady Bentham, would be if we failed to apprehend Pudsey's killer. Now do take a seat so that my wife can pose her questions in an orderly fashion. The longer it takes for you to comply, the longer this ordeal will go on."

Lady Bentham was disinclined to argue with a duke, especially one who wielded as much influence as Kesgrave, so she sent her husband a beseeching look to request that he do it on her behalf.

He obliged her at once. "My wife and I share your passion for justice, Kesgrave, and would happily submit to an interrogation if we believed it would help Pudsey attain it. But you cannot place a noose around a frayed rug and a pair of scissors that are tragically facing up. And obviously that is what happened: Pudsey tripped on the edge of the rug, landed on the blades and flipped onto his back. He had the great misfortune to die before he could remove them from his chest. It is a terrible tragedy but not a crime."

The skeptical expressions on his fellow guests' faces indicated that none of them believed in this unlikely sequence of events, and yet the other suspects in the room remained silent. Mr. Fawcett, in particular, seemed prepared to object to the implausibility, for a look of contempt swept across his features, but he, too, said nothing.

It fell to Bea to point out that Pudsey's body was too far from the border of the rug for its condition to have played a part in his death. "And furthermore, the carpet is pristine. I would not be surprised if Lady Abercrombie installed it new only a few months ago."

"Four," her ladyship said. "I also replaced the settee. I am very fond of my son and am always delighted to have him visit, but he can be dreadfully thoughtless in his placement of his wineglass. Both items suffered intolerable stains and had to be replaced."

Perceiving the futility of arguing, Mr. Fawcett led his wife to a chair and sat down. "I agree that Bentham's theory of an accident is outlandish, but I cannot understand why you would then think it is one of us. This house is full of servants who may harbor an irrational resentment against our class, or maybe the villain sneaked in through a window. It could have been a stranger, someone who was hired to end his life for reasons we do not know."

Bea agreed with this statement and allowed that both scenarios were plausible. "And that is precisely why I have asked you to remain—because we do not know what happened. The only way we will find out is by gathering information, first from you, then from the servants. We cannot do that if you leave."

"I do not possess any information," Mr. Fawcett said brusquely, "and if I did, I would rather share it with a Runner. Surely, that is who should be summoned. I beg of you, do not waste our time with a constable, who is almost certain to be useless. This investigation requires the skills of a Runner, and I urge you to call for one immediately."

"A Runner to investigate a rug?" Bentham asked scornfully. "That is as ridiculous as allowing this overstepping chit to interrogate us."

Bea ignored this insult and explained to Mr. Fawcett that he might know more than he realized. "That is the purpose of an investigation: to identify what information is important. I do hope you will be patient, Mr. Fawcett. Perhaps some of Lady Abercrombie's excellent claret? I'm sure that will ease the pain of waiting. I will just have"—a quick look around the room revealed no footmen to be present—"Kesgrave pour you a glass."

Mr. Fawcett's shoulders rounded slightly as he seemed to yield to an irrefutable reality and said, yes, a glass of claret would be just the thing.

Bentham, observing the direction of the wind, asserted that a sherry would calm his wife's nerves. "I would also not cavil at a port."

Bredbury followed suit as he and Miss Petworth took the settee across from the fireplace. "I would like port as well, and a bracing sip of ratafia would not go amiss for my niece."

Graciously, the duke filled their orders from a neat little stand in the corner, submitting to the role of butler without protest, and Bea felt an absurd impulse to giggle. Once again, she had skewered his consequence without intention.

She kept expecting the reports of her investigative skills to be his ruination, and yet it was the casual disregard she had for his position that genuinely undermined his importance.

Mrs. Fawcett was not as easily placated as her husband and glared at Bea with narrowed eyes. "You may talk about gathering information all you want, your grace, but only minutes ago you accused me and my husband of murder whilst absolving yourself. I find that highly suspect and wonder what information *I* may gather from *you*."

Flora chirped in protest of the implication, but Bea nodded approvingly. "An excellent point, Mrs. Fawcett, and I can see why the *ton* holds you in such high esteem. Your reasoning is indisputable, so let us indeed begin with me. Please present your case."

Slightly disconcerted to have been taken seriously, the society matron did not immediately reply. Having launched a rhetorical maneuver, she seemed ill-prepared to make an argument.

Nevertheless, she gamely rose to the challenge and said, "You long for acceptance. That was the point of this futile exercise, was it not, to demonstrate how worthy you are of our respect and admiration. It stands to reason, then, that if a pretend murder promotes your cause somewhat, then a real murder would benefit it hugely. We are now meant to be amazed by your deductive skills and relay that astonishment to society. Your ambition is obvious to everyone and shamefully unseemly, and I would not be at all surprised to discover that you had killed to further it."

Lady Bentham liked this line of argument so much, she shifted forward in her seat and nodded in vehement agreement. "Mrs. Fawcett's observations are indeed accurate, for you *have* benefited greatly from the many dead people who populate your world. These murders that you claim to have solved have raised you to our notice, secured the countess's support and provided entrée into one of the oldest families in England. And now another victim has appeared, conveniently as ever, and you would have us believe it is merely the result of yet another misfortune? I have been alive for almost five full decades, your grace, and never once encountered a single corpse before this terrible moment. How do you account for that?"

Flora, whose opinion had not been sought, replied that chancing upon a dead body was far easier than either lady could possibly imagine. "You probably have not been looking carefully enough."

Insulted, Lady Bentham pressed her lips in a peeved moue and announced that she was just unobservant enough not to notice impudent misses unworthy of her attention. Then she pointedly turned her head away.

A delicate blush rose in Flora's cheeks as she opened her mouth to object, and Bea, hoping to avoid a spat between the two women, asked for a clarification of the allegation. "Am I being accused of Pudsey's murder or all the murders I have investigated? If the latter, I can understand your concern, for I must be a very cunning villain to have disposed of my parents at the remarkably tender age of five."

But Bea's amused contempt was no more conciliatory than Flora's naïve sincerity, and her ladyship glared at her with a mixture of ardent dislike and embarrassment.

As neither emotion would further her investigation, Bea apologized for her comment and addressed the original point by agreeing that nobody in the room was above suspicion.

"Every one of us was in the house, and any one of us could be responsible. A murder investigation is about following the evidence. To that end, let us establish where everyone was at the time Pudsey was killed. I was in the study on the ground floor, where I remained until Kesgrave came to escort me to the drawing room."

"That is correct," Kesgrave said. "And I was shown to the room next door. I remained there for fifteen minutes before collecting my wife."

"I was in the library," Flora said.

"Which is down the hall from the drawing room," Lady Bentham noted.

Although the implication was clear, Flora kept her expression smooth as she confirmed the location of the library, observing that, yes, it was down the hall from the drawing room. "*Three* doors down," she said, before adding, "Miss Petworth, in the music room, was *two* doors away."

All eyes turned to the young beauty, who, horrified to be either the center of attention or suspected of murder, turned a faint sickly color and stammered that she had been in the music room for the entire interval. "In fact, I am sure I remained longer than the allotted time because I could not decide between Concisely and Sunshine. Concisely's motive seemed stronger to me, but Sunshine appeared more vindictive."

"If proximity to the drawing room is to be your measure of guilt, then I advise you to look at Nuneaton, not my dear girl, who is as gentle as she is beautiful," Bredbury said hotly. "He was in the room adjacent."

"That is right," Lady Bentham said, narrowing her eyes, "and there is a door connecting the two."

Nuneaton, seemingly unconcerned by the accusation, brushed a speck of dust from the shoulder of his immaculate tailcoat and looked lazily up. "I assure you, my lady, if anyone were to spur me to murder, it would not have been Pudsey, whose inability to maintain a pristine cravat was exasperating at best, but your husband, whose waistcoat is an affront to humanity. His continued good health is proof that I have resisted my baser instincts. Given his callous disregard for his fellow man, I cannot say he has done the same."

Lady Bentham huffed angrily, but her husband, displaying only amusement at Nuneaton's antics, said he had spent the interval comfortably ensconced in Lady Abercrombie's sitting room on the second floor. "Bredbury cannot say the same, for when I looked into the guest room to which he had been assigned on my way to the staircase, he was already gone."

"I was not gone," Bredbury said defensively. "I was merely somewhere else. The guest room was warm and I desired fresh air, so I returned to the terrace."

"The terrace that is off the dining room?" Bea asked.

Bredbury nodded affirmatively.

Lady Abercrombie's home was capacious, yes, but it was not palatial, and Bea thought it was likely that the dining room had also been allotted for use during act three.

"Yes," the countess said, confirming her supposition. "Mr. Fawcett was assigned to it."

"Was he?" Bredbury asked inquisitively. "That is most curious because it was empty when I passed through only a few minutes into the interval."

Mr. Fawcett colored at the accusative tone and mumbled that he had not remained long in the room because he sought to confer with his wife.

Bredbury, finding this explanation equally peculiar, asked what could have been so important that he had to discuss it with Mrs. Fawcett during the climactic moment of a murder mystery contest.

"It is a private matter," Mr. Fawcett said stiffly.

"A private matter," Bredbury repeated with scorn. "Yes, I

imagine figuring out how to kill one troublesome member of the House of Lords in precisely the same manner as Lady Abercrombie's fictional victim was killed *is* a private matter."

The flush in Mr. Fawcett's face deepened as he indignantly replied that he had figured out nothing. "And that was precisely the issue. I did not have the single notion of who might have committed the act, so I went to the conservatory to ask Mrs. Fawcett's opinion."

"And did she give it?" Bea asked.

Mr. Fawcett darted an apologetic look at his wife and then said, "No, she was not there."

Untroubled by the implication, Mrs. Fawcett confirmed that she had left the conservatory several minutes after arriving to attend to personal business. "And, no," she added with a reproachful glance at Bredbury, "it was not to attack Lord Pudsey with a pair of scissors. It was to avail myself of the water closet. I did not see anyone on my way there nor on my return to the drawing room."

Unappeased, Bredbury stated that he found it suspicious that nobody observed her passage, not even a servant.

"Did a servant observe your passage to and from the terrace?" she asked.

Bredbury conceded that one had not, and Bea, recalling the shifting of footmen during the meal, asked their hostess what mishap had occurred in the kitchens.

Although Lady Abercrombie confidently assured her that all was well belowstairs, her expression displayed just enough wariness to convince Bea of the opposite.

Again, she speculated about what could have gone amiss.

Not a second murder, for that would be impossible to hide and did not account for the staff changes during dinner.

An injury, perhaps.

Or maybe a dispute among the footmen that descended into fisticuffs.

As unlikely as it was that the drama in the servants' quarters had any bearing on the drawing room tragedy, the possibility had to be explored before it could be dismissed. As such, Bea asked the countess why the footmen had disappeared from the dining room one by one and received a petulant glare in return.

Bea expected her ladyship to issue another denial, but after a moment of extended silence she said, "It is nothing, you wretched girl, nothing at all except a gastric complaint that is causing some discomfort among the servants. It is very minor, I assure you, but you know how the staff can be. As soon as one thing is out of order, everything becomes an uproar."

Lady Bentham gasped in dismay, and Mrs. Fawcett asked if they would all perish before leaving the drawing room.

"It is not the plague," Lady Abercrombie replied snappishly. "It is a gaseous problem—an excess of flatulence, if you must know. I cannot say how three footmen came to be infected with the same issue, but I am certain you are safe from its ill effects. The biggest concern is the noxious odor emitted by its victims. Regardless, it has nothing to do with Pudsey's death and I would be grateful not to have to discuss it further."

Mr. Fawcett, however, refused to be consoled on his wife's behalf and announced that they could not remain one moment longer in a house that was afflicted by a strange illness. "I would never be able to forgive myself if she became sick."

Bredbury concurred with this statement, beckoning to his niece, still sitting demurely on the settee. "It is time to leave, my dear."

As Bea was still standing in front of the entryway, she did not find it necessary to offer an objection. They would have to physically remove her to pass through it, and she did not think that was likely to happen.

Even a drab spinster would be safe from such rough treatment.

Kesgrave, however, proved unwilling to take that chance, for he promptly told the Fawcetts and Bredbury to resume sitting. "As you are too worried about your health to consider the matter clearly, I would remind you that anyone who leaves before answering my wife's questions will be considered guilty of the crime. Since at least two of you are most likely innocent, it would be a shame if word to that effect spread through the *beau monde*."

He spoke mildly, almost with disinterest, but his words drew an immediate response. Miss Petworth, who was the most socially vulnerable of the group, shrank back against the cushion of the settee, almost as if struck.

Mrs. Fawcett smiled amiably and thanked the duke for reminding them of their duty to Pudsey. "We owe it to him to discover the truth, which I am sure will turn out to be just as Bentham said: a terrible accident."

His lordship, gratified by her faith, added that Pudsey subscribed wholly to the free movement of peoples and would be quite aghast at their being detained there in his name.

Replacing the top to the crystal decanter, Kesgrave apologized for the misunderstanding and assured Bentham that he was free to leave. "It was never my intention to constrain your movements. I was simply operating under the assumption that you were as interested in the truth as I am. If that is inaccurate, then you must act according to your conscience."

Bentham owned himself to be thoroughly enamored with the truth and said he was eager to assist the duchess in her little investigation. "I find her belief in her ability to pursue justice to be adorable. Yes, she must be allowed to proceed with her questions and draw her own conclusions. I am confident, of course, that after a diverting interlude she will realize my original supposition is correct."

Although his condescension was infuriating, Bea did little more than nod noncommittally; there was no reason to engage him further. His theory was risible and not worth the breath it would require to refute it. The countess, however, found him more difficult to ignore, and offended at the insult leveled at her drawing room, demanded that he show her the imperfection in her rug at once.

"So that I may have it repaired," she added.

"Of course, yes, happy to lend my assistance," Bentham said, striding to the edge of the floor covering, which was as pristine as the rest of the room. Regardless, he drew her attention to an area that appeared threadbare to him and remained calm when she urged him to sink to his hands and knees so that he could see he had pointed to a lotus blossom. He refused the invitation and indicated another promising swath.

It was a dragonfly.

With the founder of the Henley Sporting Club sufficiently distracted and the revolt on the wane, Bea caught Nuneaton's gaze and commanded him silently to take her place at the door. He complied as Kesgrave handed Mrs. Fawcett a glass of sherry and Flora glared at Miss Petworth for looking even more beautiful than ever in her pallid fragility.

Grateful to be free of her post, Bea stepped forward to examine the body.

Chapter Seven

I t was impossible to say who gasped first—Lady Bentham or Mrs. Fawcett—for both women inhaled sharply the moment Beatrice positioned herself next to Pudsey. She had not even lowered herself to his side before they perceived her intention and were properly horrified.

"I did not believe it," her ladyship said with arch disapproval. "When I read in the paper that she had examined Mr. Réjane without the head on his body, I assumed Mr. Twaddle-Thum was exaggerating to make his account more sensational, but clearly it is true. All of it—true!"

Mrs. Fawcett contended that she had never doubted a word. "She was, as you know, a spinster well into her twenties, and being an unattached female has a detrimental effect on the mind. Without a man to bolster her ability to reason, it begins to degrade. That is scientific analysis, not my personal opinion. Even so, I assumed she still retained the good sense not to behave so indecorously in public. My experience is limited, of course, but I think we can all agree that inspecting the corpse of an acquaintance is something one should do in the privacy of one's own home."

"Or belowstairs at the very least," Lady Bentham added.

"Yes," Mrs. Fawcett agreed, adding snidely, "if one has no other options, then the downstairs of a banker's establishment."

Her ladyship sighed audibly at this comment and lamented the questionable quality of resident that now occupied Berkeley Square. "I cannot imagine what Pennington was about, selling his house to a Fleet Street dealer."

"Following the Duke of Manchester's lead, I expect," Mrs. Fawcett replied critically.

"Ancient history," Lady Bentham scoffed. "And you cannot begin to compare the two situations, for Manchester did not sell *his* property to Robert Child to settle an outrageous gambling debt."

Nevertheless, Mrs. Fawcett felt confident her point held. "Robert Child was the scion of the Child family banking dynasty."

"*And* Lady Jersey's grandfather," Lady Bentham reminded her.

The progression of their conversation amused Bea, the way they had begun by disparaging her behavior and ended by arguing over a real estate purchase from the middle of the last century. She was grateful for their distraction because it allowed her to examine Pudsey without their interruption.

Leaning over his chest, she confirmed that the puncture that killed him was skillfully managed. There were splatters, especially around the point of entry, but by and large the wound was clean.

As she had said, the person who did this was assured and experienced.

Only someone who was confident they would succeed would dare to make the attempt during a dinner party. Had Pudsey cried out, the culprit would have been caught in the middle of the deed. Likewise, if he had missed his mark on the first try, he would be soaked with blood now.

No, this was done by an expert.

Or, she thought, landing on another possibility, Pudsey was made insensible before the scissors were plunged into his chest. Such a method was used in her previous investigation, for it was difficult to remove the head of a squirming man.

On that occasion, the murderer employed a drug to achieve that condition.

Could that have been done here?

Bea allowed that it was possible.

If something undetectable was slipped into his drink...

But the timing of that would be difficult to pin down, as the countess's murder game played havoc with the familiar dinner party itinerary. The ideal moment to administer the drug would be after the meal, when the ladies adjourned to the drawing room to allow the men to enjoy their port.

That interlude, however, did not occur, leaving the culprit with a substance he had no opportunity to dispense and forcing him to come up with another approach.

No, she thought, dissatisfied with the theory because it indicated premeditation as well as preparation. As Bredbury had pointed out, Pudsey was killed in the same manner as the fictional Lady Rambling—that implied spontaneity.

Unless their hostess had discussed the details of her play in advance of the evening.

Considering the possibility, Bea looked over to the edge of the rug, where Lady Abercrombie and Bentham were struggling to come to a mutual understanding of the word *frayed*.

"It is lint, yes, that I readily own," her ladyship said, "but I take issue with your categorizing a few small clumps of fuzz as fraying. Fraying requires some amount of unraveling of the fibers. Surely, on that we can agree."

Oh, but they could not.

Bentham, rising ardently to the defense of fluff, argued that it was a widely recognized precursor to full-fledged tattering, and Bea interrupted his tirade by catching Lady Abercrombie's eye.

With an abrupt word of apology, the countess excused herself from the conversation and moved to Bea's side. Softly, she said, "If Bentham does not stop maligning my rug, there will be a second murder."

"As painful as it must be to listen to someone impugn any aspect of your drawing room, which is perfection itself—"

"How well you understand me, your grace," her ladyship murmured.

"Bentham's obstinacy has the benefit of keeping him distracted, which is to the good."

Lady Abercrombie could not argue with this conclusion. "Very true. Now how may I assist you?"

"Your plans for this evening," Bea said. "Did you discuss them with anybody?"

"I discussed them with everybody," she replied promptly, "yourself included. How else would I have managed to gather my guests at the allotted time and place?"

"No, I mean the particulars of the story," Bea said. "Did you discuss the details with anyone?"

"Oh, I see, you mean did I tell anyone that Lady Rambling would be killed by a pair of embroidery shears driven through her heart?" the countess said. "No, I did not mention that to anyone. I discussed the three-act structure with a few people—Bentham, I believe, and Mrs. Fawcett—and I told Lady Bentham that Mrs. Simon had deigned to appear. But I never revealed anything about the story itself. Mrs. Simon only saw the script for the first time this morning, when she arrived to rehearse."

"Thank you. That is helpful," Bea said.

Lady Abercrombie nodded and, turning to resume her

argument with Bentham, stopped suddenly and looked again at Bea. "You know, I trust, that I only *imagine* running your aunt through with scissors. I would never actually do it."

Bea pressed her lips together to keep from laughing. "Yes."

"And it is not all the time," her ladyship added. "Only when she is talking about your mother. Or explaining what is best for you. Or complaining about the price of something."

As these subjects were among her aunt's favorites, Bea thought *all the time* was a rather apt description. "I'm sure," she said mildly, then returned her attention to Pudsey, incorporating the new information. As the countess had not revealed any of the details of her play in advance, she dismissed the idea of a drug and considered physical assault. The more reliable way to ensure insentience was a knock on the head. Suffocation would work but would cause a struggle and not guarantee success. But a solid thump to the skull worked wonders.

Thoughtfully, she turned his head to the left to inspect the back.

Across the room, Mrs. Fawcett squealed. "Good lord, she is *touching* him now."

"Poor Pudsey," Lady Bentham said, shaking her head piteously. "As if lying prone in the middle of a dinner party were not punishment enough for his sins. To be handled roughly as well! The poor man would simply die of mortification."

Observing nothing of note at the base of his skull, Bea moved her gaze upward.

"It is Miss Petworth," Flora said.

Startled, Bea looked up to find her cousin leaning over her shoulder. "Excuse me?"

Flora stepped forward and lowered herself so that she was

directly next to Bea. "Miss Petworth is the culprit. She did this."

Smothering a smile, Bea said, "The murderer cannot be simply the person you dislike the most."

"Yes, I know that," Flora said defensively, "for I am familiar with the mechanics of an investigation because I have conducted one myself."

"Wrested from my own hands," Bea said.

"Yes, wrested from your own hands," Flora affirmed, "so my reasoning is somewhat more sophisticated than your comment indicates. Furthermore, of the company in the room, I dislike Lady Bentham the most. Talking about us like that! She is utterly wretched."

"Us?" Bea echoed with slight confusion. "I do not recall hearing you described as a nibbly little ant."

"We are family," Flora said firmly, "so an insult to one is an insult to all."

"Unless the target is Russell, in which case it is an accurate description?" Bea asked, amused by this new vision of familial harmony.

"Well, he *is* a nibbly little ant," Flora said.

"All right, then," Bea said, "tell me why you suspect Miss Petworth."

"Her knuckles are white," Flora said.

Bea glanced across the room to where Miss Petworth sat on the settee, but her angle was such that she could not see the Incomparable's hands, only her face. "She seems calm."

"Exactly," Flora said with satisfaction. "She seems calm, and yet her knuckles are white. She is clutching her hands. Why is she clutching them so tightly? What does she fear? And why is that the only sign of her disquiet? They had a tryst, did they not? Clearly, she desires a title and assumed an older man would make a biddable husband. When he proved intractable, she murdered him in a fit of rage. You saw her at dinner, flirting outrageously with him."

"She spilled her soup on him," Bea said.

"Precisely," Flora replied, "and it caught his attention."

Since she could not eliminate anyone this early in the investigation, Bea saw no point in discussing the matter further and assured her cousin she would keep her argument in mind.

Flora thanked her for her consideration and then said, "You are looking for evidence of a whack on the head, I trust."

Once again, she found it impossible not to be charmed by her cousin's air of authority. "Yes."

"There appears to be a small wound there," Flora observed, pointing to the spot near the crown where the thinning hair seemed to be slightly matted.

In fact, Bea's fingers were already gliding over that particular area of Pudsey's balding pate and a moment later she encountered a bulge. "Ah, yes, there it is. The skin is broken and sticky with blood."

Flora inhaled deeply but said nothing.

Bea could feel her excitement, however, and although she knew it was absurd, she asked her cousin if she would like to examine the lump too.

"I would, yes," Flora said, her matter-of-fact tone reflecting none of her delight. Gently, she placed her hand over the spot and told Bea she was correct. "A bump that large could only be caused by a heavy instrument."

Considering the spur-of-the-moment nature of the crime, Bea decided the murderer most likely used something in the room to stun Pudsey. Given the countess's lavish taste, there were dozens of objects from which to choose.

Flora, drawing a similar conclusion, said that a candlestick was the obvious implement. "The staff allows for a solid grip, which makes swinging it into someone's head easier."

Bea agreed that it was a reliable weapon. Lady Skeffington had employed one with great success in the library at Lakeview Hall.

"I'll examine the candlesticks for evidence of blood," Flora announced, "and you may scrutinize the gargoyles."

The extravagant room contained few gothic elements, least of all sculptures designed to draw rainwater away from a building, but Bea found a series of solid serpent figures in the black-lacquered cabinet next to a bamboo screen. Carefully, she inspected each one for blood residue but decided it was unlikely because the furniture's glass front required the killer to open it first before grabbing one of the items.

If it was a true act of spontaneity, then the item had to be readily available.

"Do I have cause for concern?" Kesgrave asked, appearing by her side as she closed the left-side door.

Her heart tripped—just a little—but she managed to maintain a mostly indifferent demeanor as she snapped the second door into place. "If you killed Pudsey, then I think yes, for you know quite well my record of success in apprehending murderers."

"I meant regarding Flora," he explained.

"Oh, I see. In that case, also yes," she replied, silently honing her thought about the way the culprit moved around the room. If the deed was planned and executed in a matter of minutes, then the object might have been grabbed on the way from the door to the spot where Pudsey stood. "She is convinced of Miss Petworth's guilt and stands ready to hurl an accusation at her. Prepare yourself for excessive awkwardness and perhaps even some discomfort."

"I meant regarding my status as your investigative

assistant," he clarified further. "Flora seems determined to usurp my position."

Bea, who had been appraising a porcelain jug with a pagoda motif displayed on a marble column to the left of the door, looked at the duke in surprise. "Truly, your grace, your humility has gotten wildly out of hand. I cannot imagine what has caused you to doubt your own magnificence."

Kesgrave regarded her with cynical amusement. "Can't you, brat?"

The jug seemed a little too large, she thought, for the size of the lump, but its shape was right. The rounded edges would have been less likely to cause a gash, and the handle would allow for a solid grip.

She scanned the room, searching for another vessel that fit her requirements, and settled on an amphora of modest proportions resting on a side table. "I cannot, no, for you excel at everything you try. Serving drinks to the company, for example. You handled that beautifully. There wasn't a single broken glass or spill. If anyone should feel insecure about his position, it is Marlow."

"And now I am demonstrating how beautifully I excel at resisting your taunts," he explained as they crossed the room to the table.

"Taunts?" she asked, her eyebrow raising in confusion. "I just proclaimed you superior to your butler. Is there any higher praise?"

Displaying yet again his ability to withstand his wife's abuse, he ignored her comment and asked if they were looking for the blunt object used to stupefy Pudsey before plunging in the scissors.

"You draw such astute deductions and yet somehow persist in doubting yourself," Bea observed as they stopped in front of the table. The amphora looked pristine from this angle. "There is a small wound near the top of his head.

Whatever the killer used, it just barely broke skin. Flora is convinced it is a candlestick, but I think it's this lovely thing."

"A candlestick would have done more damage?" he asked.

"Having seen what it did to Mr. Otley's skull, I believe yes," she said, raising the vase to inspect it carefully.

Bea saw it immediately, the splotch of dried blood amid the decorative pattern.

"It is here," she said, handing the vessel to Kesgrave, who tilted it slightly to the side to improve his perspective.

The jar made a faint jingling sound.

"Did you hear that?" Bea asked.

But the duke was already peering inside the amphora as he shook it again. The tinkling was louder.

"There is something inside it," he said as he turned it over. A small precious stone—green and round—encased in a gold setting dropped into his hand. He grasped it between his fingers as he held it up for Bea to see. "It is a sleeve button. Half of one, actually. You can see here"—he gestured to thin strips of metal that had formed the sides of a U shape —"where it broke off from the other half. The link is worn thin."

Bea accepted the fastener and rubbed her thumb over the jewel, which glittered in the candlelight with the same luminescence as the Matlock rubies. "It is an emerald."

"Yes," Kesgrave said, his tone thoughtful. "And quite a valuable one at that. Its clarity is excellent."

"Could it have slipped off the killer's sleeve when he bashed Pudsey over the head?" she asked.

The duke allowed it was possible and observed there was an easy enough way to find out to whom it belonged.

"Look, Lady Bentham, the duchess has found something," Mrs. Fawcett said. "It seems to be a very small object. I believe that is what females of a particular bent call a clue."

"That is correct, yes," her ladyship replied. "A clue is

precisely what such a female would call an item she discovered while poking around in someone else's drawing room. I wonder if it is something of genuine interest or if she has stumbled upon a fribble one of the footmen overlooked in the execution of his duties. It is a habit of some women to find intrigue everywhere, especially where none exists."

Lauding the wisdom of this observation, Mrs. Fawcett suggested they ask her grace to show them the interesting artifact she had discovered.

"I appear to have acquired a Greek chorus," Bea said softly. "As I do not know yet what the terms are, I cannot promise that it won't return with us to Kesgrave House."

"I consider that highly unlikely," he said equably, "but in any case, we can board them in the east wing and never have to hear them again."

"Ah, now I perceive the advantages of a large house," she said.

"Now?" Kesgrave repeated with meaningful emphasis. "The pleasures of the library and the conservatory and the room that you describe as your office for cake consumption had not convinced you?"

"Rout cake enjoyment," she corrected.

"But a room reserved for more general cake consumption is available to you, which is precisely my point," he said.

Bea's reply was forestalled by Lady Bentham's reminder that she and Mrs. Fawcett were still waiting to see her discovery.

In fact, they were not.

Peeved at not having their curiosity immediately satisfied, the society matrons strode across the room to discover the answer for themselves and as soon as Lady Bentham's eyes landed on the sleeve button Bea held, she gasped. "How dare you!"

As gasps of varying degrees of outrage seemed to be Lady

Bentham's primary form of communication, Bea was not at all surprised to have elicited yet another one. She was baffled, to be sure, by the cause of this specific outburst, but she was confident her ladyship would enlighten her soon enough.

Verily, she did. "That is my husband's sleeve button—from Kimpton, of course!—which I gave him last year for his birthday, and I would thank you to tell me how it came to be in your possession. And that is only half. Where is the rest? I am not accusing you of thievery," she rushed to add, lest Kesgrave misunderstand her words and take offense. "I can think of no reason why a woman wearing the Matlock rubies would feel the need to pilfer an emerald of modest size and sentimental value. I am simply trying to understand what has transpired."

Mrs. Fawcett, however, was not as slow to comprehend the series of events that led to Bea's custody of the jewel, and her eyes grew wide as she looked at her rival. "My goodness, Lady Bentham, she found your husband's sleeve button somewhere," she said, before looking at Bea for confirmation. "Is that what happened, your grace? You found Bentham's sleeve button in a place where it ought not have been?"

As she wondered at the meaning of the discovery, Mrs. Fawcett tried to appear at least a little concerned on the other woman's behalf, tilting her head to the side and pursing her lips.

But, as Bea noted, she simply did not have the skill to make the effort appear convincing. Unquestionably, she was delighted by the unexpected turn in her adversary's fortunes and could not look anything but pleased.

Nevertheless, Mrs. Fawcett made an effort to strike a maudlin note, adding, "How exceedingly wretched for you. Now, my dear, you must not despair. I am sure it is not at all what it seems. Never say, your grace, that you found the button sleeve on Pudsey's body. You may claim that is true, but I simply will not believe it. Bentham would never be driven to murder, even if he did have a vicious row with Pudsey earlier in the evening."

Lady Bentham did not gasp again so much as gulp a large mouthful of air as she glared at the other woman. Then her expression softened, the lines around her eyes growing less rigid as she sought to affect indifference. Feigning a lack of concern, she said, "My dear Mrs. Fawcett, as much as I want to profess astonishment at your shocking insinuation about my husband, I simply cannot muster even a soupçon of surprise, for it is only to be expected from someone of your stamp. You are famously without delicacy or scruples, which is part of your appeal, so it would not be fair to cavil about it now. I am merely incapable of understanding how Lady Jersey can enjoy your company, for you are far too talkative to bear, even for a woman whose nickname is Silence."

Whatever bitter rejoinder an observation of this ilk would have ordinarily elicited from Mrs. Fawcett, she was too gratified by the unexpected turn to allow herself to be drawn into a bickering match. "Yes, dear, your understanding has always been less than exceptional, but you possess other strengths for which I have long admired you. Regardless, we must stay calm and not panic. I am certain the duchess will not have him carted off to Newgate. A man of his stature must have other options available to him. Perhaps Elba? As you know, it has a vacancy."

To her credit, Lady Bentham adopted an expression of mild good humor, revealing no hint of anger at the suggestion that her husband belonged in exile in the style of England's greatest foe. "I knew you suffered from a sense of inferiority, Mrs. Fawcett, but had not realized the situation had grown so dire you are compelled to fabricate evidence to undermine me. Bentham had no quarrel with Pudsey this evening or indeed any evening. They had a cordial relationship. Indeed, the conversation in this very room earlier was everything amiable and gentle. Not even a frown ruffled their brows."

"One may smile and smile and be a villain," Mrs. Fawcett said with a faint air of smugness, as if being able to provide an appropriate Shakespeare quote was all that was needed to settle the matter. "My husband heard Bentham threaten Pudsey's life."

As the society matrons traded insults, Bea looked across the room at Bentham, whose irritation at having his rug theory dismissed was etched on his face. Even with half his features obscured by the glass of port, his annoyance was plain.

He was, she thought, the only guest in the room who had proposed an alternate explanation for Pudsey's death and had advocated assiduously in its favor.

On its own, that fact did not argue one way or the other for his guilt, as it was human nature, she believed, to look for the most benign explanation for a tragedy. Paired, however, with the sleeve button being inside the weapon used to stun the victim, it took on a more sinister cast.

Even so, she was determined to withhold judgment. Making assumptions or drawing obvious conclusions would only lead her astray.

Although Bea appreciated Mrs. Fawcett's forthcomingness, she desired to hear the information from its source and called upon Mr. Fawcett to relate the dispute he had heard between Bentham and Pudsey earlier in the evening.

"Dispute?" he asked on an awkward chuckle, darting a sullen look at his wife before offering Bentham an apologetic grimace. "I did not say it was a dispute. A slight difference of opinion, perhaps."

Mrs. Fawcett did not appreciate his discretion, reminding him of his report. "You said Bentham was so incensed by Pudsey's refusal to listen to reason he threatened to kill him."

"No," Mr. Fawcett said sharply as the color rose in his cheeks. "I never said that. Really. What I *said* was Bentham told Pudsey that he would live to regret his actions. But possibly that is wrong because I was not listening to the conversation, of course, for it would be rude to take note of a discussion that did not include me. That was merely what I thought I'd overheard through no fault of my own."

His wife, who had already been accused of possessing no delicacy once in the past five minutes, asserted that the distinction held no meaning. "His intent was clear."

Mr. Fawcett, however, did not think the matter was so cut-and-dried and argued that it was possible to interpret those words in a variety of ways. "Provided," he added with a self-conscious cough, "those are the words under contention. I cannot speak to words I endeavored not to hear."

Bentham considered Mr. Fawcett for several long moments, allowing the other man's discomfort to grow, before confirming he had said those very words. "But I cannot believe anyone but the most miserly minded would consider them a threat to Pudsey's life. I said he would live to regret his actions—*living*, you see, is the very opposite of dying."

"It is, yes," Mr. Fawcett said, visibly relieved to be exonerated for the faux pas of eavesdropping. "Living is quite the opposite of dying."

"That is true," Mrs. Fawcett said mildly, "but as Bentham's sleeve button was found on Pudsey's dead body, I do not think the two are as far apart as he would have us believe."

More confused than startled by this revelation, Bentham looked down at his shirtsleeve, first the left, then the right, and noted that one of the buttons was indeed gone. "I do not understand. You say my sleeve button was found on Pudsey?"

Mrs. Fawcett replied yes just as Bea said no and Lady

Bentham announced that it was a fantasy devised by an unwell woman whose grasp on reality was clearly faltering.

"But you must not fear that your friends will abandon you during your time of need," her ladyship rushed to add, "for I will remain as steadfast as always and will endeavor to bring light to the darkness as you descend ever further into your twilight world."

"How kind you are," Mrs. Fawcett said softly, returning to the settee as the other woman continued to stand in the middle of the room, her smile rigid with displeasure. "And although such support is not necessary, I will gladly allow you the delusion if it will make your husband's exile to Elba any easier to bear. The very least I can do as your friend is provide a distraction."

At the second mention of the island, Lady Bentham's mask slipped and for a moment the depth of her dislike was etched in every line of her face. It was only a flash, just a glint and a flare, but staring into the glower, Bea could feel the exhausting weight of hatred, years and years of it.

Nobody else noticed.

Presumably, they were too baffled by Mrs. Fawcett's cryptic remark to pay her any heed, for Lady Abercrombie asked why anyone would be banished to Elba when the island had proved so evitable Napoleon had found his way off it after only two hundred days.

"Three hundred," Lord Bredbury said.

The countess looked at him in confusion. "Excuse me?"

"He found his way off the island in three hundred days," Bredbury explained. "Still not the durable solution we were hoping for when he was banished there but more effective than you are giving it credit for."

Mrs. Fawcett, interpreting both these comments as a rebuke of her understanding of current events so widely known that even the lowest chimney sweep could recite them, ventured that she had said Elba because it was famously less hospitable than St. Helena.

Bredbury, professing himself unfamiliar with the comforts of either locality, asked her to cite the source of her information.

As the conversation grew increasingly inane, Bentham's expression remained bewildered as he stared down at his shirtsleeve, as if trying to understand how the button had traveled from his wrist to Pudsey's corpse.

Bea did not doubt the sincerity of his confusion, for it was revealed plainly on his face. He truly had no idea how the fastener had found its way onto the dead man's body. But the actual source of his confusion was not as readily apparent. Was he incapable of comprehending how the button had arrived there in the first place or merely bemused by the fact that he had not noticed it had fallen? Surely, it behooved a gentleman in the act of executing a fellow peer to remain cognizant of the location of his button sleeves at all times.

Indeed, he should be fully aware of every aspect of his ensemble.

But the time frame he had in which to perform the deed was so slight, it would not be surprising if he lacked the attention or wherewithal to notice something as minor as a fastener slipping free of its hole.

And the vase, Bea thought. It was the instrument used to strike the first blow—possibly, Bentham had been too overwhelmed by the immensity of what he was about to do to observe anything but his victim.

It was a reasonable theory and rather likely, for there were few ways a small jewel could land at the bottom of a narrow-necked vessel.

"The button half was not found on Pudsey," Bea said loudly, interrupting Mrs. Fawcett's detailed account of Elba's uncongenial topography. "It was discovered inside a vase. I do not know where the other half is."

Although Lady Bentham felt this information definitively proved her claim about her rival's tenuous grip on reality, Mrs. Fawcett argued just as confidently that it attested to Bentham's guilt. Since neither matron was able to make a cogent case to substantiate her theory, as the presence of the button in the vase was manifestly inexplicable, they settled for raising their voices to ever-increasing heights in hopes of drowning out the other's argument.

Bentham, ignoring the cacophony, strode across the room until he was standing next to Bea and the duke. "It was in there?"

Again, Bea was struck by the look of utter befuddlement on his face and the lack of defensiveness in his attitude. He did not appear to be a man discovering he had made a fatal mistake in a crowded drawing room surrounded by influential members of the *ton*.

"How extraordinary," he murmured. "May I ask why you were examining the vase in the first place? What about it spurred your interest?"

Briefly, Bea detailed the line of reasoning that led her to that particular vessel. As she spoke, the room slowly fell silent and by the time she mentioned the stain of blood marring the otherwise pristine porcelain, she had everyone's attention.

Lady Bentham harrumphed loudly, as if to imply the logic Bea had used was either faulty or suspect, but her husband owned himself duly impressed with her ability to deduce. "You are very clever, your grace."

"Do stop fawning, John," his wife said testily. "The girl is accusing you of murder!"

"I do not think she is," he replied, his tone reasonable and sincere, with none of the mockery he displayed earlier. "At least, not yet. And since I obviously had nothing to do with Pudsey's death, I am not the least bit worried. You may continue with your deductions, your grace, with no interference from me. I only wish I could be of more help to you, but I have no idea when the sleeve button slipped out. I simply did not notice the event."

Mr. Fawcett warned his wife about the deleterious effects of rampant speculation, while Lady Abercrombie lauded his lordship for the pervasive rationality of his approach. Flora, who had meandered over to the table to inspect the vase for herself, dipped her head knowingly at the red mark and confirmed her cousin's conclusion.

"Oh, yes," she said. "That is definitely blood."

Dismayed, Miss Petworth shrunk back in her seat, and her uncle patted her hand consolingly while calling for the servants to remove Pudsey from the room. "It is a crime against humanity to subject the women to this brutality."

Bea, desiring that the body remain where it was in case she needed to ascertain additional information, asked if a cloth might be employed instead to remove the unhappy sight from view.

"That is not an adequate solution," Bredbury protested.

"No, please, uncle," Miss Petworth said, her voice shaking slightly. "I am sure that is fine."

A servant was summoned immediately, and as soon as the blanket had been laid over the victim, Bea asked Bentham what he and Pudsey were arguing about.

"But were we arguing?" his lordship asked. "I do not recall either one of us raising our voices or even glowering at the other. We did have a conversation—indeed, more of a debate, I would say—about an act he had introduced in Parliament pertaining to the treatment of horses. As would any gentleman worthy of the name, I abhor cruelty to animals and would sooner cut off my own arm than abuse one. Nevertheless, I question the wisdom of attempting to legislate something so nebulous. How does one define cruelty against a horse? Surely, the definition varies from man to man? Who is Pudsey to decide that for all of England? And I cannot pretend that it is not a troubling precedent to set. Admittedly, we all agree that horses are noble creatures and well worth our respect. But what will be next? Will Parliament decide that the meanest cur in the manger is deserving of our protection? Or the grouse in the tree? Might someday Parliament decide that the beloved tradition of hunting foxes is cruel?"

True to his word, Bentham did not raise his voice or glower at the company as he discussed the topic. His tone remained calm and even as he described the hazards of Pudsey's proposed act. "Are some of my concerns outlandish?" he asked rhetorically. "Yes, I believe they are. From where I am standing, it is inconceivable that the British government would ever think of banning such a noble sport as the hunt. But just because something seems highly unlikely does not mean it is impossible, and *that* is why I told Pudsey he would live to regret his actions. It begins with horses but will end with the smallest dormouse under the floorboards in the poorest kitchen."

"Yes, precisely," Lady Bentham said approvingly. "That is exactly the sort of high-minded debate my husband engages in regularly, and I do not doubt for a moment that Pudsey addressed his valid concerns with erudite observations of his own, for both are members of a deliberative body devoted to the elevation of ideas. Obviously, such a concept eludes Mrs. Fawcett, which is why she turned Bentham's insightful remark into a murder threat. She gave it the worst possible cast because it reflects her own way of looking at the world and how she would respond if Lord Pudsey had proposed legislation that would harm something she treasures in life.

Oh, my goodness, now that I think about it, he *had* done exactly that with his proposed levy on the importation of fluorspar. Remind me, my dear, what are the chances Prince Adriano will go through with the marriage to your daughter if he cannot sell fluorspar to the foundries in Middlesbrough for a profit? Is it zero or almost zero? I can never remember."

Mrs. Fawcett's blue eyes hardened to chips of ice, and yet somehow she managed to respond as if unbothered by the query. "Prince Adriano is delighted to join our family regardless of the minor concern of commerce. He is very devoted to Patricia. It is a love match, you see, which I do not expect you to understand, being such a rapacious creature yourself."

Lady Bentham responded to the accusation of voracity by calling Mrs. Fawcett a manipulative schemer, which earned her the charge of ravenous gluttony. Seething, her ladyship decried her as a second-rate Machiavelli.

Nuneaton, deeming the door safe, came to stand next to Bea. "If I had realized that your investigative method consisted of allowing spiteful society matrons to hurl insults at each other, I would have stopped pestering you for details weeks ago."

"It is not her *only* method," Flora said, her tone snappish in defense of her cousin. "It is one of many, and the one that is employed depends on the situation. Conducting an investigation is a very complex business that you cannot understand until you've managed one of your own."

Although Bea would not describe allowing the rivals to argue viciously with each other a method, she was in fact interested in seeing where their tempers led them. Neither one would be the first woman to utter an indiscretion in the heat of the moment.

Lady Abercrombie, expressing a sentiment similar to the viscount, asked if the mêlée was really necessary. "Mrs. Fawcett seems near to apoplexy, and while I can ride out the scandal of having one person die during one of my dinner parties, I am almost positive I cannot survive two."

Suddenly, Lady Bentham inhaled sharply—another gasp—and turned to stare at the countess with wide-eyed horror as the truth forcefully struck her. "Oh, my God, it was you! It was you! Only you knew about the scissors and where everyone was and how long they would be there. You set the stage and then you killed Pudsey. My God, *you* are the murderer."

Chapter Eight

L ady Abercrombie laughed at the allegation and insisted that if she had wanted to end Lord Pudsey's life, she would have done so in the privacy of her own bedchamber, not in the middle of an elaborate affair she had organized.

"Hosting a seamless dinner party is difficult enough without adding the additional hardship of successfully eliminating one of your guests during the brief interval between dessert and port," she said with a smile. "And even if I were inclined to accept the challenge, I would never dream of making the attempt in Beatrice's presence for she is far too clever. Inevitably, I would overlook some remarkably minor detail that she would latch onto, and it would be over in a matter of minutes. Recall, if you will, that she managed to figure out who killed her parents twenty years after their deaths, which is to say she lacked the advantage of examining the amphorae in the room where it occurred. No, if I *had* wished to revenge myself against dear Pudsey for some slight, though I cannot imagine what that would be, as he was a lovely man with whom I enjoyed spending my time, I would do it furtively at night. Truthfully, I have never given the matter any thought, but forced to consider it now, I suppose I would administer a fatal dose of some poison to ensure he passed in his sleep. Perhaps laudanum? Something gentle so that he would go quietly. It would be wretched if he made a mess."

Lady Bentham, who did not find the countess's aggressively pragmatic approach to murder persuasive, cited her cool detachment as further proof of her culpability. "How smoothly she talks about murdering her lover! How casually she discusses poisoning him in his sleep! Her indifference is horrifying. I am only relieved that Pudsey is not alive to hear it, for surely he deserved better."

Mrs. Fawcett was likewise unconvinced. "Although I know Lady Bentham's intent is to turn our attention from the sleeve button that incriminates her husband, I must concede that her argument does make sense. I know well the audacity of the Countess of Abercrombie. Indeed, I think all of us in this room know how ardently she enjoys being the center of attention, and I do believe she would perform even the most monstrous spectacle if it would increase society's interest in her."

"La, how you do flatter me!" her ladyship said with a breathless chortle. "It is a pleasure to know that one's life work has not been in vain. It is true, everything you said, for I do so relish the *ton's* attention and am much gratified to know that my efforts have not gone to waste. But that is exactly why your argument falls short, for whom would I find in Newgate to admire me? Who would gawk over the elegant loveliness of my prison cell? Would I even be allowed to decorate it in the Oriental style?" She shivered dramatically here as if contemplating a new horror. "No, a monstrous spectacle would appeal to me only if I could be certain to evade the consequences, and as I said, I would never take the risk with the duchess in the room, especially during an evening designed to showcase her particular skill at figuring out murders. And if I was set on so reckless a course, what cause would I have to harm Pudsey? Even a detestable creature such as myself must have a reason."

Although Bea did not consider a perpetrator's motive to be a central factor in any investigation, it remained a reasonable question to ask and she looked at Lady Bentham to see if she could provide an answer. Slightly daunted, her ladyship fluttered her lashes swiftly, almost confused by the query, and then turned to stare at Mrs. Fawcett, as if compelling her to supply the response of which she was incapable.

For a moment, the women gazed blankly at each other, and although neither spoke, it seemed as though many words passed between them.

Watching their silent communication, Bea decided that Flora's and Nuneaton's understanding of their relationship was imperfect, for it underestimated how much the two women actually had in common. They were opposing sides of the same coin, and she thought they rather enjoyed their games of manipulation, each considering the other a worthy opponent.

As if to prove Bea's thesis, the society matrons abruptly turned to Miss Petworth at the same time and pointed.

"There is your cause," Lady Bentham said fervently.

"She is the reason," Mrs. Fawcett replied with satisfaction.

Miss Petworth squeaked lightly at the sudden attention and rounded her shoulders, as if to make herself smaller or less visible.

"Everyone knows he has been courting her," Lady Bentham added.

Mrs. Fawcett nodded. "Yes, that's right. We all saw it on Wednesday night at Mrs. Reddington's rout. They had a private exchange on the balcony, did they not, and when she emerged, she was quite becomingly flushed."

"And how attentive he was to her this evening when she spilled her soup," Lady Bentham said, speaking more quickly as she settled into her theory. "How gentle and kind as he sought to ease her embarrassment over her terrible clumsiness."

"You could not stand it," Mrs. Fawcett said, "watching him fawn over a woman thirty years your junior in your own home!"

"A woman who is more beautiful than you ever were," Lady Bentham announced with triumphant zeal, confident that she was delivering the coup de grâce.

Mrs. Fawcett appeared to agree with the force of this argument, for she breathed in deeply and said with relish, "Oh, yes, much more beautiful than you ever were."

Their hostess laughed again, her peels ringing with genuine amusement as she assured the society matrons that her beauty had little to do with her romantic success. "It is what draws them in, I will concede, but it is my wit and experience that maintains their interest. I cannot speak of the threadbare strings that hold up your vanity, but I can assure you mine are not so weak that they can be snapped by a slip of a girl. Yes, Miss Petworth is very young, but so are Cuthbert and Thirlwall, and they have no complaints about my aging charms. If you doubt my word, I urge you to apply directly to them for confirmation."

Predictably, Lady Bentham gasped, and Bea could not decide if the reaction was spurred by the countess's candidness in discussing her lovers or her revelation that there was in fact one more than the *ton* realized.

Perhaps it was a little bit of both, for her ladyship sharply chastised their hostess for discussing such a depraved topic with innocent ears in the room. She looked at Miss Petworth with pointed emphasis, making it clear whose ears she considered to be of particular purity, but then expanded her gaze to include Flora as well.

Miss Petworth, appearing miserable, shrunk even further into herself and would have returned to the terrace at full speed had it been an option.

Her mortification would be greater still if she knew at least one person in the room considered her to be among the more likely suspects.

Thinking of Flora, Bea marveled over how differently two people could interpret the same event. Her cousin was convinced Miss Petworth spilled the soup in a desperate bid for attention while Lady Bentham ascribed it to excessive clumsiness.

Both seemed out of character for the Incomparable, whose self-assurance Bea had experienced firsthand on the night she had become engaged to Kesgrave. Boldly, she had asserted a kinship with the duchess-to-be that categorically did not exist. The determined young woman she knew the Incomparable to be would never slyly tip over her soup—not when fluttering her long, gorgeous lashes would accomplish the same goal without exposing her to ridicule or undermining her reputation for elegance and grace.

She was simply too poised to make such a novice mistake.

Indeed, she was, yes, Bea thought, suddenly struck by the strangeness of her behavior.

If the mishap with the soup was not a poorly considered attempt at flirting or a moment sincerely lacking in dexterity, then it had to be attributed to another source.

A more nefarious source?

She examined Miss Petworth's other behavior during the evening more carefully. The act that stood out the strongest —after the soup, of course—was the way she had fled from the room containing Pudsey's dead body. Her uncle said she was horrified by the ghastly sight, and she herself claimed to require fresh air.

Bea did not doubt those explanations, for it was no startling thing for a young woman to be undone by the unexpected sight of a murdered man, especially if she nurtured feelings for him.

But *did* she nurture feelings for him?

Bea was not as convinced as her cousin because she had seen the way Miss Petworth had darted to the other side of the room as quickly as possible when Pudsey arrived. She seemed unable to stand his presence.

True, but she *had* arranged to sit next to him at the table, politely declining the alternative Lady Abercrombie had offered.

Why would she desire to be near him in the dining room but not in the drawing room? Why endure the entirety of a meal when a brief conversation repulsed her?

What was unique about dinner?

The food itself, obviously, she thought, and pondered why that would be important.

She recalled also the oddness of Lady Abercrombie's inexplicably indisposed footmen and considered the possibility that the two events were related.

Surely not.

And yet it struck her as too much of a coincidence: the poised beauty suffering a graceless accident while sitting next to a man she disliked only a half hour before the footmen were struck with a mysterious gastric complaint.

Could that explain the use of the scissors as the murder weapon?

Having come prepared with poison to end Pudsey's life, she had resorted to embroidery shears when her first attempt failed.

It had failed, Bea thought, because Pudsey barely ate the

soup. He had moved his spoon around the bowl but rarely lifted it to his lips.

With Mrs. Mayhew's ability to wield a hatchet in mind, she pushed aside the question of whether Miss Petworth was capable of driving a pair of scissors into a man's chest and examined instead her behavior after the body was discovered. She had dashed to the terrace, she claimed, because she desired fresh air. But if she had just stabbed Pudsey, then she might have required the time to compose herself.

Or maybe she needed an opportunity to get rid of a few stray splatters of blood?

No, those stains could not be removed with water. Soap and a good hard scrub were necessary.

But the idea of getting rid of something resonated with Bea, and she realized that if her soup theory was correct, then the toxic substance had to have been conveyed in a container of some sort—a small vial or jar.

It was, Bea knew, an imperfect hypothesis because it failed to account for Bentham's sleeve button. Furthermore, no motive had been revealed for Miss Petworth, while his lordship's was clear and plainly stated.

She imagined many a gentleman in London would kill to preserve the fox hunt.

Nevertheless, Bea refused to allow herself to be dissuaded from pursuing the line of inquiry. She could pull only one thread at a time, and this one was firmly in her grasp now.

Of course, that did not mean she had relinquished the Bentham string, merely transferred it momentarily to the other hand.

While Lady Abercrombie pooh-poohed the use of the word *depraved* to describe her relationships, which were, she explained, all very moralistic and highly principled affairs, Bea said softly to Nuneaton, "I have an idea that I wish to pursue.

Would you be so kind as to ensure nobody leaves the room in my absence?"

Flora, either noticing a particular look in her cousin's eye or simply resenting any sotto voce conference that did not include her, leaned forward to ask what was afoot. "Do we have another clue to investigate?"

"Not a clue," Bea said quickly, "just a thought. But in order to validate it, I need your help. You must work with Nuneaton to make sure the company stays here. Do you think you can manage that? As soon as Mrs. Fawcett tires of arguing with our hostess, she will notice I am gone and try to slip out."

"Have no fear," Flora said staunchly. "I have several stalling tactics available to me, and if they all fail, Nuneaton will forcibly restrain her."

"No, I will not," he replied.

Impatiently, Flora told him that the situation was far too grave to allow his fear of industriousness to rule him.

"It is not a fear of industriousness that concerns me," he explained, "but a fear of being called out by Fawcett. He is skilled with a foil and would not hesitate to use it on me for assaulting his wife."

Flora dismissed his concern as unlikely, as it would be terribly gauche for Fawcett to threaten to run through a fellow guest at a party where another fellow guest had already been run through. "As angry as he might be with your handling of his wife, I am sure he would never allow his displeasure to overcome his decorum."

Nuneaton observed that her remark lacked a fundamental understanding of how anger functioned.

Bea left them to handle the matter and darted a meaningful glance at the duke, who caught up with her as she was exiting the room. Like Flora, he assumed she had discovered something of interest that she wished to explore further, and as they passed through the dining room to the terrace, he asked what their purpose was.

"I am not certain," she said as they stepped out into the cool night air. Briefly, she explained her theory, which sounded even more improbable when spoken aloud. The idea of Miss Petworth, with her porcelain shoulders and delicate hands, driving a pair of blades into Pudsey's chest was patently absurd.

If Kesgrave agreed, he gave no indication as he surveyed the wide expanse of dark stone pavers lined with overflowing planters on three sides and a neat hedge on the fourth. "If events unfolded exactly as you described, then I would not expect her to have been particularly elaborate in her conceal- ment. She would have seized gratefully on the first spot to capture her attention and used that without thinking too deeply on it. She would not have had the time or presence of mind to consider whether the hiding spot could be easily found."

Confidently, he strode toward the line of planters bordering the far edge of the terrace, stopped at the one in the middle and lowered his hand into the pot of bluebells and cowslips.

Amused, Bea watched the Duke of Kesgrave root around in the dirt in his evening finery, the line of his rigorously tailored coat remaining smooth, and realized with a familiar tinge of mortification that she had done it yet again— brought the highly respected peer to another new low. Not content with consigning him to the role of butler, she compounded the insult by requiring him to act as gardener.

Would it never end, the indignities to which she would subject him, or would their marriage be the slow eroding away of his consequence until there was nothing left?

It was horrifying to contemplate, the damage she could do, and now, as always, she feared what would happen when she went too far. Sooner or later, she would cross an invisible line and commit some transgression that would scandalize polite society and Kesgrave would finally know the sting of rejection.

"I've got something," he said, interrupting her thoughts as he held up a small narrow cylinder that he had found in the third planter he examined. "A scent bottle. The flowers are freshly planted, so it cannot have been out here long."

Kesgrave dropped the vial, which was decorated with an enamel pattern, in her hand and immediately turned his attention to his cuff, which was speckled with potting soil. Indifferent to the dirt, he brushed at it lightly, then straightened the sleeve of his coat. Observing the nonchalance with which he attended to the task, she was struck firmly and unequivocally by the truth: He did not care.

No, he did not care.

Truly, sincerely, wholeheartedly, and without reservation, he cared not one whit what society thought about him.

He had been saying it for months, yes, insisting with every other breath that any stance he adopted instantly became the fashion. Beset by her own insecurities, she had assumed his attitude was merely an aesthetic choice—the carefree leader of the *beau monde*—but she realized now that it was a conviction that permeated every inch of his body. He did not worry about the approval of the *ton* for the simple reason that he did not desire it.

More significantly, he did not require it.

He was complete in himself.

It was a straightforward enough concept and yet so alien to Beatrice that she had been incapable of conceiving it. It was simply beyond the scope of her perception.

As a consequence, she had been able to comprehend his standing only as she understood her own, as something buffeted by winds—of society, of fate, of selfish actors who lacked empathy or kindness.

His sails were sturdier, she assumed, and more firmly fixed to the spar but just as vulnerable to gusts.

Eventually, she thought, a strong gale would tear them down.

But it was not a matter of degrees—the fragility of her mast versus the durability of his.

No, Kesgrave was in a different category altogether.

His own category.

It was the reason why people like Bentham sought his approval so relentlessly and why the earl had resorted to creating his own organization to raise his stature. His position at the helm of the Henley Sporting Club was an artificial construct —reinforced, yes, by an arbitrary system of inclusion and exclusion but still too feeble to withstand a mildly stiff breeze.

His grace's assurance was only to be expected, for he was, after all, born to outrageous privilege and raised in its advantages. As the sixth Duke of Kesgrave, he stood at the end of a very long line of men who had used their power to gain more power. For five hundred years, the Matlock family had been cementing its influence, fortifying its authority, and it was little wonder that the heir to that inexplicable inheritance would hold himself in great esteem.

Indeed, the shocking thing would be if he did not.

And knowing himself to be superior to much of humanity in both material and immaterial ways, he should by right be insufferable.

Tavistock, whose land marched along only the northern border of a ducal family estate, considered himself so entitled to its abundance he thought nothing of destroying a young woman to get it.

And Mayhew!

That preening nodcock.

He was the legatee of a minor banking empire, and yet the small amount of prestige conferred by his situation had turned him into a pompous bore incapable of complex reasoning.

That Kesgrave managed to be neither of those things—cruel or dull-witted—had always struck her as a matter of luck. As easily as his temperament had tipped into kindness, it could have tilted toward intolerance.

But her assumption was wrong, she realized now.

Extremely, entirely wrong.

Character was not a thing that balanced on a pivot, like a child's seesaw, yielding to the greater force.

No, it was the fulcrum itself, and the beam swayed above it.

As sturdy as a rock, Kesgrave stood firmly in place, and the proof was here, she thought.

This was the proof—the small vial in her clasp, the smudges of soil on his cuff. Neither would have happened if he were a thing that teetered.

Astounded, astonished, utterly in love, she said, "I was hiding from Marlow behind the door in his bedroom."

Kesgrave, adjusting his cuff, glanced up at her with an expression of mild amusement. Then he lifted one brow with curious interest as he contemplated her in the moonlight. "Was this before or after you convinced him that leading compulsory Bible lessons was not the ideal way to endear himself to the staff?"

"As his goal was improving the tone of the servants' conversation, I merely pointed out that requiring them to read and discuss Ephesians 4:29 at length would likely produce the opposite effect and generate more unwholesome talk, most of it centered on him," she explained as his lips quirked. "And it was before that. On my first morning in

Kesgrave House. I went belowstairs to consult with Mrs. Wallace and before I could locate her office, I heard Marlow coming down the corridor. I ran to hide in what I thought was the stillroom, but it turned out to be his pantry. He and Joseph came in, so I scurried into his bedroom and hid behind the door."

"Ah," said Kesgrave, as if finally receiving the answer to a long-pondered question. "So, that is how you found out about Mr. Réjane's death."

"Yes, eavesdropping on the servants," she said. "I swore never to tell you because it is mortifying to be terrified of the butler in one's own home. For one panicked moment, I contemplated hiding under the bed and then made myself weak in the knees imagining Marlow discovering me there."

Kesgrave, wincing at the scene she described, applauded her wisdom, for if she had been found in such an awkward position, he naturally would have had to disavow her entirely. "The sanctity of the servants' quarters must be fervently professed to if not strictly honored," he explained before asking why she felt compelled to confess to the incident now. "And by *now,* I do not mean here, on the terrace during Tilly's suddenly real murder mystery party as we examine the planters for evidence. I mean, why at all?"

It was, she acknowledged, a fair question, and because she was not entirely sure of the answer herself, she paused for a moment to consider it.

What was the link between that moment and this one?

Perhaps it was the door, she thought.

Yes, that was it.

Explaining, she said, "Because it struck me as funny. That was a door and this was a door."

Her reply failed to provide enlightenment. "This?"

"Specifically, this situation. Recall, if you will, about a half hour ago. I pressed my back against the door, literally barring with my body Lady Abercrombie's carefully selected assortment of influential guests from exiting the room," she explained, as if the exchange might have somehow slipped his mind. "More broadly, this hand of fate, this instrument of my destruction. I have struggled to hide from you, Damien, the depth of my insecurity."

He opened his mouth as if to argue this point—to assure her, Bea thought with amusement, that she had managed to hide nothing from him—but rather than speak, he pressed his lips together and nodded.

Clever man, she thought.

"The servants, the houses, the social obligations—they are merely the tip of a very long sword that threatens to cut me in half," she said, running her fingers over the decorative scent bottle and noting the swirls of the enamel pattern of circles and stars.

"The pineries," he added softly.

"Yes, you see, precisely," she said with swift affirmation, as if all at once everything had been made clear. "*The pineries!* It is so tedious, is it not, having to listen to the same list over and over, having to offer the same reassurances over and over. It is deadening in its own way, and I wanted to spare you."

He assured her quite firmly that he did not wish to be spared.

"You only say that because you have not been subjected to the endless monologue that plays in my head," she replied with an unamused chuckle. "It is quite intolerable, your grace. Whole paragraphs of qualms and doubts that hum with persistence while other people talk, frequently to me. And no matter how ardently I wish to end them, how fervently I wish to silence them, I simply cannot turn my thoughts off like water from a spigot."

Frown lines etched into Kesgrave's forehead as he said with clipped precision, "Two weeks."

It was a baffling response, cryptic and curt, and she stared at him uncomprehendingly as she repeated the words. "Two weeks?"

"Yes, Bea, two weeks," he said heatedly. "It has been two weeks since we married. It has been two weeks since you assumed the position of Duchess of Kesgrave. How many years since your parents were killed?"

The second non sequitur confused her as much as the first, but she answered without quibbling, "Twenty."

"How many seasons since Miss Brougham undermined your confidence?"

Although she could not perceive the whole of his argument, she felt certain she had a glimmer of it. "Six."

"How many days since *The Sussex General Advertiser and County Express* published an article detailing the various ways you are unsuited to be a duchess?" he asked.

Bea, who had prepared to produce another by-rote number, stared at him aghast. "*The Sussex General Advertiser and County Express* published what?"

"Ah, yes, that's right," Kesgrave said with an amused shake of his head. "We managed to hide that story from you. It is a local paper with a small circulation of only a few hundred readers, and the arguments themselves fell well short of persuasive, although I will admit to being biased, for I happen to find an agile mind to be a very attractive trait in a duchess. Mr. Smarten-Muke, of course, has the right to his own opinion. Nevertheless, you cannot know how many days it is so I will supply the answer, which is four. It has been four days since *The Sussex General Advertiser and County Express* devoted a pair of remarkably dense columns to your inadequacies. And remind me again: How long have we been married?"

"Two weeks," Bea said, her tone faltering as she tried to follow his point while also figuring out how she would get her hands on the newspaper, which reported on events close to the Hyde-Clare family seat in Bexhill Downs. If Kesgrave's steward, Mr. Stephens, refused to provide her with a copy, she could always pay a call to the Addison coffeehouse and read it there.

He nodded. "That's right, two weeks. Two paltry weeks against twenty years and six seasons and four days. Your insecurities are deeply ingrained and you cannot expect simply to slough them off like a snake shedding its old skin. I know you hold yourself to a higher standard than me, but surely even you can see that expecting to overcome a lifetime of ill treatment in a single fortnight is inordinately ambitious. I have pledged to support you in your determination to investigate further crimes, but I draw the line at indulging an irrational expectation of yourself," he said firmly, before his lips quirked slightly and he added, "Well, that *and* hiding under the butler's bed. I really must insist that you continue to withstand that impulse, and should you fail and are discovered, I shall chastise your impudence horribly. As much as I love you, I will not risk the servants' wrath."

Listening to this lovely speech, Bea was not at all surprised to discover he had considered the matter deeply, for he had already demonstrated a keen understanding of her situation. His acceptance of her investigative habit, for example, was predicated on the conviction that it would give her the confidence she needed to navigate the manifold challenges of her new position.

Even so, she was slightly unnerved by the arrogance of his assumption. To believe that all she needed to overcome her insecurities was a little more time—it was a perspective she could not fathom, for her anxieties felt to her profoundly rooted, as if they could defy both time and space.

His conclusion came, she decided, from five hundred

years of social elevation. How flat the world must look from his very high perch, how easy to traverse.

And yet, had it really been so difficult for her?

In the end, it had required only a patch of soil on a pristine white cuff.

That was it. That was all it took to vanquish her fears.

A speck of dirt.

It was, she thought, a testament to the random mechanism of the heart.

"Not a higher standard *than* you, your grace, *for* you," Bea corrected with an impish grin. "I actually hold myself to quite a low standard. But that is neither here nor there, for I am happy to report that the issue has been resolved. Watching you brush potting soil from your sleeve with utter indifference to the mark it left made me comprehend in a way your repeated assertions never did that you are genuinely impervious to the judgment of others. The respect of your peers, the opinion of society—none of it matters to you."

He adjusted the cuff of his tailcoat as he stepped closer to her. "Your opinion matters."

"I am gratified to hear it," Bea said, "but I was never worried about my own derision, which I am adept at keeping in check. I was worried about everyone else's. Much of my anxiety was on your behalf, for I hated the thought of your getting the cut direct on my account or, worse, being cast out entirely."

"Would it be so terrible, social pariah-hood?" he asked softly, taking her into his arms and pressing his lips against her forehead. "Banished to the library with you and forced to spend all my time in leisurely repose with no interruptions save the housekeeper with regular meals and perhaps my steward with a document or two for me to sign. Truthfully, my love, it sounds heavenly. Please do whatever you can to ensure my expulsion from the *ton* as soon as possible."

Oh, indeed, yes, it sounded utterly divine when accompanied by a kiss on her cheek and her neck and the spot just below her collarbone that had the bewildering ability to turn her knees into water.

But his description of a secluded retreat, cozy and snug and sheltered from the world, bore no resemblance to the reality she had experienced. Her exile had been lonely, and she felt a renewed sense of gratitude that he would never know the icy sting of isolation.

Struggling to maintain some sense of decorum despite the privacy of the terrace and the warmth of his lips, she tried to order her thoughts to form a coherent response. It was difficult, however, with the duke's ardor playing havoc with her senses.

"You are forgetting the door," she insisted breathlessly.

"On the contrary, I am recalling your cool command of the situation," he said, turning his attention to her earlobe, "and it might be the single most impressive thing I have ever seen."

Naturally, Bea could not allow such elaborate praise to go unanswered, for hyperbole, when aimed in her general direction, made her distinctly uncomfortable. That said, she found it very difficult to form a coherent argument with his lips gently nibbling on hers. If anything, her protest came across as a satisfied sigh.

This will never do, she thought as her arms snaked around his neck and she leaned further into the kiss. We really must stop.

And yet she moved closer, pressing herself against him as moonlight bathed them and a gentle breeze ruffled the flowers on Lady Abercrombie's terrace.

Good lord, Lady Abercrombie!

Horrified by their behavior, Bea inhaled sharply and dropped her hands to the side. She tried to take a step backward, but Kesgrave held her in place with one arm as his fingers danced enticingly along the edge of her bodice.

Her heart beating erratically, she said, "We must return to the party."

"Yes," he agreed amiably, "but no."

Bemused, she laughed and told him he must pick one. "Even you cannot exist in two states at once."

"We shall return, yes," he said, drawing her more tightly into his embrace and settling her head sweetly underneath his chin. "But first, for a moment, stay here, just here, and let me appreciate my wife's fearlessness."

Discomfited by his praise, for his comprehension of the situation lacked a sophisticated understanding of how impetuousness worked, she acceded to his wish but added that the moment must be brief. "If we are discovered like this in the wake of poor Pudsey's death, then we will truly be banished."

Kesgrave chuckled lightly and warned her that that was not quite the inducement she thought it was. After a moment, however, he succumbed to the inevitable and loosened his grip. Taking a half step backward, he inspected her appearance. Then he straightened the bodice of her gown, laid a chaste kiss on her cheek and extended his arm. "Your grace?"

'Twas curious, she thought as she accepted his escort, how he always managed to make those words sound like an endearment when she consistently imbued them with a faint hint of mockery.

As they walked back into the house, Bea pondered the meaning of the vial. That it existed at all aligned with her theory and seemed to indicate that Miss Petworth had indeed made a first attempt on Lord Pudsey's life by poisoning his soup.

That in itself was quite shocking, for it was a most daring

act to try to murder a man in plain view of eleven other diners. She would not have imagined the young lady had the nerve.

But it was the second attempt on his life—the one that succeeded in the ghastliest manner—that required true audacity and Bea wondered if Miss Petworth had the physical capability to drive scissors through Pudsey's chest.

If he was rendered insensible by the blow to his head, then she rather thought yes. She was less certain, however, that she possessed the strength to hit him hard enough on the head to bring about the desired lack of consciousness.

But if they were romantically involved as their tryst at Mrs. Reddington's rout indicated, then she would have been able to get close enough to surprise him and perhaps do sufficient damage. If he had in fact been kissing her when she struck, that would account for the positioning of the wound, which was higher on his head than she would have ordinarily reached with her small frame.

Kesgrave, similarly occupied by the puzzle of Miss Petworth's actions, asked Bea what she thought the Incomparable's motivation might be. "Aside from their encounter at Mrs. Reddington's earlier this week, I have never heard their names linked, so I am at a loss to understand her reasoning. Could the rumor that she has long nursed a tendre for him be true and she is simply acting as a woman scorned? I know better than to judge a person solely on their appearance, but given her youth and beauty, she would have many opportunities to do far better than Pudsey even if she is determined to marry a title."

Bea, who also found it difficult to imagine a woman with Miss Petworth's physical advantages forming a hopeless passion for someone much older than she, could likewise not fathom a man of Pudsey's years rejecting her.

He was, after all, well into his sixth decade, and did not all men desire young flesh?

Kesgrave objected to this general categorization and said that *most* men desired young flesh. "But exceptions abound, including Pudsey himself, for he was also involved with Tilly. Although still exquisite, she is far from her first blush of youth."

"That substantiates your woman-scorned theory," Bea said thoughtfully as they passed through the dining room into the corridor. "Perhaps Miss Petworth was incensed that Pudsey preferred an older woman to her. I cannot imagine she has been denied many things in her life."

"Or she issued an ultimatum and he refused," Kesgrave added.

"It is a plausible explanation for the vial and the soup," Bea said, "but I am not sure it extends to the vase and the scissors. It seems odd to me that having failed to end his life quietly and indirectly with poison that her next step would be to pick up a pair of shears and drive them into his chest. Why not wait for another opportunity to ply him with poison?"

"I agree that the two actions are an uncomfortable fit," he replied, "especially as the latter required her to think quickly, for she could not have known when she entered the house that there would even be a pair of embroidery scissors in the offing."

"Or that those scissors would be the implement used in Lady Abercrombie's murder mystery play," Bea observed. "To improvise a plan during the meal while conversing with seeming calm and natural vivacity requires an agility of mind with which I would never have credited her."

"Nor I," Kesgrave said, "although I have learned from our last investigation not to make any assumptions based on a suspect's physical appearance or mental acuity or even their apparently unassailable alibi for the time of the murder. Thanks to Mrs. Mayhew, I believe all things are possible."

Bea nodded absently and wondered if the intent had been to make it appear as if Lady Abercrombie were the guilty party. "Is that why Miss Petworth set herself the challenge of using the scissors? So that we would all suspect our hostess? Even if that was her plan, how can we explain Bentham's sleeve button? It is by far our most compelling piece of evidence, and yet it does not fit into the narrative we are compiling. Could they be working in concert?"

"Miss Petworth and Bentham?" Kesgrave asked, taken aback by the possibility but happy to consider it. "He certainly nursed his own resentment against Pudsey. He may sound as if the animal cruelty act does not alarm him, but he is actually quite anxious about its passage and implementation. In order for them to be working together, however, they would have had to have settled on a plan before they arrived, and I cannot imagine Bentham allowing someone else to take the lead in any endeavor. He is always at the front of the pack."

"A valid point," Bea said, "and they would have had no opportunity to arrange a new scheme during the meal, for they sat at opposite ends of the table."

"It is difficult to imagine them secretly devising a new plot even if they had been seated next to each other," Kesgrave said as the buzzy sound of raised voices wafted into the corridor from the drawing room. "Bentham issues order like a general directing his infantrymen. It would not have been a quiet conversation."

"Speaking of unquiet conversation," Bea murmured as they approached the entrance to the room. "Chaos seems to have broken out while we were gone. I hope nobody else is dead."

Despite the loud argument currently consuming the attention of everyone in the room, all ten sets of eyes turned to Bea and the duke as soon as they entered.

"There!" Flora cried in the sudden silence that followed, an air of vindication in her tone. "I *told* you they had not left."

But Lady Bentham was far from appeased and pointed out that the word she had used was *gone*. "For they were gone—gone from the room and our presence. And now they are back."

Flora, impressing her cousin with her remarkable forbearance, did not argue further over the point and instead requested politely that Lady Bentham retake her seat. "Indeed, if everyone would kindly sit down, my sister will tell us what she discovered. You did discover something, did you not, Bea?"

Momentarily taken aback by the description, which Flora had never used before, Bea decided it was not a surprising development. If being cousin to a duchess was advantageous, then being sister was twice as beneficial, particularly now that she was about to make a startling revelation.

Smothering the surge of poorly timed amusement, Bea said, "I did, yes."

Then she stepped farther into the room as she looked at Miss Petworth, whose location had not changed during the interval on the terrace. While the others argued about leaving, she had remained quietly on the settee, her hands clasped tightly in her lap.

She looks guilty, Bea thought, or scared or remorseful or at the very least hugely uncomfortable.

Something about her interest must have communicated itself to Miss Petworth, for she looked up suddenly and, meeting Beatrice's gaze, turned alarmingly white. She rose swiftly to her feet and raised her head to a defiant angle, as if daring the other woman to make an accusation. Then just as quickly she collapsed onto the cushion, her entire body wracked with sobs as she screeched, "I didn't do it!"

Chapter Nine

Although Bea had not said a word, Bredbury reprimanded her for abusing his poor niece so terribly.

"She has clearly been made distraught by this evening's ghastly events, and your wanton disregard for her delicate sensibilities is the most appalling thing I have ever seen," he said harshly as he lowered himself onto the settee next to Miss Petworth. "It is barbaric, your treatment. Accusing an innocent girl of murder!"

"But she did not," Flora observed immediately. "Bea did not accuse Miss Petworth of anything."

Lady Bentham overcame her churlishness to agree with her recent adversary. "Miss Hyde-Clare is correct. No accusation has been lodged against your niece, and yet she has issued a passionate denial. It is most curious."

Mrs. Fawcett begged to disagree. "Rather, it is most enlightening. I believe we may take her outburst as a confession. Miss Petworth, for reasons known only to herself, killed Pudsey. How horrifying. I feel as though I am about to faint again. Lady Abercrombie, please do have one of your servants fetch the smelling salts."

Bredbury's cheeks flushed red with fury as he turned his ire on the society matron. "Are you entirely without wits, madam? Are you even aware of what you are saying? Look at my darling girl. I said, look at her! How could she stab a man a good head taller than she to death? It is physically impossible. Pudsey would have taken the scissors from her grasp as easily as taking a doll from a baby. She would be more likely to hurt herself than him," he said, struggling to contain his anger as he announced to Lady Abercrombie that he could not remain a minute longer. "I fear this event has done irreparable harm to my dear niece. She will never be able to look at a gold and jade dragon ever again without shuddering."

Bea thought few people were capable of looking at a gold and jade dragon without suffering some sort of physical reaction, but that was neither here nor there.

No, the only thing that mattered was Miss Petworth's nerves, which appeared to settle more with every angry word her uncle spewed. The tears continued to pour down her cheeks, but she managed to straighten her spine and return her hands to her lap. They were unclasped, an indication, Bea thought, that the other woman truly had herself under control.

When it seemed as though the Incomparable would refrain from hurling her torso against the cushion again, Bea said quietly, "Miss Petworth, I hope you will consent to join me in the study so that we may speak privately."

The girl's refusal—a firm no undermined by a weeping-induced hiccup—was repeated a second time. "No, your grace, you made the accusation publicly so I will earn my exoneration publicly."

"But she did not," Flora said again.

Miss Petworth continued as if Flora had not spoken, her tone even despite her anxiety. "I did not do it, your grace. That is, I did not stab Pudsey to death. That was never my intention. That is to say, my intention was never to cause him lasting harm."

"Halt!" Bredbury cried agitatedly, as if suddenly realizing the danger. "I insist that these proceedings stop at once. Do not say another word, my dear. Not even the Duchess of Kesgrave can compel you to speak."

Miss Petworth reached for her uncle's hand to soothe him and softly assured him that her silence would achieve nothing. "Her grace found my scent bottle," she said, looking at Bea. "Is that not so?"

Bea nodded, holding out the decorative vial, as Bredbury said, "Your scent bottle? What nonsense is this? I am sure whatever item the duchess claims to have found it has nothing to do with you."

"Hush, dear Uncle, all will be well, for I have done naught other than make a few of Lady Abercrombie's footmen indisposed," she said, now turning her lovely gray eyes toward her hostess. "I do hope you will forgive me, my lady, for upsetting your household and causing your staff discomfort. That was not my intent. Unfortunately, it never occurred to me that your footmen would finish the soup."

Her ladyship received this information with a narrowed gaze and asked, "What *was* your intent?"

"To kill Pudsey," Lady Bentham said with shrill satisfaction. "It is obvious to everyone here."

But her husband, fascinated by the development, asked her to reserve judgment until the duchess had finished her interview. Then he glanced at Bea and asked her respectfully to continue.

"You spilled your soup on purpose to create a distraction in order to put something in Pudsey's bowl," Bea said.

It was at once a question and a statement.

"That is true," Miss Petworth said. "But it is exactly as I said. My intention was never to cause lasting harm, I swear it. My maid procured the elixir for me, and although I do not quite know what is in it, I am sure it is as mild as she described. The fact that her ladyship's footmen have already begun to recover attests to that. I only wanted to cause him embarrassment."

Bea, whose limited familiarity with poison extended to information she had read in books, knew little of the potency of various substances. Nevertheless, she found this argument somewhat persuasive, for if the contents of the vial had been genuinely lethal, then members of the countess's staff would be in far greater straits.

But perhaps the outcome would have been different if one man had consumed the whole of it rather than three.

"Embarrass him how?" Bea asked.

"By creating an unfavorable gastric condition that he would find too challenging to overcome, causing an inconvenient disruption that would alter the cast of the room," she explained.

It was, by any measure, a detailed description, but Bea could not be certain of what. Which, she supposed, was most likely the point: obfuscation by elaboration. "Excuse me?"

"Farting," Miss Petworth replied bluntly, her face turning so brightly red it would glow in the dark like a candle. But she kept her eyes fixed on Bea, resolutely refusing to look down or away, either out of a sense of defiance or a fear of observing the reactions of her fellow guests. As one would expect, Lady Bentham responded with a horrified gasp, and Mrs. Fawcett clucked her tongue with arch disapproval.

Flora managed to remain silent, expelling not even a small peep of surprise, but her jaw fell open as she gawked at the girl whom she had suspected of murder.

Murder, yes, for it was a fairly mundane activity that human beings had been participating in for one painful reason or another for millennia.

But causing the expulsion of intestinal gas!

That was an unprecedented thing, wild and inconceivable and diabolically biological.

Bea did not doubt that it threw her cousin into a tumult of confusion, uncertain of how she should proceed—continue to resent the Incomparable's beauty or begin to worship her audacity.

Miss Petworth, determinedly persisting in her explanation despite her mortification, said, "I wanted him to embarrass himself by farting effusively during dinner and added a substance to his soup that would have ensured that outcome had he actually eaten it. Alas, I discovered too late that he nurtured an aversion to peas."

Lady Abercrombie, who had withstood the introduction of bodily gas to the drawing room conversation with equanimity, appeared deeply troubled by this observation. "Oh, my goodness, you are right. He absolutely detested them. I completely forgot. Poor Puddy. His last meal and I did not have the consideration to serve him foods he liked. I believe he was not overly fond of turbot either."

"I cannot believe what I am hearing," Bredbury said angrily. "A young girl has been so deeply disturbed by the horror she encountered in your home that her mind has resorted to elaborate fantasies in order to escape reality, and all you care about is that a dead man did not enjoy his dinner."

"No, Bredbury," said the countess, "that is not *all* I care about. I also care about the health and well-being of my staff and understanding the events that occurred in my own dining room. Your niece seems to be very well informed on both accounts."

Seething, Bredbury said, "She is not informed, she is troubled."

"You must calm yourself, Uncle," Miss Petworth said, "truly, you must, for there is no reason to work yourself into a lather. I did not kill Lord Pudsey. I brought the substance and emptied it into the soup, and when I saw him lying there with the scissors protruding from his chest, I ran to the terrace to dispose of the vial because I was fearful of how it would look if it was discovered on my person. I realize now that was a mistake. If I had been thinking clearly, I would have had the good sense to faint like Mrs. Fawcett."

Stung by the implication, Mrs. Fawcett said that her faint was not the result of careful consideration but of an overwhelmed sensibility.

Lady Bentham replied with snide satisfaction, "I believe you mean overwrought."

Mrs. Fawcett replied, "Since you are intimately familiar with the condition, I defer to your expertise."

Bea, ignoring the bickering matrons, asked Miss Petworth why she had sought to embarrass his lordship. "It was my understanding that you were kindly disposed toward him."

"Because of events at Mrs. Reddington's rout," Miss Petworth said bitterly.

"Yes," Bea replied, "because of events of Mrs. Reddington's rout."

"They were not as they appeared," Miss Petworth said with scathing resentment. "I have never been kindly disposed toward Lord Pudsey, as he very well knew, but he did not allow my dislike to interfere with his pursuit. At Reddington's rout, he found an opportunity to express his interest in the most vulgar way possible and after I managed to extricate myself with some effort, I encountered Mrs. Conwithe, who misinterpreted what she saw and eagerly shared it as widely as possible, saying that I was desperate to nab a title. And that is why I put the preparation into his soup. I wanted to humiliate him as he had humiliated me. But that was *all* I wanted. As I told my uncle, I did not want Pudsey thrashed or called out, for creating a spectacle would simply draw out the scandal."

As Miss Petworth detailed her treatment at the hands of the respected politician, Bea looked at Lady Abercrombie and Bredbury to see how they received the news. Neither seemed particularly surprised, with the latter nodding his head in vigorous confirmation.

"That is true, precisely true," Bredbury said. "My niece refused every offer I made to address Pudsey's insults in a respectable manner. There is an established protocol for handling scoundrels like him, and it does not include putting a substance into their soup. I fully intended to call him out but allowed myself to be swayed by Sophie's pleas and now look at the damnable mess in which we find ourselves. I do wish you had informed me of your plan, my dear, so that I could have talked you out of it."

Miss Petworth assured her uncle that it would have made no difference, for she had been determined to revenge herself on Pudsey in the manner she considered most fitting. "Having exposed me to the unfettered ridicule of the *ton,* he had to suffer a consequence of equal humiliation. What you proposed was excessive. If he had succeeded in his aim of harming my virtue, then perhaps I would not have objected to your running him through with a sword."

"There, you can see for yourself," Bredbury said with an air of vindication, as if something he had long sought to prove had been substantiated. "With every word she utters she reveals her inability to properly comprehend what has happened to her. *If* he had succeeded!"

Miss Petworth, whose embarrassment had begun to subside after the explication of her plan, colored slightly at this remark. Clearly, her relative's understanding of the incident varied greatly from her own, and Bea wondered to what length he would go to attain the reprisal he believed the situation deserved.

By several measures, the uncle was a much better suspect than the niece. For one thing, he possessed the physical advantages she lacked, having both the height and strength necessary to render Pudsey unconscious with the vase. Furthermore, he had the skill and experience to deliver a fatal strike quickly and cleanly. With his training, he would not have hesitated to drive the scissors directly into the scoundrel's heart.

Yes, Bea thought, he made a much better suspect—which did not, of course, exonerate his niece. They had only her word on the actual nature of the substance she had poured into the soup. Confirming her story would require discovering the source of the potion and inspecting it herself.

It was enough, however, to move Miss Petworth toward the bottom of the list.

Examining Bredbury with a contemplative expression, she said, "You wanted to challenge Pudsey to a duel with swords?"

Bredbury stiffened at the question and asked with searing contempt, "What am I—a white-livered feather? Of course I wanted to challenge Pudsey to a duel. He dared to besmirch the purity of my niece, and I longed to hold him to account. As I have just explained, I kept my temper in check out of respect for her feelings. I see now that was a grave mistake. Had I realized she planned to take her own revenge, I would have responded at once."

"Yes, I understand that," Bea said, "and I was merely confirming the instrument. You wanted to use swords, not pistols?"

"It does not work that way," Bentham said, as he strode across the room to the cabinet that held the port. "The man who receives the challenge has the right to choose, not the one who issues it. If confronted, Pudsey would have almost certainly chosen pistols, which are not Bredbury's forte."

While Bredbury eagerly conceded that he was more proficient with a sword than a dueling pistol, he begged the earl to recall that he had served as an infantry captain during the war. "I am not without a familiarity with firearms."

"But Pudsey was a prime shot," Bentham said, removing the top from the decanter and pouring the deep red liquid into his glass. "Unless he chose to delope, you would be killed almost instantly."

"I find your certainty somewhat overblown," Bredbury said calmly, "for hitting a target at one's leisure and a man's chest during the heat of battle are two different things. That being the case, I will concede the central notion of your point. It is true that if I had challenged Pudsey, the outcome was not wholly in my favor. But that just underscores the necessity of it. A man of honor cannot pick and choose the occasion for which he stands up for decency."

"But you did," Mr. Fawcett said quietly. "You chose not to act after Pudsey's disgraceful behavior toward your niece."

"Out of respect for her wishes," Bredbury replied stiffly.

"Ah, but did he?" Lady Bentham said, posing the question with a suggestive lilt that could leave no doubt as to her real meaning.

Bredbury, his temper flaring at the insinuation, spun on his heels and glared at her angrily. "No, I did not, and I resent your implying otherwise. I would never slip into a room to cut a man down whilst everyone's backs were turned. There is no justice in secrecy, only shame. If I thought to run Pudsey through with my blade, I would have done it in plain view so that his disgrace may be known," he stated firmly, then immediately retracted the statement to make it clear he would never indulge in such brutish behavior in front of his niece.

"Or any of the ladies, including you, Lady Bentham, despite your own coarse behavior tonight. But I am not surprised you have made the allegation, for you have made many this evening, going from one of us to another in a futile attempt to draw our attention away from your husband. Who will you point your finger at next? Fawcett? He is almost as good with a blade as I am."

Mrs. Fawcett objected to this observation, asserting that her husband's skill with a blade was unequaled by any in London. "He is a master of the fencing arts. Angelo himself has noted the excellence of his form."

Her husband, slightly embarrassed by the effusive praise, insisted that Bredbury's stance was nothing to scoff at, which of course made Mrs. Fawcett scoff and Lady Bentham accuse him of undue modesty.

"We all know your wife's fond habit of embellishing your accomplishments regardless of how unimpressive they are," her ladyship said, "but in this case she is actually correct. You *are* remarkably skilled with a sword. In addition, you have an excellent reason to wish Pudsey dead. His legislation levying a tax on imported fluorspar all but guarantees the end of your daughter's engagement to the prince. You were determined to stop it at any cost. Did you not arrive at the party in a fury about the whole thing? You were so impatient to discuss it with him, you tried several times to interrupt his conversation with my husband. That is how you heard their argument. Admit it!"

"I was angry over the legislation when I arrived here, yes," Mr. Fawcett acknowledged, "and I remain livid still. But the target of my wrath was not Pudsey. It is true that he is the one who proposed the bill, but I discovered today that he did it only at Bentham's urging. They made a pact. Bentham would support Pudsey's act banning cruelty against animals and ensure the members of his sporting club voted for it as well in exchange for Pudsey proposing the tariff. Your husband was intent on destroying my daughter's happiness, but like the coward he is, he did not want me to know it. If he had not let the truth slip to Mrs. Ralston, I would be in the dark even now."

Bea, whose own run-in with the notorious London gossip had caused her to teeter on the brink of ruin, knew this was a significant tactical mistake on Bentham's part. Any person determined to carry out an underhanded scheme of nefarious intent had to conceal all hint of it from Mrs. Ralston. Once she had picked up the scent of a scandal, she pursued it assiduously until every disgraceful detail had been exposed.

Bentham, aware of his misstep, had the grace to look embarrassed and muttered something about being in his cups at the Grundy chit's coming out.

His attitude, nonchalant and slightly abashed at the wrong thing, reignited Fawcett's fury. "You see! He does not deny it! Acting with what can be described only as malicious intent, he deliberately sought to end my daughter's betrothal and ensure her misery. And he shows not an iota of shame at being discovered. I arrived at the party determined to confront him, yes, and was made to cool my heels while he argued with Pudsey. It appears that Bentham had come to regret his immoral bargain and sought the removal of a provision regarding hounds from the act. Before I could get his attention, however, Lady Abercrombie began her game, and I did not manage to have a word with Bentham until we were adjoined to the dining room."

"If only it was a word!" Bentham said with amused contempt. "Alas, it was many—indeed, a whole torrent—and none of them interesting. I trust you will all understand why his outrage rang hollow to me. It is highly disingenuous to complain about receiving the very treatment you yourself have dealt. All I did was engage in the level of play as established by him when he manipulated events to ensure my own daughter's unhappiness. Now we are even. Be glad, Fawcett, that I am content to play to a draw and do not feel the need to best you because I assure you I would."

Fawcett growled low in his throat and swore that nothing was over. "I will have my revenge, Bentham, and it will be swift and without mercy. You will regret this!"

"That is a threat," Lady Bentham said triumphantly. "Mr. Fawcett just threatened my dear husband's life, and you are all witness to it. Having dispensed with Pudsey, he is now turning his murderous gaze onto my husband. He must be stopped."

"He has said nothing that your dear husband did not say to Pudsey," Mrs. Fawcett replied with an arch look at her rival, "and Pudsey is dead. Bentham is very much alive."

"Yes, Pudsey is dead and your daughter's future is secure," Lady Bentham observed calmly.

"As is your husband's sporting club," Mrs. Fawcett said.

"Ah, but the Henley Sporting Club was never truly at risk, as we all know the law, even with the provision regarding dogs, will be toothless. That is why Bentham agreed to it in the first place. And even if it was a threat, it is absurd to suggest my husband could hurt anyone but himself with a blade. He wore a sword to a masquerade ball at the Giddings' and nearly chopped off his own pinky," Lady Bentham replied with an overly bright smile. "Whereas your husband is a master. Unequaled by any in London, I believe, is the description you used."

Piqued at having her own words tossed back at her, for boasting about one's husband's skill with a sword appeared now not to be the deftest response to a stabbing death, Mrs. Fawcett pressed her lips together as she glared at the other woman. Her resentment, however, was fleeting, for only a moment later, her expression lightened and she pointed out how similar the shears were to a knife, which Bentham had much experience with, as he was a renowned hunter. "How many grouse does he gut during a typical weeklong stay at Marchbank?"

Lady Bentham fluttered her lashes as if much amused by the idea that her husband gutted his own birds. That was why one kept a gamekeeper. "Can you say the same of his matches with Angelo? I think not."

Mrs. Fawcett did not immediately reply, for she could not make that claim. But soon enough she realized she did not have to because there was still the matter of the sleeve button, which was not subject to opinion such as her husband's skill with a sword. "Do tell us again how your husband's button arrived at the bottom of the very vase the duchess identified as the one used to stun Pudsey, thereby rendering him an easy target for a man with no fencing skills."

Bentham laughed easily at the accusation, dismissing it as a fantastical story with no basis in reality, but his wife blanched, for she knew how it looked to the others in the room. She could see it in their faces—the doubt, the suspicion—and feared it would hover like a dark cloud over the rest of the season and possibly the next several years.

Even Miss Petworth, whose own behavior cast significant aspersions on her innocence, found the sleeve button to be highly incriminating.

"Do tell us again, Bentham, how your button arrived there," Lady Abercrombie said quietly, "so that we may put the matter to bed once and for all."

"Again?" Mrs. Fawcett echoed in exaggerated confusion. "His lordship failed to tell us the first time. I believe we are still waiting for an explanation."

Stubbornly, the founder of the Henley Sporting Club refused to submit to mobbish pressure, however gently it was exerted, and said he would not reply.

"I believe you mean, *cannot* reply," Mrs. Fawcett corrected.

Sweetly, Lady Bentham asked her to refrain from putting words in her husband's mouth, to which Mrs. Fawcett replied that she was happy to allow Bentham to speak for himself—provided he actually *spoke* for himself. Jeering at his silence, Fawcett observed how curious it was that a man who had so much to say to Mrs. Ralston and Pudsey was now as silent as a grave, which caused his lordship to assert it was better to hold his tongue than to sound off like an oaf.

Stiffening, Fawcett replied, "I would expect nothing less than personal insults from the man who destroyed my daughter's happiness."

Bentham, smiling sweetly, explained that he had in fact acted out of kindness, for if Fawcett and his wife had made their presentation at Prince Adriano's court, they would have repulsed everyone with their coarseness. "Now you may retire to the country without mortifying any foreigners."

Bredbury criticized this line of attack as being unworthy of a sportsman of Bentham's ilk while Fawcett sputtered and his wife asked again about the sleeve button, positing that perhaps it possessed magical qualities that allowed it to travel through space on its own. Lady Bentham gasped at intervals and avowed her admiration for Fawcett's swordsmanship. Appalled by the display, Miss Petworth tried to gently extricate her uncle from the fray and when he appeared unable to hear her, she raised her voice.

As the noise level increased, quickly growing cacophonous, Bea, like Mrs. Fawcett, stayed focused on the sleeve button. The society matron was correct in her insistence that the fastener could have arrived at the bottom of the amphora in only a limited number of ways. If Bentham was responsible, then it either slipped off when he grasped the vase, perhaps inspecting it for its suitability for the task, or when he returned it to the table.

But slipped off how so that it fell in two pieces?

Could the strike have been so hard that it jarred the link into severing?

It was possible, Bea thought, considering the wound on Pudsey's head. The blow had drawn blood, and the gold itself was worn thin. It probably would not require much force to break.

Equally baffling, however, was the state of the sleeve button itself and the fact that its condition had degraded so much in only a year. As Kesgrave had observed, the emerald was spectacular. Why spend so much money on the stones and then stint on the setting?

Perhaps Lady Bentham had run out of funds to expend on the gift, Bea thought.

Or maybe she had simply been cheated by an unscrupulous jeweler who charged her full price for poor craftsmanship or inferior gold. Neither development was unheard of.

If that was the case and the link had broken on its own from the force of the blow, then the second half of the fastener could still be in Bentham's possession.

Bea closed her eyes for a moment and pictured the series of events: link snapping, emeralds dropping into vase and...where?

Not on the rug near Pudsey because that area had been explored thoroughly, nor on the floor around the vase's table for the same reason.

Ah, but Bentham had been insistent that the carpet was the culprit. Could that have been merely a pretext so he could examine the area for the emerald without raising suspicion?

If that was the case, though, why would he have insisted on drawing Lady Abercrombie's attention to every woven strand? It had been a fairly ridiculous exercise, quite vexing to his host, and Bea wondered if that was also part of his ruse.

Perhaps he wanted to make it clear to everyone in the room that the emerald was nowhere near the victim as a way to demonstrate his innocence.

But he did that before the sleeve button was discovered in the amphora, Bea reminded herself, so he was not proving anything to anyone.

Frustrated, she returned to the idea that the jewel was still in Bentham's possession. If it had slipped inside the sleeve of his coat, it would be on him even now.

Where, then?

In his pocket, perhaps.

No, surely not. Having planned such a meticulous murder, his lordship would not be so careless as to keep hugely incriminating evidence on his person. He had had ample time to dispose of the emerald in various places in the house, and the lavish drawing room alone had hundreds of spots to conceal a small stone.

Even as she contemplated the value of launching an exhaustive search, Bea knew it would serve no purpose. Finding the second half beneath a seat cushion did not implicate anyone.

As that avenue of thought did not lead to a promising prospect, she changed direction and revisited the notion that Bentham had no idea where the fastener was. If that was the case, then his insistence on calling the constable might have been an attempt to ensure that nobody made a thorough inspection of the room. He had certainly tried to thwart her attempt to scrutinize the murder, only changing his stance when she discovered his fastener. Perhaps at that moment he realized she was not the hen-witted nibbler he dismissed her as and it was better to flatter her ego than give further offense.

'Twas an adequate theory, but it left her unsatisfied.

The weak link, she thought, was the weak link.

Although the break *could* be explained by the force of the blow, she was not sure it should. If the strike was so hard as to snap gold, then surely the vase itself would show damage: a crack in the porcelain, a chip in the paint. But the condition of the vessel was pristine.

Furthermore, even with inferior craftsmanship, the sleeve button was still too new for it to have simply snapped on its own.

Surely, it needed a little help.

Oh, that is an idea, Bea thought sharply, stuck by the possibility that the link had been broken by the same hand that had dropped it into the amphora.

It was a promising hypothesis, for it explained how the sleeve button had made its puzzling journey to the bottom of the vessel.

The question then became, Why?

What purpose could the murderer have in placing the emerald in a location so obscure its odds of discovery were almost zero?

The constable, certainly, would not have found it. If he noticed the bruise on the back of Pudsey's head at all, he would have dismissed it as an injury sustained in the fall. He would never have scoured the room for the object that had caused the wound, inspecting candlesticks, figurines, and vases for evidence of blood.

As the constabulary's lack of rigor was widely known, Bea had to assume that the killer expected it as well. He or she had chosen the amphora for a particular reason.

Maybe, she thought, because placing it somewhere more obvious would have made it too easy to dismiss or recover. Bentham, spying it on the carpet, could have slipped it into his pocket before anyone else noticed it or reasonably say that it had fallen off earlier in the evening. Mrs. Fawcett would be denied the pleasure of gleefully pointing to it every few minutes.

Verily, the killer did not want the emerald to be too easy to find. But what was the point in making it so difficult? Why go through all that trouble of stealing the sleeve button only to bury it in obscurity?

Oh, yes, she thought as the realization struck her. The killer *stole* the button. That changed the cast of the investigation entirely, for it limited the suspects to only those who had gotten close enough to the earl to commit the theft.

Of that group, Lady Bentham topped the list. She could stand as close to her husband as she desired without raising an eyebrow. Bea could not quite work her way around to believing she would incriminate her husband for murder because her own standing in society relied on his. If she destroyed his reputation, she would in effect be ruining her own.

Could she loathe him so much she would sacrifice herself?

Bea thought no, if for no other reason than she would have to ultimately cede the high ground to her rival, a situation she would find intolerable.

There was no question that Fawcett detested his lordship. Only a few minutes ago he had sworn to revenge himself on Bentham for seeking to destroy his daughter's happiness. Incriminating him in Pudsey's murder not only accomplished that goal elegantly but also eliminated the threat of the importation tax.

As Lady Bentham said, the wedding could proceed as planned.

It was no small thing, securing a prince for a son-in-law, for there were few options for advancing the fortunes of one's family, and since Fawcett could not send himself back five hundred years to advise his ancestor to acquit himself more heroically during the Peasants' Revolt, he needed the marriage to proceed.

It was little wonder he had worked himself up into such a lather by the time they went into dinner that he grabbed the earl by the wrist.

That was right, Bea thought. Fawcett grabbed Bentham *by the wrist.*

How had she failed to comprehend the import of that earlier?

Fawcett had had the perfect opportunity to steal the sleeve button.

Could he truly have been that brazen in his thievery?

Prior to discovering Miss Petworth had poisoned Pudsey's soup with the entire company looking on, Bea would have said no. But she herself had turned away, embarrassed for both men during the confrontation, and she assumed others in the room had done the same.

If Fawcett had stolen the sleeve button, then he was the culprit.

He had, she recalled, insisted several times that they summon the Runners.

The Runners, whose training and diligence would all but guarantee they would find the bloodied amphora and, consequently, the sleeve button.

He had been contemptuous of the constable, deeming him a waste of time.

It was a reasonable assessment, Bea thought, for the constable was utterly useless to him. Fawcett's plan hinged on the Bow Street Runners discovering the emerald at the bottom of the vase.

How relieved he must have been when Bea managed to display just enough ingenuity to find it.

As the facts lined up against him, she grew increasingly convinced that Fawcett was the culprit. He possessed the skill with a sword to accomplish the deed—that had been roundly confirmed by several people, including his wife—and his location during the interval could not be established to any degree of certainty. He claimed to have paid a visit to the conservatory to consult with Mrs. Fawcett, but she was absent from the room.

Yes, Fawcett made a very promising villain.

But how to prove it?

Unlike Lady Bentham, Bea did not feel comfortable lodging an accusation without having a way to substantiate the allegation. The only piece of evidence she had pointed to someone else. If she could just figure out some way to connect the broken sleeve button to Fawcett.

The *broken* sleeve button, she thought, her entire body stiffening as she contemplated yet again the bewildering fact of the severed link.

Why break the fastener in half if not to use both pieces to point to Bentham's guilt?

If one emerald hinted at his culpability, then two emeralds shouted it clearly.

Where was it then?

In a hiding spot even more cunning than the first?

Thoughtfully, Bea looked around the drawing room, with its seemingly endless opportunities for concealment.

But why hide it so well that nobody would ever find it? How diligent did Fawcett expect the Runners to be?

At some point, even the most dedicated investigator would stop and shrug his shoulders.

You are looking at it all wrong, she told herself, because you are considering the question from the perspective of an investigator. To figure out where the emerald was, she had to examine it from the point of view of the perpetrator. Here was a man who had committed a murder with so much care and precision, he did it in a house full of people during a brief interval with a hastily supplied weapon. *This* man put the emerald in one place and one place only—where it was most valuable to his purpose.

Valuable, she repeated, inhaling sharply.

Valuable.

But even as the possibility that Fawcett held on to the gemstone flitted through her mind, she dismissed it as unviable. No human being could be that caper-witted.

It simply was not possible.

And yet Kesgrave *had* marveled over the clarity of the stone and Nuneaton *had* hinted at gambling debts so immense Fawcett could not afford a hat commonly favored by coachmen.

The Bentham emerald could buy quite a few hats.

Truly, what harm could there be in slipping the precious stone into his pocket? Nobody would demand to search his person because they would never suspect him, for it was not *his* sleeve button lying at the bottom of the vase splattered with Pudsey's blood. And what if someone did decide to look in his direction? It would not matter because he would have been long gone by the time the Runners discovered the first emerald. After all, he was not so gruesome or gauche as to linger at the scene of the murder.

Oh, yes, Bea could see it clearly from his point of view and comprehended why he would have few qualms about keeping the jewel. All his assumptions were logical, and under normal circumstances, he would have been free to march from the premises in a matter of minutes.

Alas, this circumstance was not normal.

To his great misfortune, these premises contained a duchess who fancied herself an amateur Runner.

If he had just stuck to his original plan, then she would have nothing save her suspicions. But the worn gold had proven too much of a temptation, and once he realized how easily the link would snap, he could not hold himself back.

All those hats!

Now he would hang for his crime.

Aware that she was not bold enough to demand access to a grown man's pockets, Bea walked across the room to where Kesgrave conferred with their hostess. Before she could make her request of him, Lady Abercrombie raised her hands in mock surrender.

"You win, Bea, I concede the utter impossibility of making you fashionable," she said with a sigh of genuine exhaustion as the guests in her drawing room squabbled with increasing ferocity. "I really thought I had outwitted the problem by coming up with a strategy that would capitalize on your peculiarity while also showcasing your intelligence. I thought it would be a delightful evening, at the end of which you would correctly announce who the killer was—correctly because the killer would be whomever you decided it was, and to be thoroughly candid, I was looking forward to learning the identity myself—and then take a bow. But you have proved to be too peculiar for even my substantial talents, so I will leave you to wallow in your unpopularity. I am confident you will thrive there with Kesgrave's steady presence. I am only worried about what I will say to your mother when I encounter her in heaven. She is going to be quite cross with me for failing you."

Bea, who was not typically a demonstrative person, took the countess's hands in her own and squeezed them affectionately. "You must not be too hard on yourself, my lady. The depth of my peculiarity is difficult for most people to comprehend. I assure you, my aunt has been puzzling over it for twenty years."

"Cruel, your grace," Lady Abercrombie said on a choked laugh. "That was very cruel, comparing me to that awful woman. I will resent that more than your turning my dinner party into a circus."

"I?" Bea asked archly. "I did not realize I was your prime suspect in the murder of Pudsey. As I said to Lady Bentham earlier, please make your case. I am eager to hear it."

"You dreadful girl!" her ladyship said. "If you had any humanity at all, you would have let the horde leave when they raced to the door."

Genuinely surprised by her attitude, Bea asked if she did not want to find out who murdered her dead lover. "I believe your affection for him is real."

"What does it matter to me who did it? Dead is dead," Lady Abercrombie replied dismissively. "I do not think Pudsey would have cared either. He was a politician and always knew he would one day be stabbed in the back. Would he have had some complaint to make about the blade being administered to his front? Perhaps. He was most circumspect about his appearance and would not be pleased with the blood marring the immaculate whiteness of his shirt."

Nuneaton, overhearing this remark, agreed that the stain was regrettable but the greater insult was to the line of the shirt.

Flora, appearing at Bea's shoulder, said, "Are we discussing suspects? I hope we are because my doubts about Miss Petworth's innocence have only increased. I cannot believe any young lady of breeding would say the word...*that* word...in public unless she was trying to throw us off the scent. And, yes, that clever pun was entirely intentional."

"Bea was just about to tell us who did it," Kesgrave said.

Startled, Bea looked at the duke. "Was I?"

"Oh, yes, you have that look in your eye of clarity and purpose," he replied confidently. "I have seen it too many times now to mistake it for anything else."

"Obviously, it's Bentham," the viscount said. "I cannot

imagine how his sleeve button would end up in the vessel any other way."

"That is what Miss Petworth *wants* you to think," Flora said. "Fie on you, my lord, for being so accommodating."

While Nuneaton defended his stance, Bea informed Kesgrave that she may have at last found a way to ensure his expulsion from society.

"Have you?" he asked, one elegant eyebrow raised in curiosity.

"Yes, I require you to make a thorough inspection of Fawcett's person," she said.

Unperturbed by the request, the duke looked across the room at the gentleman in question, whose lips were twisted in a snarl as he issued yet another insult at Bentham. "Although hardly conventional, I do not think examining another man's pockets is the sort of thing that gets one's membership to Brooks's revoked."

"But if it is not in his pockets, you will have to continue your examination," she explained, the light in her eye an unexpected mix of amusement and embarrassment. "You will have to...um... feel his body for the item."

Kesgrave received this information with equanimity and announced he would no doubt sail through even this challenge with his reputation intact. "Indeed, it might even be burnished when I find the item I am looking for. Which is what, by the way?"

"An emerald sleeve button," she said.

If he was surprised by her hypothesis, he gave no indication, merely nodding his head thoughtfully. "I look forward to hearing how he managed that."

Flora, noticing their heads pressed closely together, broke off her reply to Nuneaton to eye them suspiciously. "Are you discussing my theory? Bea, if you have come up with a way to prove Miss Petworth is guilty, I must insist that I be allowed to participate."

"It is not Miss Petworth," Bea said firmly.

Although her cousin looked unconvinced, she did not argue and only repeated her request to take part in the plan.

Bea assured her the duke had the matter well in hand.

In fact, he did not, for he had been intercepted on his mission by Lady Bentham, who felt obligated to explain in point-by-point detail why she was unable to support his duchess in her quest for social dominance. "It pains me, of course, for I hold you in such high esteem, your grace, but such naked ambition in a female cannot be rewarded. I speak for the good of society, not myself."

Impatient with either the insult to his wife or delay to his mission, Kesgrave announced in a voice dripping with indifference that he could not care less about her opinions or her person. Then he proceeded to interrupt Fawcett's quarrel with Bentham by asking both men to be silent.

They ceased speaking at once.

Forthrightly Kesgrave said, "In the interest of discovering the truth about this wretched business, Fawcett, I must insist that you grant me access to your pockets."

To say that the gentleman was startled by the request would be to greatly understate the case. Thoroughly nonplussed, he stared blankly at the duke for several seconds as if unsure he had heard him correctly.

Stuttering slightly, he said, "I...I am sorry, your grace, did you say m...m...my *pockets?*"

"I did, yes," Kesgrave replied.

Although seemingly confused by the interest, Fawcett consented without protest and Bea, disconcerted by the ease of his agreement, wondered if he had hidden the emerald so well he had no fear of the duke finding it, or if he was simply that unabashed in his villainy.

As there was no established protocol for a guest to search a fellow guest's pockets at a murder mystery dinner party at a countess's house, Fawcett raised his hands awkwardly over his head to provide easier access.

Kesgrave started with the welt pocket on Fawcett's waistcoat, a slim gap containing nothing, and progressed to the one in his tailcoat. It was likewise empty, and Bea began to feel some of her confidence falter. She remained convinced that the sleeve button was on his person but feared the duke's dignity would take a drubbing if he had to run his hands along Fawcett's calves to look for evidence of its presence in his stocking.

Amazingly, Fawcett managed to keep his expression serene. He had to be discomfited by the duke's search, both physically, for it must be a strange sensation to have another man's hand in your pocket, and mentally, for his villainy was about to be exposed.

Failing to find the emerald in either coat, Kesgrave turned his attention to Fawcett's pantaloons, beginning with the pocket on the right side, which contained a gold watch with a hunter case. It held nothing else of note and he slid his fingers into the compartment on the left. At once his posture changed, stiffening and straightening at the same time, and a moment later he displayed the brilliantly cut emerald, glittering like green fire in the palm of his hand.

Chapter Ten

F awcett laughed, as if vastly entertained, and congratulated the duke on a very clever trick. "I would have sworn your hands were empty."

"That is because they were empty," Kesgrave answered soberly.

Affecting great puzzlement at the duke's reply, Fawcett wrinkled his brow, but Lady Bentham perceived the implication at once and gasped loudly. One gloved hand flew to her mouth as if to stifle further shock.

Her husband, also awake to the meaning, staunchly announced that he did not believe it. "Not Fawcett!"

Although the implication was staggeringly large, Fawcett continued to underplay its significance, turning to Bentham with that same perplexed expression. "Believe what? I'm afraid I am at a loss to understand what is happening. Why would his grace make a great show of discovering your sleeve button in my pocket? What purpose does it serve to pretend that the button from the vase is suddenly in my possession?"

Bea thought it was an impressive wide-eyed display, the mix of ignorance and bewilderment, and decided few people would have been able to brazen out such a scene without revealing at least a trace of fear or anxiety. It was not surprising, however, for she had noticed during dinner that he could mount a convincing performance.

She held up the other half of the sleeve button now and said, "That is not the one from the bottom of the vase."

Staring at the emerald in her hand, his confusion deepened and he laughed again, more awkwardly this time and with the first hint of dread. Nevertheless, his gaze was steady as he looked Bea in the eye and said, "I believe you are accusing me of something, your grace, but I cannot comprehend what it is. It is odd that the emerald was in my pocket. I have no idea how that came to be. I certainly did not put it there. It can have only been your husband, but that is an even stranger thing, for why would the Duke of Kesgrave wish to make it appear as though I had anything to do with Pudsey's death?"

His wife, whose face had grown more pallid the longer he spoke, shook her head slowly and then with increasing speed. "The duke would never behave with such indecency. He would never. It is simply impossible."

Bentham agreed that Kesgrave's integrity could not be questioned but remained fervently opposed to the other explanation as well.

Clearly, a mistake had been made!

"Fawcett and I have our resentments, yes," he admitted readily, "but they are *gentlemanly* resentments. I think he is a terrible shot and would not allow him within a mile of me while hunting grouse. In turn, he asserts—inaccurately, of course—that I am overly fastidious in my ways. Tempers have grown heated of late, which is only to be expected given the seriousness of the matter at stake. A royal son-in-law is a tremendous asset to any family. But what you are suggesting is inconceivable."

Frustrated and increasingly agitated, Fawcett said, "*What* is she suggesting?"

"He might have resorted to murder," Bentham continued. "I will not pretend to know what evil lives in his soul or what desperation rules his mind. Killing Pudsey might have seemed to him the only way forward. But making it appear as though another man committed the act? No! He would never behave in such a devious manner. It violates every rule of conduct, and I won't believe it of him."

Bentham, of course, did not have to believe it, for his wife was convinced enough for the both of them and announced she had known it was Fawcett from the very beginning. "It was his reaction that gave it away. He displayed almost no concern at all for poor Pudsey, which was odd, for he bore him such a very large grudge. Was it only the importation tax? I cannot say. I do vaguely recall other disagreements. Fawcett has always been a man of immoderate temper."

Troubled by this charge, Mrs. Fawcett insisted it was not true. "My husband is the most mild-mannered of men. He rarely raises his voice to anyone, not even the children when they are behaving like heathens, and I have never seen him lash out at anyone in anger."

Although they might have averted their gazes to afford the gentlemen some privacy during the awkward confrontation, everyone in the room saw Fawcett forcibly restrain Bentham by the wrist a mere two hours earlier. On the off chance anyone forgot the skirmish, Lady Bentham was ready and eager to remind them.

Arranging her features into a look of pitying concern, her ladyship added with a sad shake of her head, "Your feelings are a credit to you, my dear. Yes, you must defend your husband. It is the only moral option available, and no one here blames you for refusing to see the truth. More specifically, *I* don't blame you. Your husband's actions are his own, and in bestowing your blind faith in him, you are merely fulfilling your obligation as a dutiful wife. You have done nothing for which you should be ashamed and I am determined to support you in whatever way you need to help you get through this ordeal. You must think of your children now. A scandal of this magnitude will destroy their chances of making good matches, and you would be in no position to help them."

"This is madness!" Fawcett cried furiously.

But the reality of the situation had taken hold and he seemed to realize how thoroughly his finely wrought scheme had failed. However seamlessly it had been executed, it was unraveled now, leaving him to the consequences of his actions. He collapsed onto the settee and lowered his head into his hands.

Softly, as if defeated, he repeated, "This is madness."

Flinching at the scene before her, Mrs. Fawcett looked from her husband's crumpled form to Lady Bentham's rigidly taut one and then back again, thinking, it seemed, not only of her children but also herself. Her bottom lip trembling slightly, she turned to stare at the emerald in Bea's hand, her sharp gaze focused intently on the stone as if trying to will it to speak.

Needless to say, it remained silent.

Suddenly, as if yielding to an unbearable weight, she lowered her head to her chest and said on a great sigh of sadness, "I knew nothing of his plan."

Appalled, her husband cried out, "Harriet!"

She paid him no heed and continued. "I knew he was distressed by the law Pudsey had proposed and that he still cherished hopes of talking him out of it. I also knew he was very upset to discover Lord Bentham's part in putting it forth, but I had no idea his agitation had risen to such a tragic level. It was a mistake, I'm sure of it. An accident. The conversation must have got out of hand. Yes, he could never have done it intentionally, for he is far too gentle and mild mannered. Pudsey must have said something that incensed him and he acted without thinking. He must not have meant to harm him. Perhaps frighten him a little with the scissors. That is all, just a little fright. Is that not correct, Owen? Do tell them everything so that they may understand that you are not a villain."

But Lady Bentham refused to allow her the comfort of this fiction by pointing out that Mr. Fawcett had taken possession of the sleeve button before they had eaten. "It is the shock, my dear. It has made you incapable of comprehending the depths of your husband's iniquity. But his plan had been set well before he arrived here. He knew that his only hope of murdering Pudsey and remaining free was to make someone else shoulder the blame. It compounds his villainy, but as I said, you are not responsible for your husband's deeds—unless you continue to support him."

Mrs. Fawcett, who had no inkling that tempering her husband's murderous inclination was an act of support, disavowed it immediately and thanked her ladyship for her generosity of spirit.

"Harriet," Mr. Fawcett said again, this time softly and with sadness. "You must know this is insanity. I would never assault an unarmed man. It violates every rule of decency. I do not know how that button came to be in my pocket, but I swear to you I did not remove it from Bentham's sleeve. I had nothing to do with it. You must believe me."

Nobody did.

Bentham paid lip service to the claim, insisting there must be some other explanation, but his words lacked conviction and Bea recognized his disavowal as the perfunctory denial it was. It was, she decided, grossly ungentlemanly to believe a fellow member of White's had tried to incriminate one in a violent murder.

Bredbury, perhaps bound by the same code of conduct, asked Fawcett to provide them with an alternate explanation. "Blame the servants again if you must. We are all eager to exonerate you."

Patently, Lady Bentham was not, but Bredbury ignored her harrumph of dissent and urged Mr. Fawcett to offer a credible defense of his actions. "We are fair-minded people," he continued, "and reasonable. Tell us something in defense of your innocence."

But Fawcett had nothing to say, and it was clear to Bea that as meticulously as he had planned his scheme, he had not considered the possibility of failure. Maybe he had devised it while trying to intercede in Pudsey and Bentham's conversation during the first part of the evening, or perhaps it had struck him only in that moment when his fingers grasped Bentham's wrist. Either way, he had no plausible explanation at the ready, and Bea waited for him to realize the jig was up, for that was the way it had always gone before. When confronted with irrefutable proof of his perfidy, the murderer admitted defeat and confessed his sin.

Incapable of offering a plausible explanation, Fawcett resorted to implausible ones, alluding to the existence of mysterious forces working to destroy him and reciting brief fragments of *Hamlet*. As her husband rambled in various directions, Mrs. Fawcett lowered her head even deeper in shame, Bredbury pressed a comforting hand on the man's shoulder, and Bentham recalled the time a hound caught up to the fox only to roll around with it in the underbrush as if they were friends.

"Damned strange sight," he muttered.

Without an admission of guilt, Bea was uncertain how to proceed. It seemed to her as though she should continue to press the matter until Fawcett owned the truth fully. Allowing the lie to remain in place would serve nobody, least of all the perpetrator, whose acceptance would help him to stoically endure the challenges ahead. Imprisonment at Newgate was nothing less than a nightmarish ordeal, and insisting you had been imprisoned there in error would only increase the horror.

But she could not compel anyone to do anything, particularly Fawcett, who had begun to talk of ghosts and was just then asking Lady Abercrombie if someone had died in her home with spiritually significant business left to finish.

"Perhaps they are trying to speak through me," he said.

At a loss, Bea sought out Kesgrave's gaze and when her eyes met his she was struck by the familiarity of the moment. This always happened, too, she realized. She revealed the killer, chaos followed, and she looked to the duke to restore order.

And so it happened now.

While Lady Abercrombie assured Fawcett that the Earl of Abercrombie had settled his affairs before departing for the Peninsula, Kesgrave helped Fawcett rise to his feet and asked if he would rather find a quieter place to wait for the constable. Fawcett seemed disconcerted by the idea and appeared prepared to argue, but seeing the condemnation on everyone's faces, including his wife's, he agreed that it was better if he removed himself from the company.

"At this juncture, I would prefer to be surrounded by the servants, who are rightly too horrified by Miss Petworth's abuse of their associates to listen to nonsensical gossip about me," he said.

The Incomparable whimpered pitifully, making him instantly contrite, and as he left the room, Fawcett promised he would not say a word about her employment of poison to anyone. "Not even if Prinny himself asks me for a personal account!"

It was indeed a pathetic spectacle, a man about to be remanded to a dungeon swearing not to defame a young lady in the best drawing rooms in London. Everyone present felt it. Even Flora, whose eyes had been bright with the excitement of discovery, suddenly found herself fascinated by the stitching on her glove.

Kesgrave lauded Fawcett's gallantry as he led him from the room, and as soon as the door was closed behind them, Bentham took three wide strides to Beatrice's side and thanked her fervently for saving his life.

It was, Bea thought, a little grandiose, and she fully expected his wife to say something snide, but Lady Bentham shared his gratitude.

"I do not know what we would have done if you had not figured out the truth," her ladyship said breathlessly. "When I contemplate the alternative...when I think of my darling John being led away in manacles . . . when I imagine the condemnation of the *ton,* every bone in my body grows weak. We are forever in your debt, my dearest duchess."

Mrs. Fawcett moaned as if in pain, and a fat teardrop began its slow trickle down her cheek. Lady Abercrombie, whose training as a hostess did not include a lesson on how to console a woman whose husband had just committed murder, applied herself gamely to the situation, treating her with an affect pitched between matter-of-fact austerity and fulsome concern.

Shaking her head sadly, she sat down next to the sobbing woman and wrapped an arm around her shoulder. "You are exhausted," she said soothingly. "We must return you to your home so that you may get a good night's sleep. Everything will feel less hopeless in the morning, I promise you that. You will take a tincture of laudanum as a favor to me. Just a few drops to ensure you get the rest you need. Can you do that for me?"

Mrs. Fawcett nodded feebly, blinking her eyes rapidly in a futile attempt to stall the torrent of tears that fell.

"You are intrepid, my dear," the countess said approvingly, "and you must hold on to that courage for the sake of your children. They will need you to be strong. Now I will have your carriage brought around at once. I am sure you will feel better the moment you are alone to gather your thoughts."

Although this reassuring statement was meant to further bolster its listener, it had the opposite effect and Mrs. Fawcett began to wail. Bea did not know if it was the idea of being alone that unsettled her or the prospect of having to explain to her children why their father was absent or just the overwhelming apprehension that the world continued outside the room and she had to be part of it. There was no escaping reality.

There was nothing to be done to address the latter two concerns, but it was certainly possible to stave off isolation for a little while longer and Bea offered to accompany her home.

Mrs. Fawcett recoiled in horror at the suggestion, and although she claimed she could not bear to inconvenience the duchess in any way, Bea thought it was more likely she could not stand the notion of being in the presence of the woman who had uncovered her husband's perfidy.

If it had not been for Bea's interference, Mrs. Fawcett would be comfortably ensconced in her bed by now and the constable appropriately bewildered.

Regardless, Bea did not think it was wise to send the distraught society matron off into the dark night alone and decided Flora could go in her stead. Before she could volunteer her cousin, Nuneaton stepped forward and proposed himself.

Although she winced slightly, Mrs. Fawcett received the startling offer calmly and accepted it with a nod of her head. It was difficult for her to look dignified with red eyes and soggy cheeks, but she managed to achieve some degree of elegance as she said, "Thank you, my lord. I would be most grateful."

Taken aback by her sudden composure, Bea wondered if Mrs. Fawcett sensed in Nuneaton's sympathy the treatment she should expect to receive at the hands of the *beau monde*. If pity was enough to move the notoriously languid viscount to kindness, it might achieve other minor miracles.

Perhaps having a murderous husband was not quite the social liability she assumed it to be.

Kesgrave returned to the room just as Mrs. Fawcett was leaving, and after a brief quiet conversation in which he affirmed the well-being of her husband, she allowed Nuneaton to escort her from the building.

"The poor dear," Lady Bentham murmured after she was gone. "We will stand by her, won't we, Bentham? We will lend her our support and make sure she does not suffer because of her husband's terrible actions. Obviously, the prince cannot marry her daughter now, but I am sure that is the last thing on her mind. You were right, Tilly, to suggest laudanum. I do hope she manages to get some sleep."

Bea did not doubt that her ladyship would take every opportunity to elevate her former rival. She could afford to be magnanimous in victory.

"But for now, I am grateful she is gone," Lady Bentham continued, "for it allows me to express my gratitude to the Duchess of Kesgrave without fear of causing her more pain. You have saved my husband from the gallows, and I could not be any more grateful to you. Earlier, in my anxiety over Pudsey's death, I said some dreadful things to you. Please know, your grace, that I never meant them. I simply allowed myself to become overwhelmed by the awfulness of the situation. That is a weakness of mine, and I hope you will allow me to make amends. You are as impressive as Tilly said you are, and although I am familiar enough with your history to know you do not require my approval, I hope you will condescend to accept it."

Although Bea found the idea of personally benefiting from Pudsey's death repugnant, she made no mention of her discomfiture as she thanked Lady Bentham for her consideration. "I will."

"I see it now," Lady Bentham said affably, "your charm and appeal. You are an original, and I have no doubt you will be warmly embraced by all of society. Certainly, when Bentham and I tell the tale of this evening, you will be celebrated as the heroine you are. But I will stop there because I do not want to embarrass you with my gratitude. Suffice to say that I am ready and eager to serve you in any way possible and I hope you will not hesitate to call on me if there is some way I can lend my assistance. And now I shall take my leave of our hostess. Poor Tilly. This evening has turned out nothing like she expected, and I hope she is not too cut up about Pudsey's death. Perhaps Cuthbert's or Thirlwall's attentions can console her."

When his wife stepped away, Bentham approached, his expression slightly abashed as he apologized for his own outburst. "Unlike my wife, I cannot attribute my behavior to anxiety caused by the situation. I simply lacked the ability to believe you were capable of deductive reasoning, primarily because you are a woman and I am well familiar with the frivolity of the female mind. I am only too happy to admit that I was wrong. You are a rare creature, your grace."

It sounded like flattery, to be sure, but Bea knew better and informed the earl that he did not have to insult her entire sex in order to give her a compliment. "You may say only, 'Well done, your grace,' and it would be sufficient."

"Ah, yes, there it is," he said with an admiring tilt of his head. "That shocking intelligence. I should have had faith in you from the beginning, and failing that I should have trusted that Kesgrave knew what he was about. No milk-and-water miss for him! That would never have done. And now I suspect more young men will follow suit, choosing depth of character over youth and beauty, which will make for a confusing season. But interesting! No wonder the society matrons are up in arms about his choice. And now, like my wife, I will pledge my undying support. If ever the occasion arises where you require anything, you need only ask."

"I will, yes, thank you," Bea said, her tone somewhat tepid because she could not imagine such a situation.

Nevertheless, Bentham was satisfied and bid her good-bye.

Next, Bredbury approached to laud her cleverness and thank her for uncovering the truth about Fawcett's duplicity. "I have known him for more than a decade and never imagined what lay beneath his placid facade. As his wife said, I have always considered him to be mild mannered and kind. But it is also true, what Bentham said, about a prince being a supremely valuable son-in-law. I suppose something like that alters one's perspective. I had thought the rivalry was only between the women, but obviously the husbands got caught up in it as well. It is a tragedy," he said, pausing to sigh deeply.

Bea agreed that it was, particularly for Pudsey.

Bredbury seemed almost surprised to be reminded of the victim, but his resentment of the gentleman did not preclude him from allowing that his death was a calamitous turn for him. "And for my niece as well. Her little plan to mortify him would never have been exposed if Pudsey had managed to keep a pair of embroidery shears out of his chest."

"It seems like such a small thing to ask," Bea said satirically, "and yet!"

Either oblivious to her undertone or determined to ignore it, he added that he bore her no bitterness. "Your lack of discretion in addressing my niece was the result of your enthusiasm to discover the truth. It is unfortunate but understandable. I am sure if you had paused for one moment to think about it, you would have realized how preposterous your conclusion was. To think my darling girl could harm a hair on anyone's head."

Although Miss Petworth had been exonerated of murder, her behavior was not entirely above reproach. "She poisoned a man's soup."

"Added a harmless elixir to a potage he did not touch," he corrected.

"Three footmen were laid low by it," she reminded him.

"Ah, but have you seen these servants?" he asked. "I am sure they are slight men of weak constitutions."

"I have, yes, for they served the meal," Beatrice replied, "and they were all quite hulking. Miss Petworth is luckier than she knows, for if Pudsey had partaken of the soup as she had planned, he could have suffered a far greater misfortune than the expulsion of an unpleasant odor."

"What an imagination you have, your grace," Bredbury said with a tight smile. "It is charming. I can see why the duke finds you so amusing. I'm sure thinking up dire consequences is the reason you are so successful in your hobby, but your elaborate fictions have no bearing on reality. Do excuse me, please, for I must take my niece home. She has been through an ordeal, and my sister will be worried."

Miss Petworth, whose vivacity had indeed been tempered by exhaustion, was somewhat more gracious in her reproach of Bea, thanking her for ensuring that the faint suspicion of murderess did not follow her around for the rest of the season. "It is far better to be known for my failed scheme to revenge my own honor."

Bea suspected the Incomparable of offering a sarcastic reply, but she found no evidence of it in her somber gray eyes.

Although Lady Abercrombie would ordinarily interpret her guests' eagerness to leave as a sign of a failed dinner party, as soon as she closed the door on the Benthams, she pressed her back against it and pronounced the evening a success. But then she laughed, a slightly wild and out-of-control sound, and insisted she did not mean it. "For God's sake, Pudsey is still on the floor under the blanket. Is there a name for that? A joke that seeks to take aim at the wretchedness of the situation. We should come up with a name. Bea, you are clever. Do come up with one."

"Desperation," Bea replied as she sat down on the settee.

"No," the countess said, shaking her head, "that is not funny at all."

"Come, Tilly, sit down before you fall," Kesgrave said, leading her gently to a chair. "The constable and his men will be here any moment to arrest Fawcett and collect Pudsey. Why don't you gather a few things and come back to Kesgrave House with us for the night? You should not be alone."

"You are so very good, Damien," Lady Abercrombie said quietly, almost as if in surprise. "You have always been decent, but since aligning with Bea you have become good. Your father would be utterly appalled. I knew something was afoot when you came here that afternoon directly from Montague House. Do you recall it? We sat in this very room, and Bea looked daggers at me the whole time. You did not like me at all, did you, my dear? You thought I had my hooks in Kesgrave and you could not bear it because you were already in love with him. I was sympathetic to your plight, for I have suffered my own share of hopeless passions, but I knew it would come to naught. That was why I resolved to make you fashionable—compensatory popularity. Being widely adored has always been beneficial to my spirits."

"Fustian," Bea said mildly. "You resented my forcing you to admit the truth of your dealings with Lord Fazeley and sought to tweak my ego with mockery. The idea of making me fashionable was always an absurd lark."

Managing a faint smile, Lady Abercrombie lifted her delicate shoulders and said, "And yet…"

"Fazeley?" Flora said sharply as she sat up straighter in her chair. "You were involved in that affair, too?"

Hesitantly, for she knew how her cousin would react, Bea said yes.

At once, a look of disappointment swept across the other girl's face. "You mean to say that, after all this time and everything that has happened, you are *still* withholding the truth from me?"

Amused by her guest's predicament although she had no true understanding of it, the countess said, "Yes, Bea, are you still withholding the truth from your cousin?"

"It has something to do with Theodore Davies, doesn't it?" Flora asked. "He seems to have had his fictional fingers in every pie."

He did indeed, yes.

The law clerk whom Bea had invented on the spur of the moment to solve a tricky but temporary problem had somehow evolved into an enduring fixture in her life. She still could not say how it happened.

Lady Abercrombie spared her the necessity of a reply by announcing that for a little while she had been Bea's favored suspect. "She enjoyed sitting in that very chair and imagining me as a murderess because it would have removed me from the duke's orbit. I was very much flattered by your confidence in me, my dear, for most of society thinks I am too much of a delightful scatterbrain to accomplish anything so complicated."

Now Bea smiled. "I believe those were the exact words Kesgrave used when he dismissed my theory."

"Men have always underestimated me," her ladyship said. "Many women too. It is because of my appearance. It seems a lady can only be one thing at a time: beautiful or intelligent. Your mother saw me clearly. Oh, yes, Clara would never doubt for a moment that I could drive a knife into a dandy's back in the afternoon and present myself at Carlton House for dinner. Although, actually, she would because she would expect me to perform the deed face to face, for she put much stock in confronting one's problems head-on. Goodness, I have rambled far from the topic, have I not? You must forgive me. I seem to be more tired than I realized. To answer your question, Damien, thank you but no. I have already sent a note to Cuthbert and expect him to arrive within the hour. He will be sufficient company, and I think it is appropriate that I be consoled on the death of my old lover by my young lover. There it is, again, Bea, desperate humor. I really do think we need to come up with a better name. Something about it makes me want to cry."

"Yes," Bea agreed gently, "that is the thing about desperation."

Kesgrave suggested a bracing glass of port, which earned the countess's ardent approval, and he had just returned the bottle to the cabinet when the butler announced the arrival of the constable.

The next hour passed drearily, and although Bea had no desire to bear witness to any of it, she felt compelled to remain. Having participated in several investigations, she had somehow avoided the moment when the perpetrator was borne away by the constable. Lady Skeffington was an exception of sorts. She had been escorted from her own home in the company of a Runner, but her husband had attended to her as well and left the house prattling confidently about her swift discharge by the magistrate. There was no concern on either of their parts that her ladyship would suffer the consequences of her actions.

Not so Mr. Fawcett.

Oh, no, the gentleman who murdered Lord Pudsey was fully cognizant of the horrors that lay ahead of him and protested his situation with increasing fury, ultimately shouting for someone to alert the regent of this abuse so that he could intervene on his behalf.

"He will vouch for me," he yelled. "Prinny knows I am innocent."

The constable, embarrassed by his staff's inability to contain their prisoner better, apologized to Lady Abercrombie for the ruckus. "Ears as delicate as yours should not be exposed to such ugliness," he added disapprovingly.

That he seemed more troubled by Fawcett's rough language than he did by his horrendous deed struck Bea as deeply disquieting, and it made her realize how incredibly fortunate she had always been to be able to slip away after the denouement of her investigations.

That was Kesgrave as well, taking command of the situation and arranging matters so that she was free to leave as soon as she was ready.

He just waited for a look from her—merely a glance and they were gone, removed from the room as smoothly as they had entered it.

The privilege of that struck her quite forcibly last time, at the Mayhews, whose squalid bickering quickly revealed the rancidness of their marriage. To be able to walk away from that, to step from the degradation of their drawing room to the delights of Kesgrave's library, was a comfort she could barely articulate.

'Twas paradoxical, she thought, the way the journey had been at once long and short—a few hundred yards between and yet miles and miles away.

Lady Abercrombie, intending to ease the constable's concerns, placidly assured him that she had heard worse language. "From my own son, in fact."

Her levity, alas, had the opposite effect, and the constable, appearing to take offense at her composure, began to subtly criticize her handling of the matter, implying that she had usurped his authority by presuming to do his job. Although in actuality he would have been disinclined to identify the murderer himself, seizing, most likely, onto Bentham's theory of the ragged carpet edge as a plausible enough explanation, he spoke with convincing umbrage.

The countess, clearly wishing to speed his departure, indulged him in this fantasy.

Finally, he was gone, as were Fawcett and Pudsey, and Lady Abercrombie saw her remaining company to the door just as Cuthbert arrived on her step. He was disconcerted at being met by the Duke and Duchess of Kesgrave, but the peculiarity of the situation was enough to overcome the awkwardness and he graciously thanked them for helping to alleviate the sordidness of the evening.

In the carriage, they were subdued, even Flora, who refrained from speaking other than to observe that her mother would be horrified when she learned of the events.

"It will be my fault," Bea said on a tired sigh. "She will claim that I somehow pull murderers to me like planets to the sun."

Flora shook her head as she smothered a yawn. "That is utterly absurd, my dear. Mama knows nothing of gravitational forces."

Bea could not but acknowledge the truth of this observation.

A short time later, they arrived at Portman Square and Flora thanked her cousin for an interesting evening, then bid her good night. As she climbed out of the carriage, she added, "We will discuss Fazeley another time."

It amused Bea, the certainty with which she spoke, and she felt her grim mood lighten momentarily.

By the time the duke returned to the carriage, however, a sense of gloominess had descended again, and she pictured too easily the desolation on Fawcett's face as he was led from the house. Inexplicably, his anger had been preferable to his anguish.

Kesgrave sat down next to her on the cushion, and although he took her hands into his own, she found it was not enough.

No, she required more comfort, more contact, and in a move that would have horrified the taciturn Miss Hyde-Clare only a few weeks before, she slid onto her husband's lap and rested her head against his shoulder. At once, his arms encased her waist, pulling her closer.

"As a general rule, I do not like rose petals," she said softly.

If the duke was taken aback by this non sequitur, his response did not reveal it. "I do not believe there are any in the arrangements currently in residence. There are delphinium and peonies in the drawing room, lilies on the table in the entrance hall, scabious and nerines in the dining room, ivy and thistle in the library, and a lovely bouquet of orchids in your sitting room. But if you have any objections or particular favorites, Mrs. Wallace would be happy to know your preferences."

Bea listened to this detailed catalogue of floral arrangements with blissful delight. Of course he knew the name and location of every blossom in the house. His pedantry was one of the things she adored about him most.

"I mean for treading upon," she explained.

Naturally, this qualification clarified little. "Impossible. Mrs. Wallace would never permit a bouquet to exceed its freshness so flagrantly as to allow it to drop petals onto the floor."

Bea giggled, and feeling the relief in every fiber of her being, she pressed impossibly closer to him. "You have your uses, and although I tend to chafe at the privileges conferred by your station, I am also desperately grateful for them on occasion."

Although he could not know to what she referred specifically, he owned himself well aware of this fact. "As someone who has been banned from your office for rout cake enjoyment, I assure you it has not escaped my notice."

"'Twas one time," she replied sternly, "and it was a necessity. You appeared suddenly in the doorway in your shirtsleeves, your blond curls in disarray, your eyes glinting with mischief, and I had but one chapter left in the book. If I allowed you to enter, I would never have found out if Persephone's plan to entrap Erasmus in the forest worked. It is not my fault you are so appealing, your grace. If you have a complaint, you must lodge it with yourself."

Oh, but he did not.

Kesgrave could not find a single thing to object to in her statement and sought only to confirm that his shirtsleeves were the source of the problem. "It is important that I understand the condition fully so that I may repeat it as often as possible."

Smiling in the darkness, she said, "Ah, so you want never to enter my office for rout cake enjoyment again?"

"On the contrary," he replied deeply, "I want never to leave it."

Bea chuckled lightly and reminded him he had said the very same thing about their bedchamber.

"That is true," he said, laughter rumbling in his chest. "I do have a disconcerting compulsion to be where you are. Currently, I am content to remain in this carriage indefinitely."

"Your valet would object strenuously," she replied, "for the space is far too confining for him to make an adequate Waterfall. Poor Jenkins would not know which was worse: exposing the carriage to the elements or you to the interior of the carriage house. Marlow would be none too pleased either because he could not tower intimidatingly over us as he presented guests. Oh, and we must not forget Mrs. Wallace's discomfort, for she would be thrown into a dither over not being able to give the space a proper scrubbing on a daily basis. All in all, your staff would be miserable, which is something you typically go to lengths to avoid."

"That is true, yes," he said, resting his head on top of hers. "But it is not my fault you are so appealing, your grace. If you have a complaint, I advise you to lodge it with yourself."

Like the duke, Bea could locate nothing in this observation with which to quibble and responded with a warmth that implied a severe lack of understanding of the limits of her current environment. Indeed, she was so enthusiastic in her appreciation of his remark that the servants who rushed from the house to greet the carriage would be forgiven for thinking she had no intention of ever leaving it.

Chapter Eleven

As Mrs. Palmer threaded her arm through Beatrice's, she apologized for not participating in the prevailing fashion of wearing a decorative magnifying glass in homage to the duchess's deductive brilliance.

"It is not because I do not consider your deductions to be brilliant," she rushed to assure her. "You must believe that I am as impressed with your ability to identify clues and reason their meaning as the rest of the *ton*. Indeed, I am slightly more impressed because I consider you a friend and one should always hold their friends in slightly higher esteem than the rest of society. Rather, it is a failure of organization. You see, I do not count a magnifying glass among my possessions —a quizzing glass, yes, but that would never do—and by the time I realized that I must acquire one, they were impossible to find. London has been quite emptied of them. Naturally, I have placed an order for one with Kimpton and Cross and specified a mother-of-pearl handle in the staghorn design. As they are the finest jewelers in London, I am confident it will be quite spectacular and pair beautifully with the garnets Irwin gave me for our anniversary last year. I do think it is a charming style, wearing a modest-size glass on a ribbon along with one or two necklaces."

Genuinely troubled by this information, Bea examined Nuneaton's sister for some indication that she was teasing her, but her green eyes were serious. "I wish you had not invested money in something so fleeting," she said. "I am sure by this time next week, the fashion will have moved on to the next frivolity and you will be stuck with an unnecessary magnifying glass. The style cannot sustain. It is impossible."

Mrs. Palmer, whose open expression glinted with an intelligence only hinted at in her brother's more languid affect, said, "You sound a little desperate, your grace. Do you not enjoy being the toast of the town? All of society is aping your mannerisms. I am certain I would be much gratified by the attention."

Before she could assure the other woman that she would find it just as repellent, Bea was hailed by Mrs. Vane, who raised her hand enthusiastically to make sure her presence was acknowledged. Self-consciously, Bea waved back and wondered if was too late to hide behind a tree.

Obviously, yes, of course it was too late.

The moment she had entered Hyde Park in the company of Mrs. Palmer it had been too late to avoid notice.

As her friend had noted with wry amusement, the Duchess of Kesgrave was wildly popular. Everything she did was noticed and emulated.

Detaining them for several long minutes, Mrs. Vane gushed over the design of Bea's hat, which, being a fairly mundane creation, deserved none of the superlatives applied to it, including "thoroughly original" and "decidedly flattering."

"And I hope you will remember my garden party next week?" Mrs. Vane added. "It is on Tuesday. An intimate affair, just a few dozen of my dearest friends. I would be devastated if you could not attend, although I understand if you have another engagement. *Do* you have another engagement?"

Having had many such conversations in the past two weeks, Bea knew better than to provide a definitive response in either direction. Instead, she made a vague remark on the busyness of the season and complimented the other woman on the elegance of her own bonnet.

Blushing with delight, Mrs. Vane thanked the duchess for her kindness and allowed her to pass.

Before they could be interrupted again, Bea pointed out that society was not aping her mannerisms, for she had never held a magnifying glass in her entire life, let alone in Lady Abercrombie's drawing room. "I do not know why Bentham thought to add that detail to his tale. He is, I suspect, fond of embellishment."

"Oh, but what a tale it is!" Mrs. Palmer insisted. "Saved from the gallows and delivered safely from the jaws of injustice by the supremely clever Duchess of Kesgrave. He is the first to admit he dismissed you as an inquisitive nonentity."

"Yes," Bea said, amused despite herself, "that appears to be his favorite part of the story. He loves to linger on how he attended Lady Abercrombie's event fully expecting to find me prosaic and dull and then I shattered every preconception he had by leaping to his rescue like a tiger pouncing on its prey."

"A lion," Mrs. Palmer corrected.

Bea shook her head in amusement. "A lion, then. Either way, it is histrionic nonsense. I did not leap to his rescue. I merely followed the clues as they presented themselves. If the evidence had suggested he was guilty, then I would have pounced like a mongoose in the opposite direction."

"Do mongooses pounce?" Mrs. Palmer asked curiously.

Bea confessed to having no idea. "I was only hoping to find an animal more absurd."

"Very good, your grace. You have succeeded," Mrs. Palmer

said, before tugging Bea's arm and abruptly changing their direction. Now they were walking stridently away from the Serpentine rather than meandering alongside it. "Lady Jersey was approaching, and she had an avaricious gleam in her eye. As you already have vouchers for Almack's, it is not necessary for you to cultivate that connection. Now tell me what you can about my brother's behavior. The reports I have gotten are truly bizarre, and I cannot begin to make sense of them. They say he offered to accompany a distraught Mrs. Fawcett to her home. Did he injure his head during the evening or suffer a fit of apoplexy?"

Bea laughed at the genuine confusion in her tone. "No, he appeared to be of sound mind and body. If I had to speculate, I would say he acted out of earnest concern and generosity. I have long suspected your brother is not quite the effete aristocrat he purports to be. I would think as his sister you would really know the truth of his presentation."

"Well, yes, Michael can be quite assiduous when he puts his mind to it," Mrs. Palmer allowed, "and managing the estates is no mean feat. But also, no, because he has put such sincere effort into his image as an indolent and indifferent dandy. I cannot comprehend why he would undo all those years of hard work to assist a morose society matron about whom he cares not a fig. It is a puzzle."

"Perhaps your brother is growing bored of appearing bored all the time," Bea suggested. "Between you and me, it seems exhausting to endlessly affect ennui, all that dampening of one's spirits."

Mrs. Palmer conceded it was possible, then tightened her grip on Bea's elbow as she pivoted to her left. "Mr. Oxberry wants to show you his hobbyhorse. No, do not look. It is a very curious sight and I would advise surreptitiously examining it at some point during the season, but making eye contact with the jackanapes is fatal. Trust me, I made the mistake at Pudsey's and even though it was several months ago, I still regret it."

At the mention of the victim, whose salon she had attended in Mrs. Palmer's company, Bea offered her condolences. "I know you enjoyed browbeating him."

"Thank you, yes," Mrs. Palmer said with a sad lilt in her voice. "Fortunately, there are dozens of other members of Parliament whom I can berate for their terrible views, so I shall be fine. I will miss Pudsey, though, for he did have a particular way of humoring me, always so charming and considerate as he dismissed my ideas. Our last debate had been over his ban on animal cruelty, which I thought was a waste of time and effort. Naturally, I find the abuse of any animal abhorrent, but the idea that you could induce a man to treat his horse better by making it unlawful to whip it is preposterous. Education is the solution, I believe. Men must be taught to value their animals as living creatures and not perceive them as tools such as shovels and plows. That was a particularly frustrating evening for me, for none of the other guests believed the ban was a good idea, but all of them planned to support it because they feared giving offense. Pudsey was an important ally to have if one hoped to introduce legislation and see it pass. Politics is all conniving and no conviction."

Bea nodded, recalling what Fawcett had said about Bentham's support of the animal cruelty bill: He provided it only in exchange for Pudsey proposing the levy on fluorspar importation.

Quid pro quo, as apothecaries used to say.

"That is dead now," Mrs. Palmer continued.

Startled, Bea looked up at her. "Excuse me?"

"The ban on animal cruelty," Mrs. Palmer explained. "It is as dead as Pudsey. With him gone, there is no one to champion it. I cannot imagine it will even get a vote."

That was hardly surprising, Bea thought, considering what Mrs. Palmer had just told her and what she had learned prior to the discussion.

And yet something about it struck her as shocking.

Yes, there was an odd agitation in her limbs, an unease she could not identify, as she contemplated the advantage gained by Bentham at Pudsey's death.

But it was not really an advantage, was it, for Mrs. Palmer's point was well taken: The law could never be enforced. The local constable could barely be stirred to investigate the death of a human; he would not make a greater or even equal effort to inspect the hind fetlock of a horse.

Ultimately, the act would have been meaningless.

The fox hunt had never been in danger from the crown, which meant the Henley Sporting Club could continue its activities unmolested.

Again, Bentham had nothing to gain.

And yet it seemed a little overly confident to assume the legislation would have no effect at all. Perhaps its very existence would start to alter the way people viewed animals, such that they might indeed begin to make the shift for which Mrs. Palmer had advocated: from shovel and plow to living creature.

Hoping to soothe her disquiet, Bea sought to learn the fate of the fluorspar tax. She assumed it would also fall out of favor now that the man who proposed it was dead. Lady Bentham had insisted it would not prosper without Pudsey, which Fawcett had also believed, for his every action had been calculated to advance his daughter's prospects.

Bentham could revive it, she supposed, but what purpose would that serve? Miss Fawcett's betrothal was already at an end, Prince Adriano having decided that he would rather not align his kingdom with a murderer.

The question, however, was not as straightforward as Bea thought, and her anxiety increased as Mrs. Palmer furrowed her dark brows. "It is difficult to say because lawmaking is a capricious endeavor of constantly changing motivations, but as things stand at this very moment, it is likely to move forward. The tariff enjoys broad support in Parliament and has since the very beginning, which the broadsheets have written much about. That could change easily enough—for example, if Thornaby decided to oppose it, he could sway other members in the region—but as of now its prospects are good."

Bea shook her head as if denying the information, for it was quite troubling to contemplate what it meant for Pudsey's murder.

Mr. Fawcett acted to advance his daughter's prospect. That was the core of her argument against him.

He secured her future while striking back at an enemy.

It was all quite rational and tidy.

But if the levy had always been in the position to move forward without Pudsey's advocacy, then Fawcett's motivation was gone.

No, Bea thought, not gone—lessened.

The second aspect remained, and it was no small thing, the desire for revenge, especially if the legislation had become inevitable. In that case, the only retribution available to Fawcett was causing Bentham harm.

Indeed, in some ways, it actually increased his motive.

Yes, she thought, but why swipe at his target from the side when confronting him face to face was the far more satisfying resolution? By slaying Pudsey to punish Bentham, Fawcett had forfeited the opportunity to reveal the full fury of his wrath and to make sure the other man, poised on the edge of oblivion, knew why he was being plunged into darkness.

In doing so, he had denied himself the sweetest pleasures of revenge.

Ah, but perhaps watching your target twist in the wind—literally, in this instance—was sweeter yet.

For a man of Bentham's stamp, consignment to Newgate was a fate worse than death. Having enjoyed the best of everything, including his associates' respect and submission, he would be crushed by the brutality of a dungeon prison.

And the looming noose...

Yes, that would weigh on him too, carrying him deeper into the depths as he struggled to comprehend what had happened to him.

The button, he would think during the endless night as cold, damp misery seeped into his bones. How had it gotten there, to the bottom of an amphora he had never touched?

Over and over.

Again and again.

And it would never make sense.

That was true darkness.

Indeed, Bea felt a chill as she considered it, and she acknowledged that she would never have imagined Mr. Fawcett capable of such viciousness. Easily, she pictured him lashing out as a concerned father doing whatever he could to salvage his daughter's happiness.

But devising a plan so wretchedly cruel and precise?

He simply did not seem like the type.

According to Nuneaton, his wife was more suited to complex plots. She was, Bea recalled now, the one who had secured the prince by arranging the lucrative contracts for fluorspar in the first place.

Could the whole scheme have been Mrs. Fawcett's idea?

The agitation, Bea realized, was the unsettling sense that she had overlooked a vital piece of information. Fleetingly, she had thought it was Bentham's motive, but now she knew it was her uncertainty regarding Mrs. Fawcett's complicity. Once she had settled on proximity to Bentham's sleeve button as the deciding factor for guilt, Bea had removed the wife from the equation. She had not deliberated on the fact that she was the far more devious spouse.

It did not matter in the end, she assured herself, for Fawcett's guilt was unmistakable and did not lessen if the deed itself had been devised by his wife. The only reason she was still thinking about it two weeks later was the killer refused to acknowledge what he had done, and by implicating Mrs. Fawcett in the act she could make sense of his denial on rhetorical grounds—that was, *I* did not do it, *we* did.

Previously, she had been fortunate that the targets of her inquiries had confessed to their crime. If Lady Skeffington had subjected her to an unrestrained bout of crying and tortured protestations of innocence, Bea's investigative habit might have ended then and there.

While Bea pondered these thoughts, Mrs. Palmer revealed her intention to launch her own political salon, as Pudsey's death had left a rather large hole in the community. "I am certain I am not the only one who feels it. Poor Longridge accosted me in Hatchards the other day to complain about my stance on the income tax, and all I had said to him was good morning. As you know, I am not at all hesitant to express my views, particularly when they are in the right and the whole of the British aristocracy is in the wrong, as is the case with the abolishment of the income tax, but I swear to you I was just selecting a novel for my mother. Even I know better than to berate a peer in a bookshop."

Bea smiled as she pictured the scene. "I think your own political salon is a wonderful idea, and I will put my ridiculous popularity to good use by attending the first evening. That will ensure your success."

"That would be marvelous, your grace, for I do want it to

be a perfect crush," Mrs. Palmer said, her eyes sparkling with excitement.

"Of course you do," Bea said amiably. "The more guests who attend, the more guests you can berate over the income tax."

Her friend could not cavil over this observation, for it was patently true. Furthermore, she added, they deserved every harsh word she had to offer. "Eliminating it was the single most shortsighted piece of business since the passage of the Coercive Acts. Unfortunately, there are several other terrible decisions the House of Lords has made recently that deserve a public airing. It shall be such fun, working our way through them one by one!" she said, grinning with delight. Her expression dimmed momentarily, however, when she realized her custom magnifying glass would not be ready in time for the first event. "There is nothing for it but to delay my plan for a week. I cannot have the Duchess of Kesgrave in my home without sporting the proper accoutrement."

But Bea could not allow such an extravagant misstatement to stand, for there was nothing properly accoutrement-ish about a magnifying glass. "For goodness' sake, what am I meant to be scrutinizing so intently? The bottom of the vase for traces of blood? Pudsey's head for signs of a bruise? I was able to observe both clearly without assistance. I know! I should be examining the dust under the settee for impressions of people's fingertips, the patterns of which I could then compare against my various suspects. It is utterly absurd, all of it."

As satirical as Bea's suggestion was, Mrs. Palmer relished the prospect of an individualized fingerprint and considered the matter in some depth as they continued their stroll through the park. She wondered what other parts of the body could be used for identification purposes and theorized the possibility of the elbow possessing a unique pattern.

Although she rejected every aspect of the premise, Bea was entertained by her friend's speculation. She was further amused by the way the savvy political hostess veered jarringly from left to right and right to left to evade the many interlopers and well-wishers who desired a word with the popular duchess.

Mr. Serle came remarkably close to detaining them successfully, but Mrs. Palmer tossed her handkerchief on the ground and then apologized for running off while he retrieved it.

Taken aback by the audacity of the maneuver, Bea risked undoing all her friend's good work by standing in place giggling.

Diverted by the outing, Bea returned to Kesgrave House with a new understanding of why a duke who was relentlessly fawned upon might not mind social banishment and made a remark to that effect over dinner. They were enjoying the pleasure of a rare evening at home, having declined three invitations, one of which was a masquerade ball hosted by Alvanley. Lady Abercrombie had energetically applauded their decision not to attend, as it would never do for the Duchess of Kesgrave to appear too readily available.

"An air of elusiveness will convince them to love you more," the countess had added approvingly, as if Bea's refusal had been a decision calculated to increase her popularity rather than an attempt to spend time alone with the duke. "You should also decline Lady Tipton's rout, for she has invited the entire *beau monde*, all but ensuring it will be a wretched squeeze. I myself plan to be otherwise engaged."

As Bea could think of few things more unpleasant than passing an evening in an overcrowded drawing room, she was happy to take her ladyship's advice.

Spooning velvety mushroom soup, Bea pointed out to Kesgrave that if he had just stated with forthright simplicity how thoroughly exhausting it was to be universally adored, she would have comprehended months ago his utter indifference to public opinion. "Instead, however, you chose to be coy about it, making oblique comments and sly references. Next time, your grace, please do me the courtesy of speaking plainly."

Kesgrave's lips twitched as he contemplated her in the flickering light of the library, a grand space beset with wonderful alcoves ideally suited for quiet moments and intimate activities. Bea found it infinitely preferable to the dining room, which was comically large for only two people. Either they sat at opposing ends with a sea of table between them, or they convened at one corner like soldiers huddled in a pit.

The duke dipped his head for a sip of wine before responding to her provocation. "Am I to understand that you are now taking me to task for not being pompous enough?"

Bea lowered her spoon to the bowl as she regarded him with confusion. "Your tone implies that the charge is unprecedented, but I am certain I have commented on your undue humility several times recently. Too much modesty is as displeasing as too little."

"No, brat," Kesgrave said, returning his drink to the table, "there is nothing unique to the charge. It is only that I begin to suspect that there is no way for me to win. I cannot believe in your estimation that there is a satisfactory measure of modesty or immodesty."

Unable to smother the impertinent grin that spread across her face, she replied, "If you are only beginning to perceive that now, your grace, then I have some rather dispiriting observations to make about your intelligence."

Oh, but that was unacceptable, casting aspersions on his intellect.

She could defame his pomposity all she wanted but when

she turned her fire on his brain—well, an act of such lavish effrontery required consequences.

Sometime later, when Bea regained her composure—and, it must be said, her senses—she was perched languidly on the settee beside her husband.

Pressing a kiss against the shoulder that cradled her head, she said, "I am not sure seducing me is an effective way of convincing me of your mental acumen. It comes across as an evasive measure or an attempt to compensate for a deficiency."

"I must disagree, your grace," he said as he smoothed a strand of hair behind her ear. "From where I am sitting, it seems extremely clever indeed."

Try as she might, the former Beatrice Hyde-Clare could find no way to dispute the point. Instead, she sat up, inspected the dinner table several feet away, and deciding she was famished, arranged an assortment of meats on a plate. With her free hand, she collected their wineglasses and returned to the sofa. Settling comfortably against the duke, she wondered why she would ever leave the room, for it contained everything she needed.

Well, except rout cakes, and those could be summoned with the tug of a cord.

Why did everyone else require so much to be happy?

But she knew, yes, of course she did, the ridiculousness of the thought, for she in fact *had* so much. The lavish room, the cozy settee, the rows of books, the excellent claret, the delicious cheese, the handsome duke—'twas an embarrassment of riches, and she giggled at her careless underestimation of it all.

How quickly one became accustomed to the comforts of a duchy!

Kesgrave inquired as to the source of her amusement, suspecting, she supposed, that it might be himself, and she shook her head rather than reveal the awful truth. Despite her teasing, his ego was quite robust and admitting to the depths of her contentment would only increase his vanity.

Instead, she regaled him with a description of her stroll in the park with Mrs. Palmer and her friend's increasingly outlandish maneuvers to evade conversation with the new duchess's admirers. When Bea described Mrs. Palmer's treat-ment of poor Mr. Serle, Kesgrave clucked disapprovingly at their conduct but allowed that the gambit had been wise, for the gentleman was notorious for telling rambling stories that had neither purpose nor end.

"Castlereagh once proposed sending him to France to bore Napoleon into surrendering," he said as he selected a buttered prawn, "for he insisted he was the most tedious person England has to offer."

"I believe that distinction belongs to my aunt," Bea replied with a smile. "But if I can convince her to attend Mrs. Palmer's political salon, we can introduce them to each other and let them battle it out for the title."

"Going to give Countess Lieven a run for her money, is she?" he asked.

"I am sure her aspirations are not nearly that high," Bea said, for the ambassador's wife and patroness of Almack's held a particularly rarefied position among the political elite. "She merely seeks to simplify the process of browbeating politicians by bringing them to her home. I applaud the effi-ciency and have promised to attend the first event. Naturally, I accepted only on my own behalf. You are free to refuse. I cannot believe you would find a roomful of pontificating lords to be an amiable setting, as you would prefer to be the only one holding forth at any given time."

"Although I rarely pontificate, I assure you, my dear, that when I deign to indulge I *am* the only one in the room doing so," he said.

Bea replied that she required no assurances, for she expected nothing less. Then she added that no date had been established yet for the event because Mrs. Palmer was awaiting delivery of her own custom magnifying glass.

Kesgrave shook his head sadly and said on a sigh of disappointment, "Even she?"

But Bea was not fooled by the display of sympathy. The duke had made no attempt to hide his pleasure at her outrageous popularity. "'Tis not funny," she insisted.

"On the contrary, it is vastly amusing," he replied, grinning widely. "You may frown at me all you like, but I will not be glowered out of my delight at the idea of all of London sporting magnifying glasses in homage to my wife's cleverness. It is simply impossible for me to feel anything else. Tilly frequently achieves her goals, but this time she exceeded beyond even her own wildest imaginings. I will have to send her a token as a thank you."

Although the countess could hardly take credit for the string of improbable events that led to Bea's current success, she had not allowed such a minor detail to stand in the way of her preening. She had been restrained in her triumph, of course, out of respect for Pudsey, but there was an undeniable sparkle in her eye whenever she contemplated Bea.

"I do not think a token is called for, but if you must, please do not make it a ridiculous magnifying glass," Bea said, growing newly exasperated as she contemplated the random arbitrariness of the implement. Bentham could have chosen a teapot for all the relevance it shared with her activities. Indeed, that would have actually made a modicum of sense, for one was always plying suspects with tea to lull them into providing helpful information. "Buy her a dagger instead. She has shown herself partial to them."

"That was Sir Walter's territory and I would rather not step there. I will have Stephens select something that is appropriately shiny. He has excellent if extravagant taste," he said.

Bea pictured the reserved man who competently oversaw the duke's business. "I would never have guessed that."

"To your detriment, then. Or your advantage. My grandmother has certainly benefited from his fondness for fifteenth-century Ming dynasty vases," he said, his tone slightly disgruntled. Then his expression lightened as a mischievous glimmer entered his eyes and he added, "Sometimes, however, I prefer to do my own shopping, as in this case."

She was confused by his statement but only for a moment because she was immediately presented with a silver box from the side table's drawer. Without even touching it, she knew what it was.

The unholy sparkle of mirth could mean only one thing.

"No," she said firmly.

Her resolve merely heightened his enjoyment. "No? You have been resistant to other gifts I have given you—I am thinking in particular of a certain nightgown—but on those occasions you have at least done me the courtesy of examining the item before rejecting it."

She shook her head and insisted that the garment in question, made of gossamer silk so sheer as to render it almost transparent, had in fact been a gift for himself. "Nevertheless, I wore it."

"But so briefly," he murmured.

"That was for you as well, your grace," she pointed out. "But if that is the precedent you wish to establish, then I will comply. Give me the magnifying glass and I will wear it for ten minutes."

"A half hour," Kesgrave said as he handed her the box. "I was able to resist my baser impulse for a full half hour."

"Fifteen minutes tops," she countered, her fingers moving

lightly along the side of the smooth narrow case. "I will not quickly forget this piece of mockery and will set Stephens on a quest to find the most expensive Ming vase in all of China."

"I am reasonably sure that specimen already sits on the mantel in my grandmother's drawing room," he said. "But I am not mocking you, Bea. I offer this present with my sincerest admiration."

Although highly suspicious of his motives, she could not doubt the depth of his esteem, for he had demonstrated it many times over.

Yielding to the inevitable, she sighed lightly and opened the box. She knew precisely what it contained and yet she gasped in surprise as she beheld the item. Designed simply with a slim handle and a narrow frame that encased the lens, it was beset with sapphires clustered around diamonds, forming delicate little flowers.

'Twas exquisite.

Too exquisite.

At once, a new objection rose to her lips, for she could not imagine wearing something so delicate and valuable. It belonged on the mantel next to the dowager's Ming vase.

While she stared in wonder, he said, "The sapphires are to match your mother's bracelet."

Oh, yes, of course he would think of that.

Kesgrave always had one eye on the details.

"It is lovely," she said softly, holding the device up to the candle, where its stones glimmered in the flame. "But it is too much. I would be afraid to wear it. The rubies were daunting enough."

"And you wore them beautifully," he said.

Bea laughed. "I am fairly certain the rubies wore me."

"Again, beautifully," he replied, abstaining from argument.

Clearly, there was no reasoning with him. "Although I

cannot say it is what I always wanted, it is stunning and I am delighted to have it. Thank you, Damien."

He took a sip of wine and leaned back in the settee, drawing her toward him for a kiss. "You're welcome."

"I know. I shall wear it to Mrs. Palmer's salon so that I can see her guests' respect for her opinions, as it is so infinitesimally small," she said as she relaxed against his chest.

"An excellent plan," he replied. "I knew it would have its uses."

Thoughtfully, she watched the light flicker through the lens. "She said the fluorspar levy will move forward regardless."

"Excuse me?"

Realizing his mind had not drifted in the same direction as hers, Bea clarified. "Mrs. Palmer said that Pudsey's act instituting a tax on the importation of fluorspar will move forward despite his death because it has broad support in Parliament."

"I see," he said. "It is impossible to say for sure, but it does seem likely."

"It makes one think," she said softly.

"Does it?"

"Well, yes, because that was Fawcett's primary motive. Or so I believed," she qualified. "I am having a hard time imagining him killing one man simply to avenge himself against another. But that is the only way it makes sense in the light of Mrs. Palmer's information. And if it had worked as he planned, it would have been a diabolical punishment."

Infusing his tone with a hint of irony, Kesgrave allowed that it was distinctly unsporting. "But it was revenge against Pudsey as well, was it not, for falling in with Bentham's scheme. Had he behaved with honor, he would have refused the proposal and allowed his cruelty ban to stand on its merits."

"That is true, I suppose."

"You are still not convinced?" he asked.

Bea shrugged her shoulders. "It is merely that I find myself wondering if perhaps Mrs. Fawcett had something to do with it. She appeared horrifyingly shocked by the revelation of her husband's guilt, but a society matron of her stature would be adept at displaying the proper response. According to Nuneaton, it is she who has been playing a game of cat and mouse with Lady Bentham for years, and it was her manipulations that secured Prince Adriano's affections for her daughter. Using Pudsey to ensure Bentham's downfall seems like something she would devise. By most accounts, Fawcett is too mild mannered."

"Precisely his wife's defense," Kesgrave observed.

"Even his attempt to interrupt Bentham and Pudsey's argument was diffident and polite," she said. "As angry as he was, he did not step into the middle of them and demand attention. He hovered at the edges, waiting for an opening. He only grabbed Bentham's arm when provoked beyond bearing."

"I am confused by what you are arguing. If every action Fawcett took that night was carefully choreographed to ensure the outcome he desired, then he only appeared too hesitant to interrupt to justify grabbing Bentham's arm to steal the sleeve button from his cuff. In that case, his hesitance was intentional, not instinctual. It cannot be used to support the theory that he is too mild mannered to have concocted the plot himself."

"You are right," Bea said with a vigorous shake of her head, as if trying to dislodge a particularly stubborn thought. The truth was, she was tired of thinking about the matter, for she only went in circles, reviewing the same evidence over and over again. "I know you are right. In fact, I am not sure what point I am trying to make regarding Mrs. Fawcett. Even if she is the one who came up with the plan, it is still Fawcett who wielded the shears. It is too implausible to believe she would have the skill, strength, or stomach to drive the scissors into Pudsey's heart. And yet something about it does not sit well with me."

"His pleading on the way to the door," he replied. "That is the thing that does not sit well with you. I know it because it does not sit well with me either. I do not wish to sound as though I'm satirizing *The Rudiments of Genteel Behavior,* but if you are going to kill a peer of considerable standing in the middle of a dinner party, the very least you could do is accept the consequences stoically."

Bea shifted her position so that she was facing the duke and examined him with the magnifying glass, as if inspecting a very rare creature. "You have read Mr. Nivelon's charming tome on proper deportment?"

"Actually, I have not, no, despite my tutor's efforts to get me to memorize its dictates," he confessed. "Hartley was an anxious fellow who wore himself to a nub worrying about inconsequentialities, such as how I doffed my hat."

"I have not noticed you to be deficient in the art of doffing," Bea said, grateful for the change in subject. She did not want to think of the Fawcetts again—neither the husband with his desperation nor the wife with her manipulations. "Just the opposite, for you are remarkably proficient at ridding yourself of things."

By "things" she meant people, for he genuinely exceled at shedding sycophants and mushrooms, but the term could also refer to articles of clothing, as he had demonstrated during the brief interval of their marriage. He applied himself to the latter now, moved, it would appear, by the rare compliment from his wife.

Although Bea was not inured to the lovely sensations the duke's fingers created as they slid the gown over her shoulders, she felt compelled to clarify her statement. It would never do to allow his vanity to increase.

To her mortification, however, the deflating retort she planned to issue slipped out as a contented sigh, and when his lips replaced his fingers, she found she could not remember the words she had intended to say.

I did not mean to imply...

Doffing is not quite the...

Breathless now, she abandoned the effort, laying her new magnifying glass gently on the table before turning her attention to his shirt, which she doffed with her own enviable skill.

Chapter Twelve

Having resolved to not think about the Fawcetts again, Bea woke up the next morning with them prominently on her mind. She kept recalling Kesgrave's remark about Mr. Fawcett's poor-spiritedness of his actions and found she could not reconcile that aspect of the gentleman's performance with his cool-headed elimination of Pudsey.

Somehow, he managed to maintain his composure while driving embroidery shears through the man's chest during a brief intermission and yet collapsed entirely the moment he was called to account.

It defied sense unless one factored his wife into the situation.

Had Mrs. Fawcett, like Lady Macbeth before her, bolstered and bullied her husband into performing the deed?

The more she considered the possibility, the more likely it felt.

Even if it was true, Bea doubted that she could prove it.

Moreover, she could not quite understand why she should.

What purpose would be served if Mrs. Fawcett was to swing next to her husband?

Pudsey would not be any less dead.

Their betrayal of Bentham would not be any less cruel.

The past could not be undone and all that would be added was another dead body to the pile.

It was a chilling thought.

Determinedly, Bea pushed the Fawcetts from her mind, and casting about for another subject, settled on her maid, whose brow was furrowed as she examined the walking dress she had selected for the duchess to wear. Observing that the weather was brisk for April, Dolly wondered if a sturdier gown would not be more appropriate. Bea agreed readily, for the day looked stormy as well, and asked the girl about her family. Having previously inquired, she knew the basics— mother and father in Alfriston, a married sister in High Wycombe, a brother who worked in Lord Midhurt's kitchens in Sloane Square—but now she pried further.

Dolly did not seem to mind in the least, answering questions about her mother's health and her father's interests while she styled her grace's hair.

Bea knew, of course, that it was the prerogative of the employer to show a vulgar curiosity in the private matters of her staff and Dolly would not reveal her discomfort if she felt it. The reminder of her privilege spurred her to find another form of distraction, and as soon as she finished her breakfast, she decided to call on her uncle to continue their discussion of the Kepler biography they had both read.

Although he was surprised to see her, Uncle Horace immediately welcomed her into his study, where, he said, they could hide from her other relatives, a scheme that succeeded for a full fifty-five minutes. Eventually, however, Russell learned of her presence and appeared in the doorway with a bundle of notes about the solar system, which he consulted frequently during their conversation with haphazard success. He caused his father to sigh in despair during one particularly convoluted exchange, in which he confused Venus with Neptune.

Fortunately, her uncle's anguish was short-lived, for only a dozen minutes later Aunt Vera insisted on dragging her to the drawing room for a proper visit with tea and cakes, creating, Bea thought, an unfair burden for Mrs. Emerson, who did not keep a regular supply of pastries on hand for unexpected ducal visitors.

"You are looking well," Aunt Vera said, her tone suffused with the bewilderment she frequently displayed in Bea's presence, for she could not comprehend how anyone could thrive under the manifold obligations of an immense mansion in Berkeley Square. Her confusion was even more acute in the wake of Lady Abercrombie's party, because her niece's social success meant she had even less time to oversee the unfathomably large staff.

"I am well, thank you," Bea replied, noting her relative had arranged herself awkwardly on the settee in a familiar attempt to hide the worn fabric on the arm. The effort amused her because she had lived in the house for decades and knew every frayed inch of it. More clearly than anything else ever could, Aunt Vera's efforts represented the drastic change in Bea's status. She was now someone from whom minor imperfections must be hidden, like the dowager duchess or Mrs. Ralston.

Something about that prospect made her feel sad.

But it was only her aunt who viewed her differently. Flora had no interest in her elevated position except as something she could use to her own advantage, which she tried to do the moment she entered the drawing room.

"You must invite Holcroft for tea and demand that he listen to reason," her cousin said by way of greeting, her lips turned down in an appealing pout. "He is being beastly about Nuneaton and I cannot bear it."

Aunt Vera, understanding only enough of this information to be appalled, told her daughter that she must not issue orders to a duchess. "You should make a gently worded request and then quickly step away—metaphorically, of course, not literally, as you are sitting down and cannot actually step anywhere. And walking backward is a fraught exercise so really the protocol is to step aside. The object is to give her grace an opportunity to consider your request, which she should feel free to decline. In that case, I would urge her to do exactly that. I have no idea who Holcroft is, but any man who does not feel inveterate respect for a viscount is not worthy of her generosity."

Flora rolled her eyes at this observation and said, "You met Mr. Holcroft at Mrs. Pelton's garden party and he called here for tea."

"Oh, yes, *that* Holcroft," Aunt Vera said disapprovingly. "I thought we agreed that he is infelicitously related."

"He is reforming his disgraced cousin, which is a highly noble undertaking and should be applauded," Flora said. "We would not want to be seen as the type of people who discourage good works, would we, Mama?"

Aunt Vera scoffed at the idea that she was anything less than a charitable Christian woman, although she did note (as a parenthetical only) that the burden of supporting rehabilitation efforts fell more comfortably on august shoulders. "Nevertheless, I was referring to his godfather, who is a hardened criminal and facing severe charges that cannot be reformed away."

"I said Sir Dudley was *like* his godfather," her daughter replied with more than a hint of exasperation, "not that he *is* his godfather. I was merely trying to explain to you why you should not mention the scandal involving the Master of the

Rolls when Mr. Holcroft came to tea. As a personal matter, it is quite upsetting to him."

"Even so, it is the third thing we know to his discredit, and it is really very poorly done of him to have a reprobate for a cousin and a blackguard for a near-godfather on top of an inveterate lack of respect for viscounts. Any one on its own would be problematic but as a group it is entirely inappropriate for the Duchess of Kesgrave to bestow her attention."

"Bea does not care about his relations," Flora insisted.

Aunt Vera gasped in shock and told her daughter that she must never put words in the duchess's mouth. Flora laughed and ordered her mother to stop being such a silly goose.

"It's just Bea, Mama, the same person who ran upstairs to get your embroidery every time you left it in your sitting room," Flora said.

Bea watched in amazement as her aunt's face turned an alarming shade of purple at her daughter's comment, which was as benign as it was accurate.

And yet something about it was deeply mortifying for Vera Hyde-Clare.

To allow her aunt time to recover, Bea asked her cousin what she had done to put Holcroft's nose out of joint. "Naturally, I do not believe Nuneaton is at fault, for it would require too much effort for him to give offense."

"I did not do anything either," Flora said defensively. "Holcroft is being utterly irrational about everything. I adore his staidness. But I had to assist your triumph at Lady Abercrombie's, did I not? And it is not my fault Holcroft misunderstood what he saw in Hyde Park. It would have been rude for me not to laugh at Nuneaton's sallies even if they had been leaden squawkers. I was just being courteous, which is what any young lady of quality would do whilst taking a ride in the park with a viscount, so for him to accuse me of flirting is insupportable. What would he have me do? Sit in the carriage like a lump of coal? Lumps of coal are quite unattractive. As fond as I am of Holcroft, I will not make myself ugly and I think it is decidedly unfair of him to ask."

Bea, piecing together the disjointed narrative, concluded that Flora and Holcroft had had a falling out over the amount of time she had spent with Nuneaton in preparation for Lady Abercrombie's murder mystery dinner party. He objected, and she responded by calling him boring.

Presumably, his reaction was spurred in some part by jealousy, for the viscount was indeed handsome and established in a way that the even-keeled Holcroft was not, and it could not have bolstered his ego to hear himself described as staid.

Flora, possessing her own associations for the term, insisted she had meant it as a compliment and grew agitated at the thought that she had inadvertently issued a cutting insult to the man for whom she had many warm feelings.

"You must invite him to tea at Kesgrave House and tell him that I find him wildly exciting," she said vehemently. "And you must praise his eyes, for they are the most verdant shade of green. I can stare into them all day. You will say that, won't you, my dear?"

Well, no, Bea thought in amusement, she would not say that, but she did promise to invite Holcroft to tea so that her cousin could do her own cajoling.

Flora clapped her hands in delight and immediately began to press for a date, forcing her mother to draw attention yet again to Beatrice's altered status.

"She is a duchess now and cannot attend to you every minute of the day, Flora," she said, then colored immediately at the reminder of her own previous monopolization of her niece's time. In an effort to hide her discomfort, she began to list her grace's new duties, all of which were domestic in nature and seemed to require her chastising various servants for not working hard enough.

Bea left the house an hour later and was pleased to realize she had not thought about Mrs. Fawcett a single time.

Clearly, her family had their uses.

Shivering slightly in the cool, damp air, she walked down the steps toward her carriage and marveled at the luxury of having such a well-appointed vehicle at her command. She was about to call out to the groom when Mrs. Ralston appeared in front of her.

It was so abrupt, the way she darted suddenly from the other side of the conveyance to greet her cheerfully, and Bea could not rule out the possibility that she had been waiting for her to emerge from number nineteen. Every so often, she would catch a glimpse of her—or what she thought was a glimpse of her—lurking in Berkeley Square biding her time to strike.

Fortunately, that moment had never come.

Now, alas, it had.

"Well, now this is a lovely treat," Mrs. Ralston said, her eyes fluttering as she sought to affect genuine surprise. "Imagine running into you here of all places. How delightfully unexpected. Oh, but I see now. We are in front of your aunt's house. Yes, of course, that makes much more sense. What a remarkable coincidence, your grace, for I am rarely in this street. I am only here now because I asked my driver to drop me on the way home from visiting my brother, for I desired a spot of exertion while the weather was pleasant. I must say, your grace, you are looking very well. That bonnet is charming. Do I recognize the expert hand of Mrs. Bell? Is that an emu feather? How very clever. My compliments to your plumassier."

Not a single thing about this speech was accurate, from the feather (ostrich) to the weather (inclement), and Bea contemplated the various ways she could extricate herself from Mrs. Ralston's grasping fingers. It would not require much, for as a duchess she did not have to retain the goodwill of scandal-hungry prattlers and could issue a sharp good day as she continued to her carriage.

Nonetheless, Bea was amused by the temerity of her lies and realized that she had said one thing that was true: Their meeting *was* coincidental, for Mrs. Ralston had played an unknowing part in Pudsey's murder and Bea could not stop thinking about Pudsey's murder.

She would never have sought the other woman out for a discussion, for she had been determined to push the concern from her mind, but Mrs. Ralston was before her now, her eyes gleaming with an off-putting insatiability.

It would be foolhardy not to make the most of the opportunity.

Affecting her own delighted smile, Bea bid the woman good day and lauded her vigorous efforts. "I wonder if I could induce you to extend your exertions to include a turn with me around the square. As you said, the weather is suited for it and I would enjoy some movement before I return to my carriage."

Having spent her entire social career wedging herself into conversations, Mrs. Ralston was not prepared for a warm reception and seemed momentarily at a loss to respond. Baffled, she stared at Bea as if struggling to comprehend what was happening. She even darted her eyes to the left and right, as if suspecting someone would leap from behind the carriage with the same zeal as herself and carry her away.

Ignoring her confusion, Bea linked her arm through Mrs. Ralston's and led her across the road. "Tell me, how are Amelia and Esther?"

Hesitantly she replied that they were both well, although the slight lilt at the end of her response made it seem more like a question, as if she were seeking Bea's opinion on the welfare of her daughters.

"They are greatly admiring of you," Mrs. Ralston added as they entered the square. "They have their magnifying glasses, of course. Amelia's is a charming pendant made from beryl, and Esther wears a cloisonné brooch that is just darling. They are simply in awe of your abilities, your grace. They cannot understand how you do it—not so much figure out the identity of the murderer, for you clearly have a superior mind capable of masculine reasoning, but look at these horrible things without fainting. The chef, for instance, who was missing his head. What was staring at that spectacle like for you?"

"Ah, you see, Mrs. Ralston, this is why your daughters have an outsized appreciation for what I do—because it is based on a gross misunderstanding," Bea said, grateful for the opportunity to clear up one matter before moving on to the next. "I never saw Mr. Réjane without his head. By the time I arrived at the residence, the constable had removed him and all evidence scrubbed away. There was not a speck of blood left behind. The floor, as they say, was clean enough to eat off."

"But Mr. Twaddle-Thum said—"

"Yes," Bea interrupted firmly, "I know what Mr. Twaddle-Thum said, and if I ever have the pleasure of meeting the gentleman, I should like to twaddle his thumbs. I assure you, Mrs. Ralston, I would like nothing better than to be the woman portrayed in his scandalous account, for she sounds quite dashing. Alas, that is not I."

Mrs. Ralston was not persuaded by this display of modesty. "Goodness me, your grace, but marching into a house that is not your own and demanding answers to impertinent questions strikes me as excessively dashing."

"Ah, but is that very different from what you do?" Bea

asked archly, causing the notorious gossip to stiffen and pause briefly in her tracks. Pretending not to notice, she continued. "That is to say, what all of us do? We visit each other's houses and talk about the things that interest us most. And of course we are all curious about the lives of other people because they seem so thrilling. Your life, for example."

"My life?" Mrs. Ralston said, disconcerted by the attention.

"Yes, of course, and not just because you have raised two beautiful daughters," Bea said with calculating flattery. No one had ever gone amiss by praising a mother on her progeny. "You have a veritable talent for finding yourself at the intersection of all the interesting events in society."

Further taken aback by either the prospect of having a talent or the idea that her presence anywhere was happenstance, Mrs. Ralston said, "I do?"

"Do you doubt it?" Bea asked, feigning amazement. "Why, you were in fact central to the murder of poor Lord Pudsey."

Now Mrs. Ralston stopped firmly and turned to look at Bea, her face a fascinating mix of insult, horror, bewilderment, and delight. After grappling with the various emotions, she settled on offended and said, "That is a scurrilous lie, and I would thank you to not embroil me in that distasteful affair."

It was not surprising, of course, that the hardened rumormonger did not welcome being on the other end of the wagging tongue, but Bea was startled by her vehemence. She would have expected Mrs. Ralston to try to remove herself from the tale with a little more finesse. "It is not I who embroiled you; it is Mr. Fawcett," she said innocently. "He cited your conversation on the day of the dinner party as the event that inflamed his murderous rage."

Somewhat mollified by this explanation, Mrs. Ralston blinked her eyelashes several times and Bea imagined she was trying to figure out how best to proceed: insert herself further or withdraw completely.

Apparently, it was the former because she said with fervent agitation, "How dreadful! I knew something was not quite right, for as soon as I mentioned Bentham's shocking behavior, he grew quite silent and introspective. Only a few moments before he had been chatting happily about the prospect of Lady Abercrombie's dinner party, for he had no idea what to expect from such an unconventional affair. Truly, I am horrified to have had any hand in it at all. I wonder if I could have done something to intercede and save Pudsey from his wretched fate. I do not imagine myself to be a heroine at all, but there might have been some action I could have taken. If only I had held my tongue! It is just that I believe so ardently in the truth. I abhor secrets, for it is my firm conviction that they destroy lives. In this case, however, the opposite appears to be true. Fie on Bentham for telling me about his devious scheme in the first place! We should have stuck to the topic at hand, for nobody has ever been harmed by a discussion of hair ribbons."

Bea, who had been waiting for an opportunity to return the conversation to Fawcett's state of mind, was struck by this comment. Although the rigidity of the Henley Sporting Club's dress code indicated an interest in fashion, Bentham did not seem like the sort of man who would care for a lady's fripperies. "You were discussing hair ribbons?"

Sensing an underlying rebuke in the query, Mrs. Ralston responded with explicatory disdain, "It is what one does, your grace, when one is buying hair ribbons."

But Bentham was not buying hair ribbons when he let the truth slip. He had been enjoying himself greatly at Miss Grundy's coming-out party. That was what he had said, was it not—in a mumbled statement about being half-sprung and indiscreet?

"Yes, of course, I did not realize you were shopping when the conversation took place," Bea said candidly. "I imagined it in a more convivial setting."

Again, Mrs. Ralston shook her head and regarded her condescendingly. "My dear duchess, is there any setting more convivial than the Western Exchange?"

Unstintingly, Bea agreed, but her brain was buzzing as she sought to comprehend the sequence of events. "So it was while you were shopping for hair ribbons at the Western Exchange that Bentham told you about his agreement with Pudsey to support his animal cruelty act in exchange for his proposing a levy on imported fluorspar?"

"I detect a hint of disapproval in your tone and I cannot fathom its cause," Mrs. Ralston said. "Do you object to ribbons, your grace? I would think not since you have a lovely pink one in your bonnet. Is it the Western Exchange that troubles you? A man was stabbed to death there some weeks ago. I did not hear your name in connection to the murder but perhaps you conducted a secret investigation? I trust you would tell me if there is a reason I should avoid the emporium. Esther and I shop there frequently, and it would cause me great distress to know I had put her at risk."

Distracted by Bentham's lie, Bea waved aside this facile attempt to elicit information and sought to learn more about their exchange. "I must apologize, for I did not mean to convey disapproval. I was merely marveling at how a conversation could digress from hair ribbons to acts of Parliament. They are quite at the opposite ends."

"Ah, yes, I see now," Mrs. Ralston said with a firm dip of her head. "When one is as skilled at conversation as Bentham or I, all topics are closely related. I cannot recall exactly how we got from one to the other. He greeted us most amiably and we chatted for a few minutes about the lovely day and the delightful time we had both had at the Winslows' ball.

And then he asked if we were shopping for ribbons for Miss Fawcett's wedding. We had not been invited, but I was much gratified that he thought I should be. Then he confessed that he believed it was unlikely that the wedding would take place, and naturally I could not allow such a shocking statement to stand without some scrutiny. That was when he confessed that he had struck a deal with Pudsey that he suspected might affect the betrothal. He was very coy about it, of course, insisting his actions were spurred by concern for the country's coffers and not dissatisfaction over the prince's treatment of his own daughter. But I was not fooled. That is why I happened to mention it when I saw Mr. Fawcett the next day. It seemed only fair that he have all the information."

Bea murmured in agreement, her mind only vaguely focused on the topic at hand, and Mrs. Ralston, delighted by the attention, rambled on about Mr. Fawcett's response. It had seemed measured to her, but given the immoderation of his subsequent actions, she could only marvel at how adept he was at hiding his true feelings.

On and on she went, expressing her horror and shock, but her voice faded into a low drone as Bea considered Bentham's lie. It was no minor distinction, sharing the details of his bargain while resolutely sober versus allowing the information to slip out while in his cups. He had wanted London's most notorious gossip to know the truth so she could do what she was famous for doing—pass it along.

It was little different from the role Mrs. Norton and Tavistock had assigned her two months ago, when they tried to create a scandal to ruin Bea's reputation.

How easy Mrs. Ralston was to manipulate!

Blithely ignorant of Bea's judgment, Mrs. Ralston continued to prattle about Mr. Fawcett's duplicity. "Truly, I get a cold chill when I imagine him succeeding in his effort to make Bentham appear responsible for Pudsey's wretched demise. I must confess, your grace, that I have never heard of anything so shocking and we are all fortunate that you were there to thwart it, for when a grave injustice is committed against one of us, it is committed against all of us."

"Yes, very fortunate," Bea said cynically as she examined her own gullibility, for she had fallen in line with Bentham's plan just as easily as Mrs. Ralston. It was her interference that had made his scheme possible. Without her there to insist on an investigation, the constable would have been summoned and the situation handled with his usual incompetence. Even if he thought the victim was murdered, he would have done little more than shrug his shoulders at the tragedy.

Her lips twisted as she recalled her complacency in discovering the amphora.

Oh, yes, she had been particularly pleased with herself for that bit of deduction.

Aren't you clever, Bea, finding evidence left for the Runners.

But all along it had been for her.

Bentham dropped the clues and she obligingly picked them up.

What an utter fool she was!

That was why she had felt apprehensive yesterday when talking to Mrs. Palmer. On some primal level she recognized she had been duped.

Was it the information about the animal cruelty ban?

No, the earl had never lacked for a motive.

It was the other comment Mrs. Palmer made, the seemingly benign one about ordering a custom magnifying glass from the finest jeweler in London, that caused the agitation. Bea's mind had grasped the meaning even if it had been incapable of fully digesting it.

Kimpton and Cross was the firm that had made the sleeve buttons.

Lady Bentham had said it specifically: *That is my husband's sleeve button—from Kimpton, of course!—which I gave him last year for his birthday.*

In attempting to understand how the link had worn away so quickly, Bea had attributed the defect to either inferior craftsmanship or lesser-quality gold. But if it had been fashioned by the finest jeweler in London, then neither of those conditions could apply.

Of course they could not.

If she had not spent so much time trying to fit a square peg into a round hole, she would have realized immediately that the precious metal had been deliberately thinned to make the break appear natural. Bentham's scheme would never have worked if the second emerald had not been discovered on Fawcett's person. Naturally, he had slipped it into his pocket during their tussle on the way to dinner—a tussle Bentham provoked by avoiding Fawcett with such assiduousness the other man had no choice but to accost him to gain his attention.

And by making his confession to Mrs. Ralston the day before the party, he had ensured that Fawcett would demand it.

If Bea had not helpfully found the emerald, she knew Bentham would have devised another method for its discovery. He could not rely wholly on her ingenuity.

And yet maybe he could, for in the end she fulfilled his every expectation.

He had baited her, to be sure, with his disdain and condescension, but neither was necessary to incite her interest. She would have investigated regardless, and that was what he counted on. Her predilection was widely known as well as her skill.

It was exactly as Lady Abercrombie had said: *I would never dream of making the attempt in Beatrice's presence for she is far too clever. Inevitably, I would overlook some remarkably minor detail onto which she would latch, and it would be over in a matter of minutes.*

Bentham had very kindly provided her with an overlooked detail on which to latch.

Mrs. Ralston, finding Bea's amendment to her statement just a little too smug, modified her original thought by saying someone else would surely have uncovered the truth in her absence. "From what I understand of the situation, Mr. Fawcett was heavy-handed in his scheming."

Having learned everything she needed to know from the notorious prattle-box, Bea considered how to extricate herself from the conversation and decided to affect concern about a brewing storm.

"Oh, dear, that was thunder," she said with an exaggerated shudder. "I fear the skies will open up any minute now, and I cannot allow you to finish your morning constitutional in the rain. I must let you return to your walk."

Although no clap had sounded, Mrs. Ralston quickly grabbed hold of the fiction and owned herself worried about getting caught in a downpour. "Perhaps if you could escort me home in your carriage, I could avoid getting wet."

"And deprive you of the exercise you need to maintain your excellent health?" Bea sounded properly horrified. "I do not know what kind of monster you think I am, Mrs. Ralston, but I would never stand between a woman and her well-being. You must continue on your way and spare no thought of me worrying about you in the warm and dry confines of my carriage."

Mrs. Ralston did not know how to reply to these remarks, for they seemed to her at once too effusive and thoroughly on the mark, and the look of indecision on her face was almost comical.

Biting her lip to hold in the smile, Bea said, "Goodness gracious, another clap! Do hurry."

"Yes, yes," Mrs. Ralston said, increasing her speed as they exited the square. "I will not tarry. But this has been a delightful interlude, your grace, and I am hopeful we may do it again. I shall send my card around, and we shall find a date to have a more comfortable coze."

Bea's response was noncommittal, but she did fear that at some point she would have to host Mrs. Ralston at Kesgrave House. Although she no longer believed she would bring the duke to the edge of ruin with her behavior, there was no harm in placating one of the most accomplished gossips in London. A pot of tea and a plate of cakes would go a long way in keeping the woman satisfied. Furthermore, she was an excellent source of information and could prove useful in a future investigation should another one materialize.

As she watched Mrs. Ralston scurry to the corner, Bea laughed at the notion of using her penchant for gossip to foil a murder plot.

She imagined training her to gather only useful information and then pictured a stable of Mrs. Ralstons chattering from one end of London to the other on a mission to end crime.

Bea's smile faded as she approached her carriage and she realized she had to decide what to do next. Freeing herself from Mrs. Ralston was only the first step. Now she had to find evidence to prove her new theory.

The weak link was the weak link, she reminded herself, and climbing into the carriage, asked her driver to take her to Kimpton and Cross.

Chapter Thirteen

aving employed several ruses to gain information in
her previous investigations, Bea found it decidedly
refreshing to identify herself as the Duchess of
Kesgrave and simply state what she required. She made no
attempt to circle the matter discreetly but asked the proprietor plainly if he recalled a pair of emerald sleeve buttons he
had sold more than a year ago to the Countess of Bentham.

Patently, he did, yes, replied Mr. Kimpton, who sported a
dark green tailcoat cinched tightly around the waist and
padded shoulders that gave him a slightly shruggish appearance. "I remember every item it is my pleasure to sell."

"That is helpful to know," Bea said. "And can you speak to
the quality of the sleeve buttons?"

At this query, Mr. Kimpton furrowed his brows, which
were snow white. "There is nothing to say, for the quality of
all my wares, including the sleeve buttons, is excellent."

"What is the likelihood that the link on a sleeve button
would be so worn away that it would snap after only a year?"
she asked.

"None whatsoever," he said firmly, but his shoulders

bounced as his agitation grew. "Any piece produced by Kimpton and Cross, even the most delicate jewel, is made to withstand common little scuffs. Why do you ask, your grace? Have you heard something to the contrary? I cannot imagine who would malign my shop, but I assure you I oversee the finest jewelry establishment in all of London. We are gold-smiths to the king and hold the royal warrant. The prince regent shops here, and you know what a discerning eye he has. He would never accept inferior quality."

Although Bea did not share Mr. Kimpton's faith in Prinny's taste, she appreciated the information because it affirmed the conclusion she had already reached.

Hoping to calm his agitation, she assured him that nobody was maligning his shop. "I have heard only wonderful things. In fact, Mrs. Palmer was just telling me about the delightful piece your artisans are crafting for her. It is merely that one of the sleeve buttons Lady Bentham acquired last year was worn to the point of snapping. But I am sure that had nothing to do with you," Bea added truthfully, for she knew Bentham had worn down the link himself.

The question was, how did he do it?

She supposed it was simple enough. Gold, after all, was an easily manipulated metal, and the earl was skilled at manipulating things.

Did it rankle, how smoothly she had fallen in line with his scheme?

Oh, indeed it did, quite sharply.

Mr. Kimpton, having been absolved of responsibility, immediately began to assume it. "You must know that I stand behind all my wares and if something proves deficient against all odds, I will replace it immediately. I can hold to that policy because all our products are of superior quality. Please know that I am distraught to learn of Lady Bentham's misfortune. As I said, it is an anomaly and I hope it will not prevent you from enjoying your shopping experience. Perhaps you would like to look around now? I am familiar with the duke's taste and can recommend several items. There is a pocket watch that I think is his particular style, which is to say unadorned but beautiful."

Bea was about to say no.

Of course she could not linger to browse. A man's life hung in the balance!

Well, not quite his life because Mr. Fawcett had yet to be tried, but his mental anguish had to be acute as well as his physical suffering. It was no small thing to find yourself locked away in Newgate for a crime you did not commit.

But she recalled the magnifying glass Kesgrave had given her—too precious to carry, too lovely to ignore—and felt a desire to reciprocate.

She could not conceive how to go about it, for she had only a few shillings in her reticule. Obviously, the contents of her purse were irrelevant because the price of the object would far exceed any amount she would reasonably be expected to carry. But it was the concept itself that daunted her. She could, of course, put the purchase on the duke's account. Clearly, he had brought Mr. Kimpton his custom before and his credit was excellent. It did not seem appropriate, however, that Kesgrave stand the expense of his own gift. She would prefer that the money come out of the inheritance left to her by her parents—the stocks, bonds, and family jewels stored in a chest on the upper floor in Portman Place. But she had yet to inspect the trove thoroughly and had no idea of its worth.

The best thing to do was to give it to Mr. Stephens and allow him to figure out what, if anything, was of value among the collection.

But that was neither here nor there, and Mr. Kimpton, taking her slight hesitation as acquiescence, produced a tray of three pocket watches, each containing a fusee mechanism.

They were lovely, the trio, with their silver cases gleaming in the golden light of the shop, but she could not perceive the purpose in buying the duke something of which he already owned several versions.

It struck her then how difficult he would be to shop for. He possessed everything and denied himself nothing.

Her only hope was to find something meaningful that would resonate with personal significance.

A challenge indeed.

But, no, actually it was not, for all she had to do was reciprocate.

"I would like to order something custom," she said. "Sleeve buttons in the shape of magnifying glasses decorated with sapphires and diamonds arranged in tiny flowers. Is that possible?"

Delighted, Mr. Kimpton assured her it was and lauded the expert work of his craftsman, who could produce any design at any scale. "And I guarantee the quality of the links, which will hold for many decades without showing wear."

"I am pleased to hear it," Bea said as the proprietor retrieved a slip of paper and began making a sketch to her specifications.

Fifteen minutes later, she left 21 Ludgate Hill, climbing into her carriage as her thoughts returned to the difficult matter of Bentham. Confirming her theory was good, but it was not enough to secure Fawcett's release or his lordship's imprisonment. In order to do that, she would need to prove he was guilty.

And therein lay the rub.

Citing Kimpton and Cross's craftsmanship would get her nowhere. Even the most accomplished worker turned out an inferior piece once in a while, and Bentham had taken the time to wear the link away. If he had used a faster method, such as splitting it in two with a sharp tool, then the break would have been clean—but that would not have served his purpose. A clean break would have alerted her at once to the suspicious nature of the fracture.

As the carriage rolled along Ludgate Hill, which quickly turned into Fleet Street, she wondered how long it had taken Bentham to wear away the link.

The answer, she supposed, depended on the method.

A sporting man, he had probably acquired several arcane skills in the pursuit of his pleasures, but would any provide him with the knowledge of how to wear down gold?

Unlikely, no.

It might have occurred to him to soften the metal with heat, but the fire would have to burn very hot to make an impact.

Prohibitively hot, she thought.

And even if he managed to raise the coals to the necessary temperature, how would he have held the sleeve button over the flames? Specifically, what tool would he have used and how would he know how to use it?

The same questions applied, she realized, to every method of which she could conceive. A file could wear down gold with far less fuss than fire, but that was not an implement an earl would have on hand. And again, he lacked experience manipulating small items.

Verily, she imagined Bentham spending months with a tiny file pressed up to his nose as he tried to smooth away the gold, the sleeve button held between his thumb and forefinger popping out of his grasp again and again.

If he had months to master the skill, perhaps he could have achieved it. But Lady Abercrombie did not give him months; she gave him one week.

That meant only one thing: Someone did it for him.

Moreover, someone found the someone to do it for him.

Bea considered whom on her staff she would ask to arrange such a thing for her. Marlow, for one, because he exuded competence in all matters and would magically sort it out. Jenkins, too, because he oversaw the horses and would know the best blacksmith in the city.

The butler and the groom, yes, Bea thought, and perhaps the valet, for he was entrusted with all kinds of intimate tasks. Bentham could have made up a story to explain his strange request, such as he detested the new sleeve buttons but did not want to give offense to his wife, so if some way could be found to render the item unwearable....

Confident that one of Bentham's servants knew something, Bea turned her attention to figuring out how to identify that person. She could not march into his house and demand to interview his staff, for he was not a *bourgeoisie* banker to be easily cowed by her consequence. It would require stealth and planning, maybe even a disguise.

Proving that Bentham had arrived at the party with a broken sleeve button in his pocket would probably not get him arrested for Pudsey's murder. Men of his standing were given a tremendous amount of leeway, even in matters as serious as murder, but she thought it would be enough to gain Fawcett's release. Her influence might not sway the magistrate, but a duke's privilege exceeded an earl's and his preference would be abided.

Fawcett's freedom would have to be sufficient.

And the revelation of the truth.

Word of Bentham's manipulations would spread quickly, especially when Mrs. Ralston realized she had been instrumental in the destruction of an innocent man.

The carriage arrived at Kesgrave House, and Bea, inquiring about the duke's location, discovered he was away from home, seeing to business. Mr. Stephens, however, was in residence, and she met with him to discuss the cache of documents left to her by her parents.

He agreed it was something he could deal with ably, and grateful for his competence, she thanked him for his help and reminded him that she would like to see Mr. Smarten-Muke's item in *The Sussex General Advertiser and County Express* as soon as he attained a copy of the newspaper. Then she wrote a note to her aunt requesting the chest and sent a footman to retrieve it.

After settling the matter with her inheritance, Bea retired to her office for rout cake enjoyment to enjoy rout cakes and plot Bentham's downfall. As keenly as she felt the injustice done to Fawcett, she could not allow herself to act impulsively. She had to have a solid scheme.

Bea considered the relative merits of donning a disguise, which she thought she could do with more success now that her options were all but unlimited, thanks to Kesgrave's wealth. But what identity could she assume that would induce a servant to talk freely with a stranger? Perhaps if she presented herself as a stable boy seeking a position, she could angle the conversation toward metalwork.

Even so, it was a very great distance from forging a horse's shoe to severing the delicate link of a sleeve button.

Indeed, the distance was so great, she wondered if the better plan was to assume the work had been done by an experienced smith. In that case, she could avoid the Bentham residence entirely and call directly on the various smiths in London without the bother of a costume.

Or, she thought, contemplating the resources at her disposal, she could remain at home and send the servants to ask the questions for her.

That would certainly be more in line with her social standing and spare the duke some talk.

Similarly, she could dispatch letters to every blacksmith,

goldsmith and silversmith within a twenty-mile radius with the promise of a generous reward for information.

But if money was the solution, she could simplify the process by bribing Bentham's servants for the evidence she sought. She could not imagine he paid them so handsomely that they would refuse an offer of a dozen guineas.

Yes, having access to the resources of a duchy opened up many encouraging avenues.

Bea made a list of ideas in descending order of viability to share with Kesgrave later, and by the time she was done, it was almost five o'clock.

As she and the duke planned to attend the theater that evening, she rose reluctantly to her feet to return to her bedchamber to prepare for the outing. Although she genuinely desired to see Robert Elliston perform *Hamlet,* the thought of staying exactly where she was and finishing Elizabeth Thomas's autobiography was equally appealing.

Marriage to the duke had provided all the repose such a union had promised, for the running of the house required very little effort on her part, but the unexpected popularity conferred by Bentham's machinations had proved quite onerous. It was baffling to her that anyone would seek out a condition that consumed so much of one's reading time.

Would not everyone else also rather be alone in a room with an engrossing tome?

Well, no, obviously not, for such a fate would appall her cousin, she thought with a grin as she stepped into the quiet corridor. Flora would consider it a horrible punishment indeed to be forced to spend an entire afternoon by herself with a book, engrossing or otherwise.

Returning to her bedchamber, Bea summoned her maid, who promptly laid out her dress for the evening—a violet-blue satin slip with a polonaise robe of white crepe—and helped her change.

Although Dolly made no comment to the effect, Bea knew very well she had chosen the gown based on its color, for it was almost the exact same shade of blue as the sapphires in the magnifying glass Kesgrave had given her.

How very clever, she thought, conspiring with her maid.

Deeply reluctant to wear an item that paid homage to her own ingenuity, for it seemed off-puttingly smug, she allowed that the activity for the evening tempered the awkwardness. Drury Lane was not a crowded ballroom, where she would be surrounded by dozens of people. Instead, they would be tucked away in Lord Hartlepool's box—not hidden, certainly, but also not fully on display.

She was not naïve, of course, for she knew half the purpose of attending the theater was to inspect the other attendees as if animals in the royal menagerie, and to be inspected in return. It was a play within a play. The exposure was minimal compared with other outings, and knowing it would please Kesgrave, she did not find the prospect completely horrifying.

Mostly horrifying, yes.

When her maid finished curling her hair into ringlets, she secured the style with a jewel-dappled bandeau. Bea, inspecting her appearance in the mirror, was, as always, taken aback by how lovely she looked. It felt to her both too simplistic and too complicated that all it required to turn her drab appearance into an elegant facade was a sure hand, a little skill, and great piles of money.

"Thank you, Dolly," Bea said, turning away from the mirror. "You have outdone yourself."

Pleased, the girl smiled and proposed an unadorned strand of pearls to complement the lush extravagance of the magnifying glass. "If you were planning on wearing it," she rushed to add. "I do not mean to make any assumptions, your grace."

"That is an excellent suggestion," Bea said, although in fact she did not know to which strand Dolly referred. The appalling truth was, her maid was much more familiar with the seemingly bottomless hoard of jewelry that accompanied her position as Duchess of Kesgrave.

The pearls were beautiful, of course, luminous and bright and perfectly matched, and when paired with the magnifying glass, which descended several inches past on its own glittering chain, assumed an added luster.

It was disconcerting, the weight of the piece as it pressed against her chest, but almost comforting, for it felt real in a way the Matlock rubies had not. The magnifying glass was, she realized, the first thing she had worn since becoming a duchess that she could imagine handing down to her own daughter.

"Lovely," Dolly observed.

"Yes," said Bea, grateful to have a maid who did not feel compelled to overpraise or exaggerate her mistress's appeal.

Dolly asked if she needed anything else, and Bea, noting it was a few minutes before six, said that she did not. After dismissing the maid, she retired to her sitting room. It was surprising, yes, that Kesgrave had yet to appear, for they were to leave for the theater by seven. But she was also grateful for the extra time to devote to her book and settled comfortably in the overstuffed armchair by the window.

Perhaps she would be able to finish *Life of Corinna* after all.

With only two chapters to go, it struck her as a likely prospect and she was focused so intently on her goal, she did not realize the duke had returned until she heard the floorboard creak. Marking her place with her finger, she raised her eyes to greet him just as a hand closed over her mouth and nose.

Stunned, she inhaled sharply, but there was no air to be

drawn and her lungs burned with effort and terror, causing her panic to rise as the desire for breath became a compulsion.

The pressure increased, the weight of her assailant dropping fully on her chest, and she flailed her legs as she twisted her torso, her fingers clawing at the fine wool of his coat to dislodge the arm that deprived her of air.

Clawing, tugging, pulling, shoving—all were useless.

Utterly useless.

His grip was too strong, his arm was too solid, like the branch of a tree.

It could end here, she thought, so easily, so quickly, a flame guttering and dying in a soft breeze, and an image of her mother flitted through her head—an image she had not seen in twenty years, it was so clear and precise, her eyes brimming brightly with laughter.

She could hear it now, robust and sweet, an echo of something long forgotten on the edge of rediscovery.

Bentham was silent.

Fast, efficient, sure-handed—he wasted no time in chatter, expended no energy in explanation.

Was this what it was like for Pudsey?

Barely a moment to acknowledge the end before it was over.

One thwack.

Bam.

And then he was on the floor, a creature wounded and exposed and ripe for disposal.

But Bea was not down, not yet, and she continued to writhe wildly, her mind screaming frantically as her lungs convulsed in excruciating depravation, her arms swinging fitfully to the sides.

If she could just grab something...something...something.

...

Her hands clenched air, then swung upwards to rake the flesh of his cheeks.

Did she draw blood?

What did it matter?

The assault continued, the pain in her lungs mounting, and she slammed her fist against his nose, felt the cartilage give way to her blow.

And still his hand remained steady, unyielding, indifferent.

He was a rock, a boulder, the whole bloody mountain, she thought madly, her shoulders jerking forward in rage even as she fell back in depletion, the magnifying glass bounding gently against her chest, a reminder of all that was lost and all that would never—

Stupid girl, eulogizing yourself when there is a weapon at hand!

Her fingers in a frenzy, she felt for the magnifying glass, fisted her hand around the fat of the lens, tugged with everything inside her and felt her entire body shiver with relief as the chain snapped. Raising the implement, she jammed its handle into his eye.

He recoiled.

Air poured into Bea's lungs like water bursting a dam, and she released it again on a high-pitched scream that pulled from every corner of her being.

Noise, she thought. Noise, noise, noise.

Because his plan had been predicated on silence.

Kill her wordlessly, leave the house soundlessly.

No one would ever know what happened.

Bentham staggered back with a shout of surprise, his good eye blinking in stunned confusion, his bad eye dripping blood around the object lodged there. It didn't matter, though, his bewilderment, and tucking his head under like an animal about to attack, he charged forward. Bea, her back pressed against the inside wing of the chair, clutched the arms for support, raised her foot and thrust it between

Bentham's legs, ramming it into what Aunt Vera had once described in blushing mortification as a man's most sensitive region.

He fell to his knees with such force, the magnifying glass dislodged from his eye and landed with a thud on the rug as she let out another ear-splitting yell. She leaped to her feet to run from the room just as the door opened and Dolly barreled in followed by Lila, then Joseph and Marlow.

They stared at the scene, all of them uncomprehending, for several humming seconds. Then Mrs. Wallace huffed into the room, screeched in horror at the sight of Bentham hunched in agonizing pain over a bloody magnifying glass, and the spell was broken. Marlow crossed the floor in three wide steps, dragged the unresisting lord to his feet and propelled him toward the door.

Although the butler's expression was as placid as ever, revealing none of his thoughts, Bea could feel his rage and knew it to be twofold: at the attack on her life and the violation of his territory.

"Thank you, Marlow," Bea said softly, striving for outward composure. There was nothing to be gained by turning into a watering pot now, especially when there were decisions to be made. If left to Marlow, Bentham would be deposited in the cesspit beyond the house or simply tossed into the Thames with other detritus of human waste. Rough justice, however, would not suffice. He needed to be handed over to the authorities so that Fawcett's release could be arranged and he could endure the consequences of his murderous actions.

Drowning in the Thames was too lenient.

"Please secure him tightly and bring him to the drawing room," Bea said.

Mrs. Wallace, dissatisfied with the suggestion, asked sharply, "The drawing room, your grace?"

No, of course not, Bea thought, smothering an overwhelming urge to laugh, which she recognized at once as hysterics. We must not host ruthless killers in the drawing room.

Alas, they did not have a drawing and quartering room.

What would such a room look like, she wondered, trying to marry the elegance of Kesgrave House with the brutal inhumanity of a dungeon and arriving at manacles chained to a thistle-patterned wall in the richest red.

Or maybe a cerulean blue to mimic the sky, for red was a little too on the nose for a room devised to torture its inhabitants.

Oh, my, yes, she was hysterical.

Constraining her thoughts to the present situation, Bea bowed to the sensibilities of the housekeeper and reviewed the other rooms of the house. If the drawing room was out of consideration, then so was the library and the conservatory and her office for rout cake enjoyment. Kesgrave's study was also too felicitous.

There was, she recalled, a room in the back of the house beyond the music room that had an unfavorable color scheme of brown and green and received very little sunlight.

Hesitantly, she suggested the back parlor and grew more confident in her proposal when Mrs. Wallace nodded in approval.

"Yes, do, Marlow, wrap him up tight and deliver him to the back parlor so that I may interrogate him," Bea said with a particular note of authority in her voice to preempt disagreement. "And please send someone to fetch the constable."

"Joseph has already gone, your grace," Marlow said.

Glancing toward the entrance, Bea realized that the small crowd of curious servants had dispersed. Only the butler and the housekeeper remained.

'Twas a well-run establishment of the highest quality, she

thought with amusement, when the staff did not linger to gawk at the grisly site of an earl with his eye gouged out by a magnifying glass.

Ah, yes, the magnifying glass, she thought, looking at the lovely implement that had saved her life. It was dappled with blood.

Mrs. Wallace, following her gaze, stepped forward as if it to block the object from her view, and told her not to think of it now. "We shall clean it up and it will be like new."

Touched by her concern, Bea thanked the housekeeper.

Mrs. Wallace nodded pragmatically, as if overseeing the scrubbing of gore from sapphire-studded gold were an everyday occurrence, and Bea thanked her again. She stood there, in the center of the room, for a few seconds more, feeling as though there was something else she should be doing. Realizing, however, that she was actually in the way, she announced that she would be in the library.

"I trust you will alert me as soon as Bentham is settled," she added.

In truth, it was she who needed time to settle, and as soon as she entered the library, she poured herself a fortifying glass of port, which she consumed in one indecently large gulp. Feeling none the better for it, she took another swig and observed with a strange sort of detachment that her hand was shaking.

It had been close, the thing with Bentham, in a way that it had never been before. For the first time in her life, she had felt halfway dead.

'Twas an illusion, she thought, created by the sheer physicality of the attack. She had been just as near to death when Latham had held a double-barreled flintlock to her chest, but it was different, not being able to draw air. She had felt the sensation once before, when an assailant briefly wrapped his hands around her neck, and yet how different that had been

—a momentary threat, a fleeting menace. But Bentham's palm had been remorseless and unrelenting, and the second he pressed it against her nose and mouth, the clock had begun to tick. All at once her life had a clear and irrefutable end point.

Even now, she could not say how close she had come.

These thoughts did little to calm her, and Bea lifted the bottle to refill her glass yet again. But she paused before pouring the wine because it would never do to get thoroughly disguised before interrogating a murderer.

What about a trifle disguised? she thought, staring into the dark liquid.

The door opened, announcing the presence of Marlow, and resolutely, she straightened her shoulders, returned the port to the table and turned to address him.

But it was not the butler.

No, it was Kesgrave, striding toward her, his blue eyes glittering fiercely, his well-sculpted lips grim and tight, and seeing him she felt all the fear she had fought so hard to restrain overcome her. Now, suddenly, she could perceive it all, envision it clearly, the moment he found her lifeless form hunched over in the armchair, and it terrified her more than death itself.

She refused to succumb.

Having staved it off while Bentham's hand was pressed brutally against her mouth, she would not crumble beneath it now. Instead, she curled her hands into fists to stop them from shaking and said with exaggerated calm, "Impeccable timing, your grace, for I was just about—"

On a feral growl, he cut her words off at the source, tilting her head backward and clutching her arms tightly and kissing her hotly.

The force of it overwhelmed her, the way he seemed

determined to devour her wholly, to subsume her fully, to obliterate the space that separated her body from his.

It went on and on until she feared the sheer overload of sensation—relief, happiness, terror, desire—would cause her to collapse like the insipid heroine of a gothic.

And then it changed.

Slowly, gradually, inexorably, his lips softened, his grip loosened, his panic lessened, transforming the embrace from an act of affirmation into a tool of seduction. Bea responded in kind, her muddle of emotions coalescing sharply into lust. Effortlessly, she could pull him down to the floor of the library.

Just a tug, she thought, and she would feel whole.

But she knew there was a reason she must not, even if it did not seem vitally important at the moment, and when she heard Kesgrave breathe a word that sounded like *Angelo* against her lips, she realized she was impaired beyond sense.

Then he whispered, "Jackson."

Wait, no, she thought, her mind clearing as the strangeness of the duke's soft utterances struck her.

He was listing names.

Why?

They were not warships from the Battle of the Nile, were they?

No, one could not wed the Duke of Kesgrave without knowing that the first two ships to enjoin the battle were the HMS *Goliath* and HMS *Zealous*.

Confused, she leaned back to inspect him properly.

Kesgrave, however, was not prepared to cease his activity and, tightening his hold, kissed her again.

But the inexplicable affliction continued, for gently he said, "Cresswell."

Now Bea extricated herself from his embrace, stepped back and asked with some concern if she should summon the physician, for he did not seem in full possession of his faculties.

The duke laughed without humor and said, "Yes, you provoke a murderer into trying to kill you in our home, but *I* am the one who is mad."

Naturally, Bea could not allow that comment to stand, for she refused to be held responsible for the actions of a depraved villain. And furthermore, she had done nothing more rousing than pay an innocuous call on a jeweler—who had, she recalled now, promised to make amends to his patron immediately.

Perhaps she should have made an attempt to determine exactly how many minutes and hours constituted an immediate response rather than blithely assuming it meant days.

Even so, the charge was decidedly unfair, and regardless, she had been attacked in the comfort of her very own sitting room, a place where she should have been perfectly safe no matter what violence her questions unintentionally provoked.

Kesgrave blanched when she pointed this out, then resumed his incoherent catalogue. "Manton, Zimmer, Melbourne."

"The good news is, no one among the *beau monde* will be surprised you have grown completely daft," she said matter-of-factly, "for they already believed you half-mad for marrying me."

"I am outlining your training schedule," he said soberly. "Angelo for swords, Jackson for pugilism, Creswell for pistols, Manton for shooting, Zimmer for fisticuffs, and Melbourne for speed."

"Oh, I see," Beatrice said, although in fact she did not. "You are turning me into a proper Corinthian. Very well, I accept, but only because I have always wanted to drive a team of four. Do tell me, your grace, who shall provide instruction on developing a steady whip hand?"

But Kesgrave did not respond to the humor in her tone.

Instead, he frowned more deeply, gripped her shoulders tightly and said with severe determination, "You will learn how to protect yourself, Bea. If you insist on continuing with this insanity, then you will acquire the skills necessary to ensure your welfare. You will not die on me."

It was an astounding statement, and Bea stared at him agog for several silent moments as she sought to comprehend the depth of his respect.

Any other husband in England—no, on the planet—would have used this near-deadly incident as an excuse to demand an end to all investigative activities.

But not the Duke of Kesgrave.

Oh, no, his solution to unfathomable mortal danger was to provide her with more power, not less.

Humbly, almost reverentially, Bea pledged not to die and to diligently take instruction and to practice her lessons as much as necessary, even if it greatly impinged on her reading time.

"Especially then," she murmured, punctuating each word with a gossamer-soft kiss, "for it will prove how devoted I am to mastery."

But it could not last, the sweetness of the embrace, and her kisses grew more heated and passionate until she was actually trying to tug him to the library floor.

"No, no, no," he said, resisting her efforts. "Bentham may have failed to retain your interest, but I assure you he still holds mine. I will speak to him now."

Bea stepped back and replied that the earl had not slipped her mind. "I merely believe it is the victim's prerogative to make her assailant wait as long as she sees fit. But if you are eager for a confrontation, do let us go interrogate him. I have pieced together most of his plan, but there are a few details I would like explained to me."

Nodding curtly, Kesgrave marched out of the library so quickly Bea had to scurry lightly to keep up and his pace increased the closer they got to the back parlor. By the time she crossed the threshold, she was running and entered the room just in time to see the duke apply himself to the ropes securing Bentham to the chair. The earl, whose injured eye had been bandaged with a handkerchief, glared at the duke with a furious expression.

Confused, Bea asked him why he was releasing her prisoner.

"Because I can't punch a man who is restrained," Kesgrave explained reasonably. "It is unsporting."

"But I have questions," she protested.

Pulling Bentham to his feet, the duke reminded her that he had questions of his own. Then he turned his lordship around so that he could unfasten the knots binding his wrists.

"I cannot ask my questions if you render him unconscious," Bea pointed out.

"Then you will have to wait until he wakes," he replied.

It was infuriating, Bea thought, how smoothly he spoke, as if his words were in fact sensible. But it was madness to suggest that he knock out the earl only to make her cool her heels until the villain revived. It had been a long day and she wanted this part to be over. Just being in the same room with the man who came so close to ending her life made her queasy.

Consequently, she said, "Correct me if I am wrong, your grace, but it goes HMS *Goliath,* HMS *Audacious,* HMS *Majestic.* Is that not accurate?"

Now his visage changed, revealing a flicker of impatience. "Yes. What of it?"

"I am merely confirming that in this house we follow maritime tradition," Bea explained. "That means we proceed in order of appearance in battle. As the first shot was fired across my prow, I go first. You must wait your turn."

Kesgrave's brows lowered as if he was prepared to argue, but then he shook his head and smiled faintly. He pushed Bentham back into the chair and removed the cloth over his mouth. "Very well, HMS Beatrice, you may ask your questions."

"Thank you," she said before turning her attention to Bentham, whose eye, she realized, was secreting a thick, milky substance. Although she saw no sign of it in his face, she could only assume he was in a great deal of pain and wondered if they should call a physician to examine the wound. She did not want him to die from an infection before his trial. "Since the duke is eager to interrogate you as well, I will keep my own portion brief. As your actions indicate, you are aware that I have figured out that you killed Pudsey. You provoked Fawcett into confronting you so you would be able to slip the emerald into his pocket and dropped the other into the amphora because you were reasonably certain I would find it. We both played into your hands beautifully and you should feel gratified at how well you conceived your scheme. It was truly remarkable. Alas, as Mr. Kimpton has informed you, I simply could not make sense of the worn button link. That baffled me, and baffling me is frequently a mistake. Now I will cease pontificating and ask the first of my three questions: How did you know the murder weapon would be embroidery shears? Lady Abercrombie insists that she did not tell anyone the details of her play, only its structure."

The milky substance oozed from beneath the white cloth on his eye as Bentham stared impassively at her, and recalling how silently he had gone about his task of snuffing the life out of her with his bare hands, she shivered.

"Disinclined to answer?" she asked tauntingly. "Determined not to satisfy my curiosity? How very discourteous of you, my lord, when I obligingly complied with all your requirements. Very well, then, I shall speculate. Please tell me if I am wrong. In fact, you did not know the murder weapon would be so ideally suited to your purpose and brought your own hunting knife with you."

His expression remained blank, so Bea said, "No, a knife would have ruined the lovely line of your coat. Rather, you planned to use one of the knives from Lady Abercrombie's collection, which is known to be extensive."

Still, he revealed nothing.

"Ah, but a knife taken from one of the rooms in her house would reveal information about the killer and you could not risk that," she continued thoughtfully. "I know, you intended to use a knife from the dinner table."

Slightly, he narrowed his one good eye, and Bea, taking the faint gesture as confirmation, asked how he had ensured that Mrs. Ralston would pass on the information to Fawcett in time for the dinner party. "Everyone in London knows she can be relied on to gossip freely, but you somehow managed to get her to gossip according to your own schedule. That is very impressive, my lord. A masterstroke. Do tell me how you managed it."

Bentham said nothing.

Here, Bea was not as confident she could fathom the answer by herself, for she had spoken only the truth. His manipulation of Mrs. Ralston was masterful. Nevertheless, she came up with a series of thoughtful scenarios as she tried to figure out how she herself would try to control Mrs. Ralston's movement. Alas, each one was less plausible than the last and when she devised a scheme involving an ill-disciplined dog and a chimney sweep, Kesgrave stepped in.

"I would deny no man the petty-minded pleasure of refusing the woman who bested him the satisfaction of answers," he said mildly, "for he has few joys remaining. That said, I must warn you that if you continue in your refusal to speak, I will deny your daughter my support. It is unlikely that she will make an excellent match after these events, but she could still find a suitable husband. Do not let your depravity ruin her life as well."

Bentham winced at the mention of his family, and Bea suspected the duke would help the girl regardless of how her father responded. As Lady Abercrombie had said, Kesgrave was so very good.

The earl, however, did not know that and explained without further prompting that he had had a package addressed to Mr. Fawcett delivered to Mrs. Ralston's address. "There was always a chance she would give it to a footman to properly deliver, but it was more likely that she would bring it to the house herself and wrangle an invitation to tea, which is indeed what happened."

Yes, a masterstroke, Bea thought again before asking her last question. "Why a magnifying glass?"

Bentham pressed his lips in confusion as the duke said her name with a mix of impatience and annoyance.

"No, truly, Kesgrave," she said firmly. "I want to know why he wove a magnifying glass into his extravagant tale of my rescue of him. It is most curious because in doing so he gave me the thing I needed to save myself. Had I not had it to plunge into his eye, he would almost certainly have succeeded in ending my life."

That Kesgrave had not yet been apprised of this fact was apparent in the startled expression on his face as he took one step toward her, then held himself forcefully in check, turning instead to Bentham, whom he ordered to answer.

His lordship complied immediately. "I had to act quickly and feared in my haste I had not ensured there was enough blood on the vase to draw you to it. I thought if only you had a magnifying glass. That is how I arrived at it," he said, then looked at the duke. "I have two other daughters as well, both still in the schoolroom. I hope you will lend them your support as well."

Kesgrave acknowledged the request with a curt dip of the head, then asked Bea if she was done. "You said three questions."

She was finished with Bentham, yes, very much so, she said, and he was now free to pummel the earl with as much fury as he saw fit. Her nerves frayed and her mind exhausted, she longed for nothing so much as the quiet of the library and the comfort of a third glass of port. Before allowing herself either, however, she looked once more at the man who had sought to end her life in the same way Wem ended her mother's and professed regret at gauging his eye out. "For it means you will see only half of the misery you are suffering in Newgate and I wish for you to see all of it."

Then she pivoted sharply and left the room.

Bea had barely stepped into the hallway before Kesgrave was beside her, grasping her hand, all thoughts of striking Bentham gone, and announced he would have Mrs. Wallace send dinner to their bedchamber.

"Unless you would prefer to eat in the library," he added.

It was astonishing, she thought, how much he understood, and she tightened her grip on his hand as her mood lightened. She did not require the library or the port, only him.

"Our bedchamber is perfect," she said softly.

"Good," he said, dropping a kiss on the top of her head.

It was sweet and fleeting, no more than a peck, but she felt it in every inch of her body, and as they turned to climb the stairs, she marveled again at the paradoxical journey from degradation to delight—at once long and short.

A few hundred yards and yet miles.

About the Author

Lynn Messina is the author of more than a dozen novels, including the Beatrice Hyde-Clare mysteries, a series of cozies set in Regency-era England. Her first novel, *Fashionistas,* has been translated into sixteen languages and was briefly slated to be a movie starring Lindsay Lohan. Her essays have appeared in *Self, American Baby* and *the New York Times* Modern Love column, and she's a regular contributor to the *Times* parenting blog. She lives in New York City with her sons.

More Mystery!

Some Romance!

Anything can happen in Regency London, as five headstrong and passionate women defy propriety and find love with powerful lords as determined as they are.

***

Love Takes Root series

Book One: The Harlow Hoyden

Book Two: The Other Harlow Girl

Book Three: The Fellingham Minx

Book Four: The Bolingbroke Chit

Book Five: The Impertinent Miss Templeton

Made in the USA
Coppell, TX
11 October 2021

63846683R20156